ROMANCING THE LEOPARD

A CARY REDMOND-TIGER SHIFTERS CROSSOVER NOVEL

KAT SIMONS

Their world is not what it seems...

Dylan Jones planned for this solar eclipse for two years. He got a prime site at one of the best locations in Oregon, and he intends to savor his last taste of freedom before he has to settled down and finish his Ph.D. thesis. He's at the festival for sun pictures and maybe some all-night skywatching. And if he can manage it, some much needed time in his leopard form. He's not there for a weekend fling. But the sexy genius in the site next to his proves too tempting to ignore. Something about Cat's scent calls to his leopard, pulling him in like catnip, and he just can't resist her.

Catalina Donovan came to Oregon for the solar eclipse, and only the eclipse. Getting away from New York and the constant pressure from the tiger shifter males to choose a mate only increases her determination to enjoy the festival. And the super hot guy in the camp site next to hers only adds spice to her vacation. There's something about Dylan that draws her, something she can't quite put her finger on. For someone like Cat, unraveling the puzzle of him is as tempting and enticing as his sexy voice.

But there's more to Dylan than Cat knows. And more to their new relationship than Dylan wants to admit. As they countdown to the eclipse, and things between them heat up, Dylan must decide how much to admit to Cat, how much he dares tell a human. When tiger shifters show up to lay a claim to her, Dylan realizes he might just have to fight for her.

And a future neither of them expects.

For my family, both found and biological.

The sky was already starting to dim by the time Dylan parked his pickup truck in his allotted camping spot. He'd intended to get here Thursday, but had gotten delayed at his parents' house and hadn't gotten on the road until midday Friday. The traffic coming into Madras had been horrific, and an accident earlier on the highway had slowed him even more. But he was here. Finally.

Oregon SolarFest.

The first total solar eclipse to cross from coast to coast in the United States in ninety-nine years. His mother might have been alive for that last one, although she wouldn't have been in the US at the time, but he hadn't and he didn't want to miss this one.

He'd been planning for this for more than two years. And still almost hadn't gotten a spot in the lot. He ended up with a 20' x 20' camping spot in SolarTown, on a flat expanse of field provided by a farmer who'd agreed not to plant that year. This was the bigger of two campsites designated for the event—the other being the main fairgrounds where NASA engineers had even set up some exhibits. He'd head up there tomorrow. For tonight, he just wanted to settle in and start hunting up the best place to set up his big telescope on Monday.

And eat, his stomach reminded him. He'd missed lunch and his shifter metabolism had burned through breakfast hours ago. He needed food soon.

Around him, tents, campers, and motorhomes filled the open field, neatly laid out in rows with dirt "roads" running between the rows to provide car access. Families with shouting kids, amateur astronomers with their scopes already out, bigger groups arranged to make up one large combined site, young college students and aging hippies all wandered the grounds. The place smelled of grass, dirt, mud, humans, sweat, and barbeque. There was a large tent for concessions to one side, including a beer tent, two large tractor trailers fitted out with showers, porta-potties scattered all around the site, and two hot air balloons for taking people up over the grassy fields.

Those fields stretched out toward the western horizon, with a brilliant view of Mount Jefferson's snow-capped peak in the distance. There were few clouds overhead, the air was starting to cool off from the August daytime heat, a comfortable breeze hinting at a cooler night ahead. The stars would be out tonight, clear and bright.

Perfect.

And now that he was here, he had two full days to enjoy the celebration and ensure his telescope and photography equipment were set up and everything worked so he wouldn't miss a moment of the eclipse. They were directly in the path of totality here, and promised a full two minutes plus of totality. He couldn't wait.

He'd also get some precious nighttime observations in. While he studied stars for his Ph.D., he rarely had time to just sit outside, away from the light polluting city around his university, and stare up at the wonder of the universe. He'd be starting the new semester soon. This would be one of his last chances to relax before the final push to get his thesis done.

He pulled the tailgate down on the flatbed of his 4x4 and dragged out his tent from under the mesh holding everything down. He was at the edge of the site, near to the open field, which suited him. He'd have liked a location with more trees, so he could go for a run in his leopard form. That wouldn't happen here, though. Not with so many humans gathered in the site, and so much open space between the grounds and the nearest clump of trees. But he could get in a run in human form through those fallow fields if needs be. He'd managed some time in his leopard form at his parents' house, near Eugene, which had released some of the building tension. Since he spent most of his time around humans at college, he didn't get to let his animal side out much and after a while he got restless. But the time in the woods surrounding his family home had helped. He was too excited about the eclipse to bemoan spending more time without shifting.

As he set up his tent in his designated patch of low cut grass, he took in the humans surrounding him. The couple to the left sitting on top of their four wheel camper, drinking beers and laughing too loudly. Across the stretch of dirt road, a group of maybe six adults sat outside another impressively large motorhome, the shade rolled out from the side of the monster vehicle to cover a table filled with food. The scent of barbeque came from that group and the smell made Dylan's stomach growl. He hoped that concessions tent had something with meat.

Opposite Dylan's spot was an older man perched in a camping chair, reading an astronomy magazine next to a nice telescope set up. He had a domed tent staked to the ground in front of his rental car. Next to the older man a couple of younger men were backing a small collapsible camper into their spot, with some difficulty and a lot of cursing at each other. On the other side of the young men, several tents had been set out with blankets for shade strung between them and a family sat on the grass between the tents playing a game of cards. To Dylan's right, another rental car with a single-person peaked tent staked on the ground beside it, but no sign of the occupant.

People passed as he finished getting his tent up, lots of chatter and laughing and conversation. He was used to cities, used to tamping down his shifter senses, so he actually enjoyed the bustle. Even with the site still half-empty there was energy in the air, a sense of moment. The eclipse deserved nothing less in his mind.

He swung back to his truck to grab the last tent poles just as his neighbor to the right came out of her tent.

And Dylan just…froze.

She was tall and thin, with a mass of blond hair decorated with blue and purple streaks, all of it pulled up into a high, messy ponytail. The hairstyle highlighted her pixie face, all angles and sharp lines. Glorious brown eyes which tipped up a little at the corners surrounded by thick lashes.

And her mouth. He couldn't seem to look away from her mouth. Full, lush, her bottom lip plumper than the top, made for biting. His pulse hammered at the thought and his leopard growled a little in his head. He held very still for a long moment as every nerve in his body jumped to life, desire thick and hot flooded his system. His nostrils flared, even though the breeze was wrong to catch her scent. Heart pounding, he took one step toward her.

And blinked.

Whoa. His reaction was so far over the top, he frowned. She was pretty, very pretty, but not the sort of stunning beauty that stopped men in their tracks. Still…

He couldn't look away.

He abruptly turned back to his truck before she caught him staring, giving his head a little shake. They'd be camped next to each other for a couple of days. He didn't want to make her uncomfortable on the very first day and set a bad mood for the rest of the event.

Even so, as he finished with his tent, he remained hyper aware of her shuffling around her site. She called a greeting to someone, and the sound of her voice brushed over him, making the hairs on his arms stand up in reaction. It took an act of will not to turn back to her. He glared at his tent, the last couple of tent stakes nearly forgotten in his hand, reining himself in, flexing his fist a few times to release some of the tension.

Where the hell had this come from?

He glanced at her again, unable to resist, and his frown deepened. She was young and bright, glowing and smiling. And yes, she was pretty. And yes, there was an energy in the way she moved, a sort of contained spark of electricity. Magnetic energy that felt like life itself. Hard-to-resist energy that emanated from her in waves. But…

But what? his leopard asked.

What the hell? he answered.

Which wasn't really an answer.

He gave himself a full body shake and went back to staking down his tent, attempting once again not to stare. He even tried to keep her out of his peripheral vision. That failed miserably. He caught flashes of movement, the bounce of blue and pink hair, glimpses of torn baggy jeans and her bright purple t-shirt. The soft growl he released when she bent over, giving him a tantalizing view of her ass, was too low for a human to hear, but even that much slip in his control shocked the hell out of him.

He stalked to his truck for his sleeping bag, watching her while trying to look like he wasn't. He never reacted to women this way. Not on first sight. Not without some build to the attraction. The breeze moved away from him, so he still hadn't caught her scent. The fact that he was having a difficult time staying by his own damned tent, that he could barely resist staring at her was baffling. What was it about her?

She hefted a large telescope out from her car trunk and carefully placed it onto a sturdy tripod. She smiled a lot, he noticed. A full, gloriously bright smile. And when she focused on adjusting her scope, she nibbled at her bottom lip.

The gesture made Dylan groan. He concentrated on snapping open his sleep bag and pushing into place inside the tent. Not that he'd need it for warmth. Between the mild August night temperatures and his shifter metabolism, he wouldn't be even a little cold tonight. But a sleeping bag helped him maintain the illusion of being a normal human, so he always had one with him when he went camping.

The breeze shifted but still didn't move in the right direction to bring the woman's scent to him. Probably for the best. If he was reacting this way to just her presence, he was afraid to find out how his leopard reacted to her scent. And yet he still found himself hunting the air for hints, for something of her essence under the stronger smells of charcoal fires and dirt. Maybe if he could analyze her scent, he'd be able to explain his reaction to himself.

He *had* been too focused on his research lately. And when his twin had teased him about his recent monkish existence, he hadn't completely dismissed the idea of a hookup during the festival if he met someone free and willing. He wasn't here for that, and he'd assumed the probability was pretty low, but he wasn't opposed either. He just hadn't expected to feel like he'd been hit between the eyes with a tree trunk at just the sight of a stranger.

As he settled his tent flap closed, contemplating his thunderstruck reaction, the older man from across the dirt path ambled over and gave Dylan a small wave. Dylan jumped at the excuse to focus on something, anything other than his captivating neighbor.

The man was probably in his mid to late sixties in human years, with a bushy gray beard and mustache, thinning gray hair, pale skin, and horned rimmed glasses that made his brown eyes look too large for his face. His scent was a mix of human musk, some sort of medicinal chemical, and breath mints. And just under that, Dylan was pretty sure he smelled gin, but faint, as if the man had enjoyed a glass last night.

"Here to gawk or to study?" the man asked with an amiable smile.

For a split second, Dylan thought the man was talking about the woman, and the way Dylan had been having trouble *not* gawking at her. But then the man glanced up in the general direction of the setting sun, and Dylan realized he was talking about the eclipse.

The entire reason they were all here.

He released some of the tightness in his shoulders and said, "Little of both." He nodded to his truck cab. "Got a ten inch scope for the sun and a smaller one for the night sky."

The man's smile turned into a grin. "Wouldn't mind a look through that ten inch once you get it set up."

"No problem."

"Sun spot activity should be good." The man glanced up again. "Gonna be a good night for stargazing as well."

"You here to gawk or study?" he asked, echoing the man's question to him.

"Little of both." He smiled. "Have you been up to the fairgrounds yet?"

"Not yet."

"Don't miss it. Got lots of fun stuff set up for us eclipse chasers." The man rocked back a little on his heels. "Where you from, son?"

"Oregon. Eugene originally."

"Well. Not too far to travel for you, then."

"How about you?"

"East coast. New Jersey at present."

"Nothing closer to home?" The path of totality would stretch from coast to coast and there were events going on all around the country.

The man waved that away. "I wanted in on this as early as possible."

"Can't blame you for that." First landfall was here in Oregon, and Dylan had jumped at the chance to be one of the first to see the event as well. "Name's Dylan by the way."

The man took his outstretched hand and gave it a firm shake. "Tom. Tom Baxter. Good to meet you, Dylan."

"You too, Tom."

The woman in the neighboring site ducked into her tent, which Dylan noticed despite his best intentions to ignore her. When she came back out again, she laughed suddenly, the sound sonorous and deeper than he'd expected from such a pixie face. And he was right back to staring at her again. She was laughing at a passing group of three adults and two kids wearing tinfoil hats. She clapped and the group waved to her. She waved back, like she greeted people wearing tinfoil hats every day.

He should introduce himself.

Wait, what? No. He needed to stay away from her so he didn't get any more distracted by her. He needed to finish his site setup and then go get some food. He needed to get his bearings and settle in.

Tom leaned close and clapped Dylan on the shoulder. "Be nice when you say hi and I bet she'll smile like that for you."

Dylan blinked, but before he could respond, Tom winked and walked away, chuckling under his breath.

Dylan faced the woman again. Apparently, he did need to introduce himself to his neighbor because he didn't hesitate in taking Tom's advice.

She bounced on her toes as she moved around her scope, adjusting the base and eyepiece, before turning her attention to the tablet in her hand. She was all energy and spark, in constant motion. What would all that energy be like in bed? He stopped that line of thinking in its tracks. Better get her name first before he leapt to fantasies of tangling in a sleeping bag with her. Not that he hadn't already made that leap.

When he was within a few feet, he cleared his throat to get her attention, and so he wouldn't startle her. She looked up, blinking at him, and he smiled a greeting.

Her mouth hung open a little before she snapped it shut.

Okay, so maybe he had surprised her. "Hi," he said, making an attempt to look harmless and take Tom's advice to be nice. "Guess we'll be neighbors for a few days." He stuffed his hands in his pockets so he wouldn't reach out toward her. He could pretend he was just offering to shake her hand, but he knew what he really wanted was to feel the texture of her skin. "Thought I should introduce myself."

She shook her head and said, "Oh, yeah. Yes. Sorry. Hi. I guess we will." She blinked. "Oh, the sun's going down."

He chuckled. "Tends to happen this time of day."

This close he finally got her scent, carried to him clearly on the shifting breeze. The scent made his leopard sit up and growl. It was rich, full of complex flavors—human, something sharp and tangy like lemon mixed with sweet, smoky nutmeg, musk, and…he almost wanted to say sizzling ozone, like the way the air tasted after a lightning strike. Not like magic, though that was a similar electrical scent. She wasn't a magic wielder. This was different. He'd never smelled anything quite like her before. No human he'd met had that flavor. He liked it.

His leopard liked it a lot.

Too much. Her scent was catnip, a flavor he wanted to soak up and explore. But he still couldn't explain why he reacted to her so strongly. Still, with her scent hanging in the air between them, it took an act of will to stay on his side of the imaginary line separating her little camping lot from his.

She bounced on her toes again, humming a little under her breath. He probably wasn't supposed to hear the hum it was so quiet. She sounded like she was chanting, "Focus, focus, focus," as she stared at her scope. Was something wrong with the eyepiece?

He didn't want to disturb her or make her uncomfortable, so he should step away, give her some room. They'd be here a few days. He had time to get to know her a little better, figure out why he couldn't stop staring at her. He started to turn away when he realized he hadn't even gotten her name yet.

And despite his better judgement, he reached out a hand toward her when he said, "I'm Dylan by the way. Dylan Jones."

2

Cat had never experienced so much trouble focusing. At least, so much trouble focusing on something she loved. When she was in her element, contemplating the delights of particle physics and the effects of quantum mechanics on the universe, getting her to *stop* focusing was usually the problem.

But the man who'd parked next to her in the field was definitely a distraction. A gorgeous, sexy, hot-as-hell-with-a-voice-like-sin distraction. She felt a little blindsided. What sort of human being looked like that? All hulking muscles, dark brown hair, blue eyes, a face like it was formed by some sort evil genius intent on making people melt with lust.

And his voice! If sin and sex had a voice, it was this man's.

Not that she thought there was anything sinful about sex. She was all for sex. Enthusiastic even. But…this guy's voice brushed across her like a dark fire that made her burn inside, and the instant lust went well beyond anything she'd felt before, paling all her past sexy thoughts.

Focus, Cat, focus. She repeated the chant in her head that she'd breathed out loud moments ago.

But how the hell was she going to concentrate on the eclipse—on anything!—when all she wanted to do was drink in the gorgeousness next to her?

It took her an amazingly long second of helpless staring, during which she contemplated the relativity of time when faced with a sex god, for his introduction to sink in.

She should probably do something about his extended hand before things got any more awkward. She took a few steps closer to him, shook his hand in two hard pumps, and released quickly because touching him made everything inside her dance and tighten. His hands were warm, and large, and his fingertips were a little rough, and all she could think about was how that roughness might feel scraping over her skin.

Her head was going to explode.

She scurried backward those couple of steps she'd taken closer to him and said, "Catalina Donovan. Cat." Because despite herself, her mother and then her sister, had insisted she adopt socially acceptable manners. Sometimes she even remembered to use those manners.

His smile deepened, and for maybe the first time in her entire life, Cat couldn't think. Her mind went absolutely blank.

Wow.

She mentally shook herself. She'd always admired good-looking men, but unless she knew they could vaguely keep up with her mind, the attraction didn't usually last long. She didn't want to spend time with a man who made her feel like she had to dumb things down for him. Her sister had raised her better than that. She hadn't exchanged more than a few words with Dylan Jones. He could be a complete idiot for all she knew. A sexist frat boy. A misogynist. He could be gay and not interested in her. He could be straight but still not interested in her. There were all sorts of options that would make her sexy feelings irrelevant. He could be…

He could be an asshole like the stupid tiger shifter men who wouldn't leave her the fuck alone.

She probably needed to exchange more than a few words with Dylan, get to know if he was one of the assholes or not. That would help. Right?

And yet…her brain seized. The experience was so rare, she found herself studying it. This was what happened to other people, huh? They had moments when their brain didn't do anything and they could just exist without the constant stream of ideas and thinking. No actual thoughts. She realized those *were* thoughts she was having. That she *was* thinking. But now she was thinking about thinking, and that should have been distracting enough to allow her to hold a conversation…

Nope. She had nothing. No idea what to say to the stunning Dylan Jones. She couldn't stop staring at him. But she also couldn't seem to find a comment.

"I have a sister named Caitlin," he said, returning his hands to his pockets. "We shorten it to Cate, though. I like Cat."

"Uh huh," she said. She really wasn't used to feeling tongue-tied. This was weird. "My sister's name is Amy."

"How many siblings?"

He was good at small talk. Damn it. "Just one. Her name's Amy," she repeated, then winced. "She's married." Why did she feel the need to say that? Small talk. This was what other people did. They made small talk with strangers they'd just met and didn't know. Wait, was this small talk? She was so off center she wasn't sure about anything anymore. "Did you know we can test Einstein's theory of gravity during the eclipse? Need pictures obviously, but measuring the lensing of the stars behind the sun should be possible."

She blinked. *What, Cat? What?* She knew for sure that wasn't small talk. Everyone had told her, more than once, Einstein's theory of gravity wasn't small talk.

And yet, she didn't stop. "During totality. I was thinking of trying it. Getting pictures of the lensing. Working out the math. For the fun of it obviously."

"Obviously," he said, his voice quiet and amused.

She didn't even pause in her rambling. "It's been done a lot. Since 1919. Einstein, right. Lots of confirmations. But still, it could be fun. Seeing the lensing through our little scopes. Being able to prove it. Well, my scope is little. Haven't seen yours yet." Her cheeks heated.

Cat Donovan, stop already! She really wanted to shut up but words kept pour out.

"I'd actually intended to take pictures that would let me see the lensing for myself, too," he said.

And she finally stopped talking.

"Relativity isn't my specialty. I'm more of a spectroscopy kind of guy. Studying stars for my thesis. But who doesn't love reproving Einstein, right?"

Her jaw went a little slack. "You study stars?"

"It's the focus of my thesis," he said. "Been work on spectroscopy comparisons of stars off the main sequence. Nothing ground breaking, just adding to the data, but I like the precision of it."

Wow.

"So, not just an amateur astronomer, then?" she asked.

He grinned. Her knees actually weakened. Like, she might just fall down. That was… Wow.

"Well, since I'm not making my living at it yet, I guess you could still call me an amateur."

"Me neither," she said, still trying to get over his smile. "Not working yet. Finishing my Ph.D. Second one. I have some job offers." She winced. More rambling.

Usually, she didn't mind her rambling. It weeded out the people she didn't want to talk to. But right now, she felt too out of control, too stunned, too… Entirely too eager to strip him naked and spend the next few hours exploring that stunning body while he talked about stars. She was pretty sure if he said spectroscopy again she was going to have an orgasm.

Focus, Cat, focus. This eclipse was a rare opportunity and she didn't want to miss out on any of it. Not that eclipses didn't happen all the time. They did. All over the world. In all kinds of phases. But having totality pass over the US hadn't happened in almost a century, and since she was busy finishing her second Ph.D. and had to finally settled into a job and a research topic soon, travelling around the world to watch eclipses wasn't high on her list of "need to"s. At least not yet. Someday maybe she'd have the money and time to traipse around the world watching the moon block the sun's light.

The reminder that she had to pick a focus for her research, and choose from her current job offers soon, made her stomach tighten—not for good reasons. Yes, it was nice having job offers. A lot of her friends and acquaintances from college didn't, and had massive student loans that needed paying back. She'd been lucky with scholarships and a rare mind that research universities knew would draw grant money.

Sometimes, though, all that choice got to be a little overwhelming, emotionally speaking. And overwhelming emotions could make her shut down, hide in her own mind, and not get around to making those decisions.

They were decisions about her entire life and…well, she wasn't sure how to make those choices yet. Which was why she was giving serious thought to a third Ph.D. instead of accepting any of the jobs. Her sister would kill her if she did that, though.

And just to add insult to injury, she had the whole tiger shifter shit to deal with.

She shook off the worry as Dylan spoke in that sex-on-a-stick voice again, capturing her full attention. He could definitely make her forget her worries.

"Second Ph.D., huh?" he said. "That's impressive. What's your focus?"

"First one was particle physics. This one is quantum mechanical effects around black holes." Those were the overview answers she gave most people because most couldn't understand the specifics of what she was working on. Words like black holes and particles were common enough people's gazes didn't tend to glaze over.

She had a weird feeling she could discuss the specifics with this guy and he wouldn't blink. He still might not understand everything she said—not even her professors could always follow her thinking—but he might actually understand enough to keep from getting bored.

"Impressive," he said again, his voice lower and deeper.

Her stomach danced at that sound, her thighs tightened, and she wanted to wrap her legs around him and lose herself in all his sexiness until morning. Maybe for the next few days. The eclipse wasn't until Monday.

Without her permission, her gaze traveled over the breadth of his shoulders, the way his t-shirt fit tight across his chest and biceps, the sinew and strength in his forearms, covered with a dusting of dark hair. He still had his hands in his pockets but her thoughts jumped to that roughness on his fingertips again. She had a lot of sensitive spots that would enjoy feeling the rub of that roughness.

She gave herself another internal head shake, trying to clear her thoughts. But he was still smiling. It was impossible to think or focus when he was smiling. If she didn't look away now, she wouldn't have to worry about unfiltered sunlight burning out her retinas. Staring at Dylan Jones would take care of that.

Her stomach tightened when his gaze locked with hers.

She could think of worse ways to go.

If Dylan had thought the woman was magnetic before, he'd been wrong. Being this close to her, talking with her... She dazzled him.

And everything around them sort of fell away. The sounds of all the human conversations, the scents of barbeque, the dust as a car eased down the dirt path between camping spots, the darkening sky. It all just dropped off his radar. All his attention zeroed in on Cat Donovan.

She rambled, hopping subjects, but beneath that he heard the genius, and it was everything he could do not to close the space between them and claim that gorgeous mouth. He held his place a couple of meters away, hands firmly in his pockets so he'd keep them to himself, and watched her talk. Something about a smart woman who smelled like lightning.

Catnip.

There was more to her, too. More in her scent. It tickled his nose, teasing him with hints of... He wasn't sure. He couldn't really pause to analyze that tantalizing mystery. He was too busy trying to keep up with her thoughts on how the discovery of the Higgs boson was just the start to what particle physics could do to help unlock the connection between quantum physics and relativity. At least, he thought that was what she was getting at. There was something in there about the singularity at the heart of black holes, too.

It took a lot of concentration to follow her thoughts, and even then, he wasn't entirely sure he understood what she was saying. He had a base knowledge of physics and chemistry for his specialty. But Cat Donovan took the conversation to the next level.

It was the sexiest thing he'd ever heard.

She blinked a few times, refocusing on his face, and a delicious blush crept up from her chest, across her cheeks. "I'm sorry. I got a little off topic there," she said.

"Not really." He grinned. "We didn't have a topic to get off."

"Uhm."

Well. He'd managed to render her speechless. He bet that didn't happen often. "Do you know which job you'll be taking after you finish this Ph.D.?"

Her face pinched in a frown, then she shook her head and said, "I'm still deciding."

"The big research facilities must be beating down your door."

He should probably end this conversation and leave her alone. At least for a little bit. She kept blinking at him like she didn't quite know what to do with him. He could offer some suggestions, most of which involved one of their tents and a lot less clothing, but it was probably too early for that.

And really, he shouldn't be getting this distracted by a woman. He had plans for the next few days. Late nights that involved star pictures, not fucking his neighbor. He could already feel himself slipping away from the event, his whole focus on her, and if he didn't shake himself loose soon, he'd miss the whole damned thing.

His twin, Julia, would never let him live that down.

Cat looked away from him finally, glancing at her telescope. Giving him the mental space he needed to realize she probably wanted to get back to what she'd been doing before he introduced himself.

He opened his mouth to say he'd leave her to her work now, but instead he said, "I was going to find some food. Want to join me?" Then before she could turn him down because she'd *just* set up her scope and wouldn't want to leave it sitting out, he said, "Or I could bring something back for you."

His leopard growled in approval. His leopard side loved feeding women. Especially this woman. Which was something Dylan probably needed to think about more when he could think clearly again.

She opened her mouth, and he was pretty sure she was going to refuse his offer—her expression and scent both confirmed she was hesitating—but then she said, "I could eat."

Her eyes widened as if her response surprised her.

He hid his smile. "What can I bring you?"

"I'll go with you," she said.

And her eyes widened more, so wide the expression might have made him laugh but he was too busy quieting his leopard's surge of triumph. She'd just agreed to a walk, he reminded himself, and getting some food from the concessions tent. Not a date. Not an offer to slip into her tent for some hot, sweaty sex. Just two acquaintances going to get some food in the middle of a big field with hundreds of people wandering around doing the exact same thing. He hadn't achieved anything here. She hadn't agreed to anything more.

But his leopard viewed this as a first step.

A first step toward what?

"I just need to put my scope up," she said, quickly turning to take her scope back off the tripod.

He returned to his truck to lock up, tossing a blanket over his gear still on the backseat even though they were at an event where a lot of people had telescopes and he probably didn't have to worry about theft. He kept his back to Cat so he could think a little, but he was so aware of her moving around behind him that trying to analyze his reactions to her was impossible.

For once, he'd have to let his analytical side go and just trust his leopard. Something about her called to him.

He might as well find out what.

3

By the time Dylan faced her again, she was closing the trunk of her rental car with a hard shove.

"Ready?" he asked.

She nodded and smiled hesitantly, crookedly, not moving closer.

He turned toward the dirt path, giving her the space she seemed to need, despite wanting to get closer, and nodded vaguely toward the concessions tent. Then he started walking, letting her make the choice to join him or change her mind. He picked up hints of her scent in the breeze, and she was nervous, a twist of musk in her lightning lemon scent. So he gave her plenty of room.

When she jogged the few meters to catch up with him, he resisted the urge to growl with that little triumph.

Tom waved to them as they passed, and while Cat wasn't looking, the older man gave Dylan a wink.

They wove through the neat rows of campsites toward the large white canvas tents stretched out at one side of the grounds. Dylan's stomach rumbled as the smells finally reached him over all the other olfactory assaults. He was acutely aware of Cat next to him, the way she fast-walked with a purpose, weaving around the obstacles, including running kids and one father daughter baseball toss, like a pro.

He stretched his legs to keep next to her and smiled at that. He usually had to slow way down for humans.

But she wasn't talking. And he found himself craving the sound of her voice.

"Tell me more," he said. "About your research," he clarified when she shot him a startled gaze.

"You weren't...bored?"

"Not even a little bit. Fascinated. I'm not sure I can keep up, but don't let that stop you. I'll ask questions if I get lost."

That surprised a little gasp of laughter from her. Oh, he could spend nights trying to get her to do that. A challenge he'd relish.

The breeze swirled around them, blowing gently against his face, bringing the cooler night air and the grassy scents of the surrounding fields. He pulled in a deep breath. The distant mountain, the open fields called to his leopard again. But not as strongly as Cat did.

There was an irony in her nickname being Cat, he was sure.

"I'd rather hear more about your research," she said.

Surprising him this time. No one in his family was particularly interested in what he did. At least not the specifics. "Like I said, it's nothing groundbreaking. I spend a lot of time pouring over tables and star charts and spectroscopy graphs."

She shivered when he said spectroscopy. That was interesting. Especially since the shiver was accompanied by a spike of desire flavoring her scent. He liked that flavor.

"Lot of time analyzing data already collected by other people," he said, filing away her reaction as they neared the concessions area. Under the white canopy, booths with food ranging from burgers to vegetarian fare lined one side of the space, and long bench tables filled the central area providing places for people to eat. To one side, a beer tent served local brews—the scent tickling Dylan's nose and tempting him. He liked craft beers, but after food. He needed something with meat in it soon. "I've gotten to spend a little time at Mount Wilson, do a few observing runs," he said, "but mostly, I'm in the lab working on analysis and doing some modelling."

"Modelling?" she asked, sounding a little choked.

He glanced at her again. "Computer models."

"Oh! Of course." She laughed but it sounded jittery. "My brother-in-law is a life model. For some reason, I thought that's what you were talking about. You're handsome enough to model. So, I thought…" She trailed off. "Good way to make money," she finished with a shrug and a little frown.

He bit back his grin. "Thanks. I think. Your sister's husband is a life model?"

"And an accountant."

"That's a…unique combination."

She waved a hand. "Not really. My sister is an artist and has a business degree. They're both too practical to just do art. Well, my sister sort of had to be."

"Why?"

She blinked at him, the frown deepening. "Oh. Uhm, she had to raise me after our parents died. Accident," she said before he could ask.

"How old were you?"

"Twelve. Amy was nineteen and had to grow up fast to keep us together. She even dropped out of college for a while, then went back. That's when she switched to a business degree. She wouldn't listen to me about going back to art school. She insisted she needed a degree that would help her make money."

"Practical," he said.

"She's too good an artist, though. She should have gone back to art school. But it's worked out now. She had a gallery showing in New York last week, even. That's where we're from. New York."

"Oregon originally," he said. "California now for college."

"One of my job offers is at Cal Tech," she said brightly, then blushed.

He wasn't sure why she'd blushed, but it didn't matter. He was too charmed by the color in her cheeks to care why she'd been embarrassed by the Cal Tech offer.

"Good research school," he said. "Would they make you teach?"

She shuddered. "I hope not. I'm a terrible teacher." She glanced at him from the corner of her eye. "I have trouble…explaining things in a way other people understand. I *am* good at lecturing, I'm told."

That made him laugh. She grinned.

"But apparently, no one really understands my lectures," she said.

"I suppose it's hard for us mere mortals to keep up with your genius."

She shrugged and looked back to the crowds around the food booths. The lines were, unfortunately, long at every single one, despite the campsite still being only about half full. He sighed. Guess their timing was off tonight. But the next couple of nights were going to be bad. They might have to find somewhere else to get dinner.

He ignored the fact that he was thinking about where he and Cat could get dinner together, as if that would be a foregone conclusion.

"I don't know," she said, sounding very serious as they neared the row of food booths. "I think people *could* understand what I'm saying if I could just figure out how to explain it right. I'm just not good at putting my thoughts into words. Better at math." She glanced at him again, her mouth quirked. "I failed English so many times I had trouble finishing my bachelor's degree."

He laughed, loud enough to draw attention from a passing family and a disapproving scowl from the mother as she pulled her teenage daughter closer to her. He didn't understand the gesture, but he was too delighted by Cat to worry about it.

"The professor kept making me write about things that weren't interesting to me," she said, with mock offense. "If he'd let me write about interesting topics, I'd have passed a lot easier." She said all this with a lot of hand gestures to emphasize her words. She was so animated when she spoke, it was like watching a dancing spark of electricity.

"Bet he wouldn't be able to understand the subjects that interested you," Dylan said, still chuckling.

She grinned. "That's what my sister used to say."

Her smile grabbed him hard and brought his full attention back to her mouth. All the things he could do with that mouth…

He gave himself a little shake and nodded at the food stands. "See anything you like?"

She paused long enough he glanced down at her again. She jerked her gaze away from him, her eyes wide. Then she gave herself a full body shake and pointed, seemingly at random, to the booth selling burgers and fries.

Not a vegetarian then. For some reason, he felt the need to file that information away as if her food preferences were of utmost importance.

"You obviously passed eventually," he returned to their conversation as they joined the back of the line.

"I had to hire a tutor. A science writer who could help me translate my thoughts into sentences. She was very patient. I wouldn't have gotten through the stupid class without her. But I will never look at contemporary social theory in post modern fiction the same again."

He snorted. "I'm not even sure what contemporary social theory in post modern fiction means."

"Thank you!" She slapped her hand against her thigh in emphasis.

The gesture brought his attention to her long legs. Her jeans were a little baggy, with holes in the knees, held up by a thick belt. He shouldn't have found those jeans sexy. They weren't skinny jeans, the denim didn't cling to her slender curves, but the way they dipped low on her hips made his pulse pound. He couldn't seem to pull his gaze up from her legs. From contemplating the shape of her under the denim. When he started to wonder how sensitive the skin on her upper thigh might be, he swallowed hard and faced the line in front of him.

"I love fiction," she said, fortunately missing the way he'd ogled her legs. "Especially Mysteries and Romances. But to this day, I don't understand the need to dissect it. It's for fun, right? Like, my sister can dissect a piece of art. And I sort of understand that because it means she'll learn something or maybe discover something, or just figure out what works for her and what doesn't. But I'm not trying to write anything outside of research papers so why do I need to know how to dissect *The Great Gatsby*. Which I never liked anyway. Gatsby was an ass. And..." She trailed off and looked over at him. "Sorry. Guess that's a hot button."

He waved away her apology. "Never liked Gatsby either. I did like Daisy. But I'm more of a science fiction fan. I'm surprised you're not."

"Oh, I do like them. I just prefer guaranteed happy endings. Mysteries have to be solved. Romances have to end with a happily ever after." She shrugged. "I like that part. Makes it easier to sink into a book without getting distracted by the stress of it all."

"I never considered reading might be stressful." The line moved forward, taking them with it as more people joined behind.

"Sometimes. I use it to distract myself, but then I worry about the characters. And that starts me thinking again. Too much. And then I'm back to thinking about science. And I like thinking about black holes and particles. But sometimes even my brain needs some down time."

"So Mysteries and Romances. Makes sense."

"Thank you. My colleagues don't always get that either." She made a face. "Some of the guys..." She rolled her eyes. "Having someone stupider than me trying to explain something he doesn't understand to me when it's my field of expertise is just..." She sighed. "Anyway."

He nodded in agreement even though he couldn't relate directly. He wasn't usually the smartest person in the room. But he'd heard similar tirades from his sisters, even witnessed a few incidents, so he got what she was saying.

"I shouldn't have called them stupid," she said after a minute. "They're not, technically. I just get pissed off." She winced. "Men can be a real pain in my ass sometimes."

He wasn't sure whether to laugh or wince at that.

He knew she wasn't talking about him—it was in her scent. But he certainly didn't want to be a pain in her ass. He wanted to do other things with her ass and that required she like him. In fact, his leopard was very very insistent that he ensure she liked him. The flavor of her attraction to him was there in her scent, which was delicious. But his leopard was pushing for...for something else. Something more? He wasn't sure. He knew he liked her. A lot. That probably should have surprised him. Attraction was one thing. Full blown crushing on a woman he'd just met was something else. But something about her...

Just. He couldn't place it. Every part of him felt drawn to her, even beyond the electric attraction.

Something about her scent…

He pulled his attention away from analyzing her scent when she said, "This is probably a weird conversation to be having with someone I just met." Little lines formed between her brows. "Hmm?"

"You okay?"

"Fine," she said, waving at him without looking at him. "Weird." This she murmured to herself, so quietly he probably wasn't supposed to hear her.

The wind shifted again, away from all the food in front of him, so he was one against assaulted by other scents from the campsite at his back. Cooling grass, dirt, warm vehicles, humans, and…

His head came up. Tigers.

As subtly as he could, he sniffed the air. Yeah, definitely a tiger shifter nearby. Actually… He pulled in another deep breath. Three of them.

That was odd.

Not that he didn't think tiger shifters could be interested in the eclipse. Everyone else was. There were going to be thousands of people here this weekend. He wasn't sure why he was surprised by the tigers' presence.

Maybe because tigers were notoriously isolated from the rest of the shifter community. They didn't interact with other shifters much, kept to themselves. So much so, he hadn't ever met one before. Having three coincidentally at the same site felt odd.

They'd likely get his scent as soon as the breeze changed directions again, if they hadn't noticed him already, and keep to themselves. He'd probably have to be careful if he did decide to go for a run, though. He knew this area wasn't in any tiger's territory. He hadn't just picked this location because it was directly in the middle of the path of totality. No other shifters had claimed any lands in this area as their specific territory. Still… He didn't want a run-in with other shifters this weekend.

He glanced at Cat from the corner of his eye. He'd rather spend his time talking with her.

4

Cat scowled at the food booth, still too far away, as the scents of grilling burgers made her stomach growl. Why the hell was she talking to Dylan about this stuff? It was one thing to talk about her research. To talk about books. Those were the kinds of things you talked about with people you'd just met. And were getting food with. Even though it wasn't anything like a date. This wasn't a date. She was eating. Everyone had to eat.

She still wasn't entirely sure why she'd said yes to coming with him for food except that she loved food—when she remembered to eat —and her traitorous stomach had reminded her she'd forgotten lunch the minute he mentioned food. She had to eat, so this was fine. And not a date because they'd only met. Barely knew each other. Which meant she should keep the conversation to general stuff. How many siblings do you have? What part of Oregon did you grow up in? What college are you at in California?

Not *too many men are a pain in my ass*. Talking to a man she wouldn't mind seducing about what a pain in the ass *other* men were seemed both ludicrously personal and…counterproductive.

Dylan Jones was essentially a stranger. She knew his name. His research focus. That she could listen to him say spectroscopy all night.

And that his laugh shouldn't be allowed out in public because it was a danger to all humankind. She hadn't missed the expression on that mother's face after he'd laughed, the wide-eyed awe, and then the woman having to pull her teenage daughter back when the girl had gone all starry-eyed as well. He hadn't even done that on purpose. He'd just laughed—and Cat was trying really hard not to preen over the fact that she'd been the one to make him laugh—but the sound had been so deep and rough and rich it was like walking sex. Really, his laugh should be against the law.

Still, her strong lusty longings for him did not mean he was a confidant. So why did she keep feeling like she could tell him stuff? She kept slipping into the conversation like she knew him better. Like she could tell him anything. And it was really disconcerting. She didn't just *talk* to people about her personal life. Especially since her sister had gotten involved with the man that was now her husband.

Which brought Cat around to her most grievous almost-mistake. She'd nearly slipped and told Dylan about the tigers. The thought that she'd come this close to revealing something so personal and secret to a stranger was a little breathtaking. But not in the good way like when he said spectroscopy. She couldn't believe she'd nearly slipped. And so easily! But talking about men who were a pain in her ass led her very naturally to the subject of the tigers—and all the pain in the ass tiger males she'd been dealing with since she turned twenty-three.

For the last six months the males had been... She huffed. They technically weren't *stalking* her. They weren't allowed. And she knew they wouldn't hurt her. They also weren't allowed. But they just kept showing up everywhere. All the damned time. Talking *at* her. Not threatening so much as pressuring her to pay attention to them. To give up some of her precious thinking space to their mere presence. And she didn't have time for any of it.

Honestly, she didn't want to make time for them. She love her brother-in-law. And his extended family was great. But she didn't want to slot herself into the tiger shifter world. She didn't want to get dragged into all that...stuff. She'd agreed to think about their reproduction problems, and she did let her brain mull over the possibilities, occasionally talking with one of their top geneticists. But outside of that, she had no interest in taking a tiger "mate" and having babies. Or trying to. She didn't want kids or the usual family stuff at the moment anyway. Maybe one day. She wasn't writing it off all together yet. It was just something way far out in the distance that she wasn't in the mood for thinking about yet. She was way too young to worry about family stuff. She had work to do. Research. The universe to study.

But the tigers were *obsessed* with reproduction. Their whole society was set up around it because they were on the verge of extinction. And yes, the extinction part sucked. She understood the basic biology driving them. She might have even been more sympathetic to their plight. If so many of the stupid males hadn't started pestering her at every turn.

She heard her sister's voice in her head scolding her for using the word stupid and mentally corrected to asshats. Which made her grin. The fact that Amy was good with asshats, but not with stupid—especially coming from Cat since most people weren't as smart as her—always amused Cat.

The line moved forward by a leap, getting them close enough to the food stand Cat's stomach growled again. She bounced on her toes in anticipation.

"Hungry?" Dylan said, amusement in his voice.

She relaxed enough to grin at him. "Starved. I forgot lunch." Again. But she didn't say that out loud.

His amusement turned to a slight frown but then he shrugged. "I got caught in traffic and missed lunch, too. I could eat the entire booth right now."

She chuckled. "Do you suppose there's somewhere around here to get... I don't know." She hunted down the rows of food stands. "Cake?"

"Cake?"

His grin made her stumble a little as they moved forward again. It wasn't just his laugh that should be illegal. The man's smile was also a danger to women kind. Probably men kind too. And person kind. All kinds. All kinds should be protected from that spectacular grin.

"What? I like cake," she said to cover her stumble.

"I do too. I just wouldn't have thought about it. We can look, though."

She nodded and tried not to look too pleased. The fact that he'd go hunting for sweets with her after dinner boded well for a friendship between them. And if he kept smiling at her that way, maybe more.

They finally reached the booth and ordered. She'd long since dumped any self-consciousness about the sheer quantity of food she could eat—when she remembered to eat—because her brain needed the fuel and fuck anyone who looked at her funny for it. But after ordering two burgers and a large fries for herself, Dylan ordered twice as much food, including chicken tenders, burgers, and two large orders of fries.

She blinked up at him. "You really are hungry." His order reminded her of the way her brother-in-law ate, had to eat because his tiger shifter metabolism meant he churned through calories really fast.

Dylan shrugged. "I hate missing meals. I have a lot of ground to make up for that lapse."

The food, when it arrived, smelled divine. She thanked the man behind the counter and gave the woman at the grill a grateful wave as she stuffed a few fries in her mouth before pulling out money from her pocket. Before she could hand over the bills, though, Dylan had already paid.

"You didn't have to do that," she said. This wasn't a date or anything. She might be a poor student, but she could pay her way. She'd been saving for this event for two years.

And Amy and Ethan had ensured she had enough cash to eat because Amy worried about her like a mother hen.

"You can get the next one," he said without looking at her, his attention on gathering up all his food.

He said it so casually, easily. She wondered if he realized it implied they'd be eating together again. He'd *assumed* they'd go get food together again. If he'd been a tiger, she'd have shut that line of thinking down immediately. But he wasn't a tiger. He was just an ordinary man here to watch the eclipse, same as her. And with Dylan, she liked the casual assumption. She liked the idea that they'd spend more time together over the next few days. Enough time that *of course* they'd be getting food together again. That she'd have plenty of opportunities to buy him a meal because this was the first of many meals they'd share. She didn't just like the idea. She loved it. It felt…inevitable. Natural. Obvious even.

That should probably be terrifying, though, shouldn't it?

She stuffed a few more fires in her mouth as she considered her feelings on this topic. He gathered up his change and all his food, then turned and scanned the long tables behind them. Most were full but people were coming and going, spaces clearing and then filling quickly. The area near the beer tent seemed the busiest, she noticed. Maybe if they couldn't find cake, they could try a beer. She liked tasting new craft stuff. She wasn't a big drinker because it dulled her brain in a way she didn't always like. But the flavors possible in a good beer did appeal to her.

Still, given she already felt a little tipsy with Dylan, cake would be better. "Keep your eyes open for a sweets booth or any place selling cake."

His chuckle made her knees wobble. "Would funnel cake do?"

"Not quite the same, but I'll take it." She perked up. "Why did you see something?" She looked around but they were in the middle of a crowded area around the tables and she couldn't see past the all the people, so she glanced back up at him. He was tall enough to see over the crowds.

But he was searching the tables, not looking at the row of food stalls when he said, "Thought I caught the smell of sugar near where we were. We can explore more after we eat." He glanced down at her. "Unless you'd rather get back to your scope, I mean."

"Cake first," she said firmly. "The stars will be out all night."

He grinned and Cat felt that grin to her toes.

He led the way to where two older women deep in conversation were just leaving their spot near the end of a table. She and Dylan would have to sit next to each other instead of across the table, which meant she couldn't look at him easily. That was probably good. She'd have an easier time eating if she couldn't get distracted by his gorgeousness.

But then he slid onto the long bench next to her, his heat seeping into her, and she realized this wasn't better. In fact, it might be worse. Now she was hyper aware of his closeness, his warmth, the fact that with just a little shift, an inch to one side, and she'd be pressed against him, feeling all those lovely muscles against her arm and side. It would be very easy to brush her leg against his, and the thought of his thick thighs captured her entire attention for so long, she nearly forgot the food in front of her.

She started tapping her toes, the leg opposite Dylan bouncing as she forced herself to pay attention to her food and not how yummy Dylan smelled. Oh god, he smelled good, though. Like heat and musk and warm earth. And trees. She could practically smell the forest on him, which was strange since they weren't in the forest. But it was a good smell. She wanted to bury her face in the curve of his neck and drink him in. Maybe lick his skin to see if he tasted as good as he smelled.

She shoved some more fries in her mouth to keep from actually drooling.

The salty fried deliciousness distracted her just enough she was able to move on to her first hamburger. And while she was very very aware of Dylan right there, so very close, her hunger pains finally got the best of her. Lusting after Dylan was one appetite that would have to wait. Her girly parts might be fully engaged with that lust, but her stomach was hollow and objected to the delay in hamburger consumption. She hummed under her breath, savoring the tasty burger as juice dripped down her hands. Messy, but very good.

She was onto her second burger before anyone spoke, a focus on his meal that she appreciated. She broke the silence with a question about his university, and they chatted easily about their respective research and universities and all the ordinary things people just getting to know each other talk about. Well, okay, she did slip into lecture mode once. But only once. And he seemed to enjoy the change up in conversation so she couldn't regret it. He asked questions, just like he promised he would, and made her think a little harder about what she was saying, and it was one of the most relaxed science conversations she'd ever had. Just…comfortable.

She blinked when she realized she'd finished her food completely and was bouncing a little in her seat as she spoke, her usual hand gestures constrained by the person on the other side of her—her sister had taught her enough manners she knew better than to wallop a stranger while talking—but she couldn't seem to help her animation. She enjoyed talking to Dylan.

Enjoyed it as much as she enjoyed her food. Apparently, since she'd finished without noticing.

"You're done eating?" she asked when she realized she hadn't seen him bring food to his mouth in a few minutes—she'd been paying way too much attention to that. A glance at the table confirmed he'd managed to eat everything too. He'd had substantially more food than she had, yet there wasn't even a left over French fry in any of the paper boxes neatly piled in front of him.

"I could eat more, to be honest," he said ruefully. "But I wanted to save room for cake."

She laughed and bundled up her trash. "I hope you're right about there being something with sugar in it around here. Be a shame to waste such a lovely evening on disappointed sweets dreams."

He opened his mouth to say something, but then paused. And she was struck by the sudden change in his expression, the way his face went from pleased, with a hint of something hotter in his gaze, to a slight frown. Every part of him tensed and grew alert, but not in a very obvious way. If she hadn't been watching him so closely, she would have missed the moment. Because that tension, that coiling of muscles only lasted a blink before he relaxed his frown and smiled again.

"You ready?" he asked, which she knew wasn't what he'd originally intended to say.

Whatever had distracted him, it had changed his mood. Subtly, but there. And her curiosity was peaked.

Somewhat surprisingly for her, though, she didn't ask. She wanted to study him more first, decide if she *could* ask. And she was a little afraid to reveal how closely she'd been watching him and studying him already by admitting she'd noticed his mood change.

They tossed the remains of their dinner into the trash and recycling bins set up at the rear of the concessions area, then plunged back into the fray near the food booths, in search of dessert. Almost as if he'd known where he was going, Dylan led them directly to a small funnel cake stand. The sweet scent of fried dough and powdered sugar made her mouth water.

But he hadn't gone hunting for it, even though he'd said earlier he hadn't seen the stand, he'd walked directly to it without any hesitance. He must have seen it while they were sitting down.

"My treat this time," she said as they reached the front of the line and ordered four funnel cakes.

Which was more than any two people who didn't want to be buzzed all night on sugar should get, but since she wanted to stay up most of the night stargazing, she didn't mind. She'd already broken off a piece of the hot dough and stuffed it in her mouth by the time Dylan got his two cakes. She imagined she had powdered sugar all around her closed-mouth grin, but she didn't care.

"Good?" he said with a smile.

"It'll due." She broke off another strip to eat, humming under her breath at the sugar rush.

He chuckled and looked around the bustling tables. "Want to just go back to our campsites? I'm not sure we'll get lucky with seats again."

"Perfect." She was too involved in her first cake—which was technically more of a donut but she was too happy to split hairs—to worry about where they sat.

She tried not to startle when he set a hand gently to her arm to guide her around a large family jostling for table space. The contact, his slightly roughened fingers against her bare skin, sent a pulse of heat through her. Instantly. Like he'd touched her with an electrode and lit her nerve endings up. It was surprising enough to make her forget her cake. The moment didn't last long, he didn't keep his hand on her after they'd passed the worst of the crowds and stepped outside the tent. But even that brief instant shook her. Because she wanted his hands on her again. She wanted his heat seeping into her skin. She wanted…privacy and less clothing between them.

Wow. If she reacted that way to a simple touch to her arm, what would happen if he touched her in other places?

She almost tripped at the mere thought and had to concentrate on where she was walking so she didn't fall on her face. Outside of the embarrassment, she didn't want to lose her cakes.

5

Motorhome lights, lights from the concessions area and shower trailers, and a few streetlights from the main road cut through the darkness on their way back to their tents. But their spot at the edge of the neat rows of campsites, beside the open field, meant a lot less of that light disrupted the night sky. Overhead, the stars shone brightly against the blackness, and later, when more people turned off lights to sleep, Cat was sure those stars would shine even brighter.

She never got this view. There was no place in New York City where the light pollution didn't obscure the night sky. Oh, she could see the planets sometimes. And obviously the moon. But no giant blanket of Milky Way. No overwhelming, sparkling grandeur.

Good thing for the sugar high. She might not sleep tonight, just so she could enjoy all of it.

She pulled her camping chair close to the invisible line that separated her site from Dylan's and he pulled out a similar chair from the bed of his truck, snapping it open one handed in a way that made her eyebrows pop up. She'd have teased him about showing off, but the move also gave her an impressive show of muscles flexing and shifting over his forearms and that was too much of a distraction. Because it led her to contemplating the rest of his arm, the thick, bunching muscles along his bicep, the strong curve of his shoulder under his t-shirt. For an academic who spent his time analyzing charts and data, the man had the most glorious body she'd ever seen.

When she started wondering what that body would look like without the t-shirt—or the jeans—she dropped her gaze to her funnel cake.

He settled next to her and leaned back, his gaze going to the stars the same way hers had, even as he devoured his first cake. They remained silent for long moments, both of them eating and watching the sky. Normally, Cat found that kind of stillness uncomfortable. And she wasn't good with silence around strangers, although she was good at silence if she was thinking. She wasn't really thinking right now, though. She was being. She didn't do that very often.

It felt good.

But stranger still, it felt good just being with Dylan.

Again that little voice in her head suggested that this should probably worry her more. She still didn't know much about him. This level of comfort around another human being usually took Cat significantly longer to accomplish—when she bothered to make the effort. She liked people. She just didn't often think about…well, accommodating them into her life. It took time and effort. She had friends but they were all driven and focused on their passions, like she was, which meant they could go for weeks at a time without speaking to each other and none of them made a big deal about it. The only person in her life she made a concerted effort to see and speak with regularly was her sister. Her sister was also one of the very few people on the planet she could be still and quiet with without it feeling weird and making her itchy.

The fact that it didn't feel weird with Dylan was, in and of itself, pretty weird.

She should probably make some small talk. But she didn't want to disrupt the quiet just yet. So she finished her second cake as they watched the stars overhead bloom into a glorious spectacle.

Licking the remains of powdered sugar off her fingers, she finally, quietly said, "I don't get to see this many stars normally. You can forget how perfect it is sometimes."

"Perfect," Dylan murmured.

"Must be fun, studying stars."

His chuckle drew her gaze to him. He was still looking up. "Most people who aren't in the field complain to me that it takes away the romance, knowing what the stars are made of, how they live, how they die. What we know—and don't know for that matter—that just makes it all the more wondrous for me."

Cat couldn't help it. She sighed. Knowing the mysteries, explaining them and then realizing how much was still unknown… She found that wondrous too—awesome and overwhelming and inspiring. The explanations they *did* have only made the entire workings of the universe more spectacular for her. She'd never understood why people found ignorance, or a lack of understanding, more romantic. When you knew a thing, when you glimpsed how things worked, it made the fact that they *did* work so much more impressive.

"Agree," she said on another sigh.

He finally glanced down and smiled directly at her, and Cat's breath caught. Something else she wanted to understand—that smile. The man wielding it. Would he be even more impressive if she learned how he worked?

She broke the stare first, as the intensity started to overwhelm her. "I'm probably not going to sleep tonight," she said, looking up again so she could steady herself. "Too much to see."

"I had the same plan."

She smiled but didn't look at him again. Too easy to get lost in him. Too easy to forget they'd only just met. "Will you take pictures or just look?"

She had a camera set up on her scope because she wanted to record the eclipse. But she had a smaller scope just for star gazing that didn't have a camera or any of the techy tracking stuff she had on her bigger telescope. She'd have to set the other one up tomorrow, make sure it was ready and everything worked and had survived the airplane trip. But for tonight, she just wanted to watch the sky change.

And maybe look at a smudgy galaxy or two.

"I'm set up for pictures on my smaller scope," he said, "so I might.

Depends on what I see. But I spend so much time pour over star data, I might just watch them tonight."

"It's a little scary how much we think alike," she said before she could think about the words. She'd meant them lightly, casually. But they hadn't come out that way. They'd sounded more serious when she said them aloud. They did think along very similar lines. And that was pretty scary.

Fortunately, he didn't seem to notice her slip and took the words as she'd intended, as a light joke. He chuckled. The sound shivered across her skin like a caress, but it was also a relief. She couldn't understand her reaction to Dylan and she needed to think about it more. That's what she did. She thought and analyzed. She hadn't had time to do that yet and she kept…feeling things. Things she didn't entirely understand. Beyond lust. The lust she understood. Who wouldn't lust after him? The man was sex incarnate.

But her comfort with him, the way she kept saying things she wouldn't normally say to someone she didn't know… Yeah, she needed to think more about that.

Although, with him up all night alongside her, sitting out here watching the sky, she wasn't sure she'd be able to think. She was just so aware of him. So…drawn to him.

If she didn't drag him into one of their tents tonight, it would only be through sheer stubborn will. But a part of her kept asking why she should bother resisting her impulse. Why not seduce him and spend the next few days enjoying him as well as the celestial show?

Her only answer to that was that it would be too hard to say goodbye to him if she did that.

And that, after a few hours acquaintance, was truly terrifying.

Dylan tried not to spend more time looking at Cat than he did his own telescope but that proved a lot more challenging than he'd have thought just twelve hours ago. They'd set their scopes up close enough to each other so they could still talk quietly as the night wore on, though they both seemed to have found a peaceful sort of silence that fit their stargazing activity. Her scent came to him easily with only a meter between them, and it filled his head with things he couldn't name.

There was a possessiveness there that defied the amount of time they'd spent together. A comfort, too. And yet a touch of… He could only call it edginess. But he couldn't quite place the reason for the edginess. He'd have been tempted to call it lust a few hours ago, because there was a significant amount of that brewing in his blood. Watching her lick sugar off her fingers earlier had nearly done him in. Funnel cakes might not have been the wisest choice. But he couldn't have refused her the treat—or anything at all really.

Which was kind of terrifying.

He adjusted his scope a little, moving it manually to follow a galactic nebula he was trying to enjoy watching. Focus and concentration were not his friends tonight, though. Well, he could focus and concentrate, but only, apparently, on Cat.

Every time she moved, sighed, murmured under her breath, his body strained toward her, all his attention on her and what she might do next. It was…

A little irritating. He hadn't spent more than two years planning for this event only to spend all his time obsessing over the little movements of a woman he'd only just met.

She fascinated him, though. Everything about her. The contrast between constant motion when she was talking and absolute stillness when she was deep in thought. The flash of her grin, the sound of her laugh, the way her dark eyes lit up when she was discussing one of the subjects she loved. The scent of her desire when she looked at him.

That last… That was the real kicker. The knowing came close to overwhelming him. Especially since his leopard saw no reason to resist her.

Yet he also caught her hesitance and confusion. She was uncomfortable about her reaction. It was there in her scent as well as the way she'd hurriedly glance away when he caught her staring at him. He'd have had a harder time not at least kissing her if it weren't for that faint flavor of confusion.

Cat didn't strike him as the kind of woman who was easily confused. But since he couldn't explain his own draw to her, the deep primalness of it, he understood how she felt.

She made a faint sound, just a longer than usual exhale, and he turned to her without thought. She was staring through her scope, a slight smile curving her delicious lips.

"See something interesting?" he asked quietly.

Around them, the campsite had darkened and quieted as the night wore on. There were still groups awake, some talking, the clink of bottles here and there. But as the night deepened, so did the silence. The couple in the motorhome next to Dylan's site had gone to sleep an hour earlier. The family opposite Cat had all disappeared into their various tents as well. The two young men across from them were still quietly drinking beers. And the older man, Tom, had set up his own scope and was silently enjoying the night sky.

The air had cooled off significantly as the night wore on, too. Dylan loved the chill in the air. Outside of helping to cool his blood, it called to his leopard, the need to stretch and run just under his skin. Not that he wanted to leave Cat's side. Even his leopard felt that pull stronger than the desire to run free. The colder air had driven her to pull on a sweatshirt, and he'd had to resist the urge to offer himself as a way for her to keep warm. She still had her hair pulled up in a messy ponytail and the stripes of purple and blue darkened her otherwise blond hair in the low light.

Everything about her profile as she stared through her scope's eyepiece just mesmerized him.

Her smile widened at his question. "I'm just looking at Saturn. Why do those rings make it so much more fascinating and beautiful than the other planets? They're just dust and ice particles."

"They reflect light and glitter if you look just right," he murmured. "They're unique, so bright and apparent. Of course they're beautiful." Saturn wasn't the only outer planet with rings, but none of the others had anything like those spectacular streams of rushing layers. He might be more of a star guy, but he had to admit, Saturn through a scope was pretty awesome.

She smiled at him, the look spearing him through the chest, before she turned back to her scope. He had to breath very slowly and flex his fists to keep from going to her, making her smile just like that again right before her kissed her…

He swallowed down a low growl and faced his telescope.

"She'll set soon," Cat said. "But it's nice being able to see her like this."

He wasn't sure why, but he hadn't expected his genius physicist to be so romantic as to anthropomorphize Saturn with a gender—and a female one at that.

A movement from across the dirt road caught Dylan's attention. He turned in time to see Tom wandering toward them.

"Thought you two might like a drink," Tom said, his voice also quiet, honoring the darkness. He held out two bottles of beer. "Don't like to drink alone," he said to Cat with a wink.

She chuckled and took the beer.

"It's one of the local brews. Nice and smooth. Good for a night of stargazing."

"Thanks," Dylan said taking the offered bottle. "You up for the night too?"

Tom stuck his free hand in his pants' pocket and glanced up at the sky, his own bottle of beer dangling from his fingers. "Likely," he said on a sigh. "Gotta love the clarity at this altitude. Not a cloud to interfere. Not even a sliver of moon until just before dawn." He sighed again and sipped his beer even though he was still staring up. "Lovely."

"Yes," Dylan said, though his gaze jumped to Cat as he said it. She was grinning at Tom, the expression soft and sweet. She looked even more like a pixie in the low light, that soft smile on her face.

"Have you seen Saturn?" she asked Tom. "I can sometimes see the planets in New York, but too many city lights for much else. I can't remember the last time I've looked at a planet through a telescope."

Tom chuckled, still looking up. "I can sometimes sneak away from the lights in Jersey, but not with so much time on my hands. Didn't get a look at Saturn yet. I'll swing the scope that way now." He tilted his beer in a little toast toward Cat. "I'm Tom, by the way," he introduced himself to her. "Tom Baxter."

"Cat Donovan. Nice to meet you, Tom. What do you do in Jersey?"

"Teach high school science. A thankless job if there ever was one," he said with a laugh.

Cat's grin kept distracting Dylan, though he tried to pay attention to the conversation. Still, every time she chuckled or smiled, his gaze went to her. Watching her throat work as she sipped her beer had a low growl rising in his own throat and he had to take a quick gulp of his own drink to swallow down the reaction.

"How about you?" Tom asked.

"Grad student at NYU. Physics."

"What's your specialty?"

"For this Ph.D., I'm working on black hole physics."

"This Ph.D., huh?" Tom whistled. "Just don't get stuck teaching at the high school level. The little devils are a menace to society and science."

Despite the words, Dylan heard the fondness in Tom's voice. He had a feeling the older man liked his students more than he wanted to admit.

"How about you?" Tom asked Dylan.

"Grad student, too. Only on my first Ph.D., though. Studying stars off the main sequence."

"Ah, to be young again," Tom said. "So many good questions to ask. But I don't have the energy for all that work anymore. I'll leave the research to the young and just read the results."

"Oh, I don't know," Dylan said. "You still seem pretty spry to me. Bet you could tackle some of the big questions if you wanted to."

Tom saluted him with his beer bottle. "I'll tell that to the Princeton grant committee. No doubt they'll hire me next week." He chuckled and nodded to them. "You two enjoy your star gazing. And that beer." He winked at Dylan before strolling back to his own site.

"Thanks again," Cat called. "He's nice," she murmured when he was out of earshot. "Funny him being from the east coast too."

"What brought you all the way to Oregon for the eclipse?" Dylan asked her, curious now that she'd brought it up.

"Probably the same thing that brought Tom here," she said, her eye against her eyepiece again. "See the eclipse as early as possible."

"Why not go to Lincoln City or somewhere on the coast?"

She shrugged without looking at him. "I worried about clouds. This hasn't happened in almost a hundred years. I'd hate to miss it after all the excitement because the sky didn't cooperate."

"That's why I didn't go that direction either."

And he'd never been so grateful for any decision he'd ever made. If he'd gone to stay with friends on the coast, fellow leopards who would have given him a room without hesitance, he'd have missed the chance to meet Cat. For some reason, even the thought of that left him hollow, like he'd have missed out on something…

Important.

He faced his own scope as he analyzed that thought. His leopard definitely considered meeting her important. Vital even. Like he'd have lost something precious if he hadn't found her.

But why?

And what happened when they parted ways after the eclipse?

6

He scented the tigers again just after three a.m., moving closer to their site than they had all evening. He'd caught their scents earlier in the night, during dinner in the concessions tent, and later after he and Cat had returned to their campsites. But the three shifters had kept their distance, never approaching Dylan or even getting close enough for him to see.

In fact, they seemed to be keeping carefully out of sight. Purposefully getting near enough and hovering upwind so he would be able to scent them but remaining behind crowds or at a distance.

He wasn't entirely surprised they weren't willing to approach him, given their species' notorious reticence to interact with other shifters, but the fact that they kept getting close… He kept expecting them to acknowledge him in some way, to set the truce for this territory. But they never got near enough for that.

He wasn't sure whether to be worried about them or not. Three tigers definitely outnumbered him. But his people weren't fighting with tigers. Cougars… Well, he'd have been on higher alert if there'd been cougar shifters nearby. His people and the cougars in this part of the country did not get along. He'd even go so far as to call them enemies, though they'd finally settled another truce with his mother a few months ago. But tigers weren't enemies, not even on the radar as shifters to avoid. So their strange approach-and-avoid behavior had him leery.

Dylan glanced down the road toward the two large blue portable toilets. Cat had excused herself a few minutes ago. He'd had to fight his leopard's offer to walk her there and back. In the human world, that would come across as creepy. But with the other shifters around, his leopard was feeling overly protective and he was uncomfortable with her being out of his sight. Especially this late at night, with most of the camp asleep, only a few late night stragglers like he and Cat still either staring at the stars or quietly drinking and talking. Tom had disappeared into his tent a couple of hours earlier, with a friendly wave to them both. The two young men opposite them had also finally headed into their camper just a few minutes ago.

Everything was quiet and sleepy in their section of the site.

Which meant having the tigers wander close felt even more…deliberate.

And without Cat sitting right next to him, Dylan was more than a little edgy. He kept his ears perked, his attention on his surroundings, listening, scenting, watching. His night vision, without all the usual city light interference, ensured he could see around the darkened camp almost as well as he could see during daylight. He'd see even better if he shifted, but he didn't think that would be a great idea, even with almost everyone around them asleep now. The tigers might take it the wrong way.

He tracked their movements as best he could through their scents, but then the wind shifted and he lost them. He mumbled a curse. His gaze went in the direction of the portable toilets again. He could clearly see them from here, would be able to see when Cat emerged, and would be able to see if anyone went into the portable bathroom next to her. So far, she was the only one there.

But now that he couldn't detect the tigers anymore, for some reason, his leopard desperately wanted to lope up the road and ensure she was safe and had an escort back to her site.

He gripped his camping chair's armrests, the soft material

collapsing in his fists. He would almost certainly scare her if he did that. He'd promised to watch her scope, implying he'd remain here until she got back. Yet his every instinct screamed to go to her and ensure she was safe.

When she finally stepped out of the plastic box, he sucked in a deep breath and eased his grip on the armrests. He didn't watch her as she returned to camp because he was a little afraid his eyes might be glowing in the dark now, his leopard had risen so close to the surface. He set his eye to his eyepiece, and saw the glow reflected back at him through the small glass. Yeah, he'd better not look at her just yet. The darkness would make that glow more apparent.

He did listen carefully as she approached, though, tracking her movements and any other movements around her. Continuing to test the air. Looking out for the other shifters who—for reasons he couldn't quite fathom—felt like a threat.

Strangely, his leopard was insisting they were a threat to Cat, not him. Which couldn't be even close to right. He was likely conflating his attraction to her and the sense of threat. Tying the two together in a way that wasn't a reflection of reality. His leopard was all instinct and reaction and really didn't *get* logic sometimes.

When Cat eased back into her chair, he let his shoulders relax. "Any problems?" he asked.

"No." She chuckled. "I hate porta-potties, but needs must, right? I am glad for my cellphone's flashlight though."

"No lights inside?"

"If there was, it broke because the box was very dark. Hopefully, they'll fix that tomorrow."

From the corner of his eye, he watched her adjust her scope to a new section of the sky. He'd intended to take the shuttle bus to the festival grounds tomorrow, after getting a few hours of sleep, so he could see what the NASA engineers had set up. He hadn't discussed tomorrow with Cat at all. They'd spent the evening either silent or talking quietly about space and science, and a few times about food— all of which had thrilled him. He loved that they could talk but also be silent together, and it felt really comfortable. When was the last time he had that with a woman? Maybe never. At least with anyone outside his family. And most of his family had no interest in astronomy. He wasn't sure *why* he was so comfortable around Cat, but he wasn't inclined to argue with the feeling. At least not tonight.

And maybe not tomorrow either.

"I was going to head up to the festival grounds tomorrow after getting some sleep," he said quietly, keeping his gaze on his scope even though his attention was entirely on her. "Want to join me?"

She adjusted in her seat, also kept her gaze on her scope. "Yeah. That would be great."

He smiled, and his leopard purred in satisfaction.

One of these days, before the weekend was out, he'd have to really consider why his leopard was so attached to Cat. But in the meantime, he intended to enjoy his time with her, whatever time she'd give him.

He caught her yawn in his peripheral vision and finally turned to face her. His animal side had settled and he knew his eyes no longer glowed. Having her accept his invitation for an outing tomorrow had helped immensely.

"You should get some sleep," he said. "You had a longer travel day getting here."

"Two days," she said with a shrug, but she did face him. "I stayed in Portland one night before driving up today… Oh, yesterday now, huh?" She grinned but her eyes drooped a little, and she yawned again. With a chuckle, she said, "Yeah, maybe I should get some sleep. This was so much fun, I hate for it to end."

He did, too. "We'll have tomorrow night and Sunday for more star watching."

He didn't add he hoped they'd spend those nights doing more than just star watching, but his gaze dropped to her mouth without his permission and his thoughts turned to things that had nothing to do with stars. At least not the ones in space.

Her lips curved in a soft smile and when he met her gaze again, there was something in her dark eyes, a flavor in her scent that started his heart beating harder. Maybe he wasn't the only one thinking about other ways they could spend the next couple of nights.

She pulled in a sudden deep breath and broke eye contact, turning to her scope. She stood abruptly and pulled the scope off her tripod. "Thanks for a nice night," she said, her voice still quiet. "It was…" She met his gaze. "I liked having company for this. Made it…better."

He nodded. He felt the same.

She hurriedly put her scope and tripod into the trunk of her rental car. Then turned back to him. He wondered what she was thinking. There was a lot in her scent, but the breeze was moving in the wrong direction and he wasn't getting enough to read her clearly. Her hands fluttered a bit at her sides, as if she wanted to say something—her hands were almost always involved when she talked—but after a moment of this, she gave her head a little shake and said, "Goodnight."

"Goodnight."

She practically threw herself into her tent and zipped up the flaps with a snap.

He listened to her settle, waited another fifteen minutes to ensure she was okay, before he finally disassembled his own scope and locked everything up in his truck. He paused outside his own tent, watching hers for another few moments. She was silent now. Probably asleep already. He hesitated to go inside, though, for reasons he couldn't quite pinpoint. He wanted to…

He wanted to keep watch over her and ensure she stayed safe. To protect her from… What? He had no idea.

Giving himself a shake, he ducked into his tent. He was acting really weird. Maybe spending more time with her wasn't the wisest idea. It would only make his strange possessiveness and protectiveness worse.

Still, as he settled onto his sleeping bag, he knew he wouldn't back out. He wanted to spent time with her. And if that triggered a little more of his leopard's protective instincts, well, he'd deal with that. They only had a few days together. He didn't want to miss out on a moment of it.

Even if he was running headlong into a disaster.

7

The fairgrounds were filled with people by the time Cat and Dylan arrived. She had tried to sleep in but by ten am, she was wide awake, the noise outside her tent keeping her from settling back to sleep. Not that she'd slept well in those few hours. She'd spent entirely too much time thinking about Dylan, and how close he was just a few meters away in his tent. How, in the dark, it would be easy to ignore the fact that they'd just met and go crawl into that tent with him.

She'd finally fallen asleep but her dreams had been restless and she woke with gritty eyes and a resigned sigh. Seeing Dylan as he emerged from his tent, looking all gorgeous and ruffled from sleep had gone a long way toward improving her mood.

The shuttle dropped them off at the entrance of the fairgrounds, and it took them a few minutes to navigate the crowds, but now they were inside. They'd already gone to the map of the world, where people were putting pins in to show where they were from—Tom Baxter had suggested it before they left. She was a little surprised how many pins were from the east coast and even more surprised by the number of pins from other countries.

After that, they'd made their way—without having to discuss it—to the pavilion where one of the NASA engineers was in the middle of a talk. While most of what he discussed was geared toward amateur stargazers, it was still fun and interesting. Almost interesting enough to distract her from the man sitting next to her, close enough for her to occasionally brush up against him.

Every brief contact sent a shiver through her, a need to lean in closer and draw out that contact. She'd never realized how tantalizing just bumping into a man's arm could be. But since Dylan had excellent arms, and she was afraid she might be a little obsessed with his forearms, she couldn't really be blamed for her reactions.

They got food from one of the many vendors set up around the grounds—she got tacos, he got chicken and French fries—and instead of taking up a space at the crowded tables under the dining tent, they found a shady spot under a tree off to one side of the grounds. They weren't the only ones picnicking in the area, either. The place was active and full of a buzzy kind of excitement that made Cat grin.

"This is fun," she said. "Thanks for inviting me. More fun with company." She stared down at her tacos so he wouldn't catch her expression. For some reason, her cheeks felt very warm. She probably needed a drink.

"Thanks for coming with me," he said, his voice quiet and otherwise unreadable.

Oh, she wanted to search his expression, to see if she could gauge what he was thinking. She was fascinated by the way his face sometimes revealed his thoughts, especially when he was discussing something he loved, how open and enthusiastic he could be. And then there were other times when he seemed guarded, and she couldn't read him at all.

And then there were those moments when she caught the heat in his gaze, when she thought if she leaned in and kissed him, he wouldn't object. Those moments left her a little breathless.

She was afraid he could read her too easily, though. Afraid of what she was giving away in her own expression. Because she wasn't just physically attracted to him. She *liked* him. A lot. She enjoyed spending time with him, even when they were silent. He didn't *feel* like a stranger anymore. To be fair, they had talked a lot in the last twenty-four hours. She'd learned a lot about him and his life, so she felt like she did know him. At least a little. Enough to know she wanted to know more.

Which was a little terrifying because by Monday afternoon, all this would be over.

She was just glad he couldn't read her scent the way the tiger shifters could. She had no idea how Amy dealt with that, knowing her husband could gauge her mood and practically read her thoughts just through her scent. If Dylan could have read her scent just then, he'd realize just how much she wanted him, how much even his little gestures drew her attention, how much more she was starting to feel. Given how much her expression likely gave away, she couldn't imagine how revealing her scent probably was. That would be embarrassing.

She gobbled up two of her three tacos before she realized it and made an effort to taste and enjoy the third. Too busy thinking, she acknowledge with an inner groan. Too busy lusting after Dylan.

Too busy worrying about wanting more than lust.

She shook herself out of her revere when she sensed him tensing beside her. She glanced at him. His head was up, his gaze narrowed. He was frowning at something but he didn't seem to be looking at anything. She tried to follow the direction of his gaze, but there wasn't anything but a crowded line to one of the food trucks there.

"You okay?" she asked. "Something wrong?"

For another long moment, he held perfectly still, his gaze on the crowd, his body tense and coiled, almost like he was ready to leap up. Then he gave himself a shake and looked at her.

She frowned a little. Wow. In the shaded sunlight, his blue eyes had a funny glow to them so they looked almost green…like there was a bit of yellow in the blue. Had to be a weird reflection of the light. But for just a split second, that glow reminded her of the tiger shifters. Which had to be her imagination.

"Sorry," he said, but his smile seemed a little forced. "Thought I saw someone I know."

"But you don't like very much," she guessed.

"Why do you say that?"

"You got all tense and…I don't know, serious." That sounded silly. And also kind of revealed how closely she'd been watching him. Oops.

Fortunately, he didn't comment on that. "It's nothing," he said.

He did stare off into the crowd again for a moment, then turned his attention back to her and changed the subject. There was another NASA talk during the afternoon they wanted to go to. And she'd seen a few craft vendors she wanted to explore to see if she could find a present for Amy.

In the middle of discussing their afternoon plans, though, she yawned. A big, loud yawn.

"Unless you're too tired," he said. "We did stay up most of the night. You want to go back?"

"No," she said, sitting up straighter. "I want to stay. I'm having fun." She grinned. "The food left me a little sleepy, that's all. I'll be fine once we start walking around again."

"You want to take one of the hot air balloons up?" he asked suddenly.

She glanced in the direction of the two balloons at the far end of the fairground. There were two at their own site as well, but she hadn't considered actually getting in one. "I've never been in one before," she said. But the physics of them was pretty cool. "That could be fun." She grinned back at him.

He reached out a hand and helped her to her feet, with an ease that drew her attention to his forearms again. She tried not to stare at the flexing muscles, she really did. But he had such nice forearms. Solid and hard and dusted with dark hair. His t-shirt clung to him, ensuring there was no barrier to her admiring his chest and shoulders either. She had to swallow a little moan when she reached her feet standing close enough to pull in a deep breath of him. He smelled wonderful, like nature and musk and male. How the hell could he smell that good in this heat?

And the feel of his hand engulfing hers was a shock of deliciousness. Those slightly roughened fingertips scrapping over her skin. His thumb brushed softly over her inner wrist, and she sucked in a sharp breath, a shiver racing along her spine. She was sure he hadn't done that on purpose. But the brief caress sent a surge of warmth and melting need right to her core. All he'd done was help her get up from the ground. But it felt like he'd caressed her in places that would be inappropriate in public.

Her heart hammering, she looked up at him. His gaze was intent, and focused on her mouth. His thumb brushed her inner wrist again. She couldn't hide her reaction, the small gasp, the way she leaned in a little closer to him.

There were people everywhere, they were in the middle of a crowd full of families and scientists and tourists and locals. They weren't alone. And this moment felt like it belonged in private, somewhere she could feel free to rise onto her toes and press her mouth to his…

She gave herself a little shake and leaned back from him, forcing a light smile that didn't match her rapidly beating pulse or the way she was breathing a little too fast. "Thanks." She released her hold on his hand reluctantly, shivering when his fingers scraped over her skin again as he let go. She gathered up her trash and worked hard not to let her mind roam through fantasies of what other parts of her she'd like his fingers to scrape across.

Her cheeks felt hot as she faced him again. She kind of hoped he wrote that off to the day's heat, and once again she was glad he wasn't like her brother-in-law. She had no doubt Dylan could tell she was attracted to him. But it would be so much worse if he could scent it. At least this way, she could pretend she hadn't nearly melted from just the brush of his thumb over her wrist.

"You ready?" she asked. Was that her voice? She sounded a little breathless.

He murmured a yes, but his gaze hadn't left her face and she could feel herself coiling inside with need, with that tight draw of desire she really didn't want to resist.

She hurried off to the trash bins before she got caught in his gaze again. The intensity of whatever was happening between them took her breath away. She couldn't explain it, but if they hadn't been in the middle of a crowd just then, she wasn't sure she'd have been able to resist it. She didn't actually *want* to resist him.

And that would be fine if she didn't also *like* him so much. Because this would end. They'd return to opposite sides of the continent on Monday. She'd probably never see him again.

She dropped her trash in the mesh-metal can, frowning a little. Why the hell did the idea of never seeing him again…hurt?

8

Dylan flexed his fingers into fists to keep from reaching for her again. He could pretend the gestures were casual—his hand on her back to guide her through the crowd, a brush against her arm to get her attention to tell her something, his fingers on her elbow to help her over a stack of wires covered by a plastic guard to prevent tripping.

But there was nothing casual in any of that. Every touch just made him want more.

He'd suggested the hot air balloon ride as a distraction, because he'd been thinking too much about the fact that the tiger shifters were here, worrying about them and trying to explain away their continued presence, the way they kept coming to his attention but never getting close enough for him to see. He knew it had to be a coincidence. Of course they'd come to the fairgrounds. Everyone from their campsite seemed to be here today, enjoying the weather and the various exhibits. There was nothing nefarious in their presence.

But every time he sensed them close, picked up their scents on the breeze, his instincts went on high alert.

The way they hid from him, the way they always seemed to be where he was, yet never revealed themselves… Every time it happened he had a harder time writing it off as coincidence. If they'd shown themselves, acknowledged him and then moved on, he'd be less suspicious.

A part of him thought if he could get the higher ground in the balloon, he might even finally catch sight of the trio. And he'd been thinking about that when he'd reached out to give Cat a hand to her feet.

Then his world had exploded into sensation and need and desire so consuming he'd forgotten to breathe for just a moment. All fed by her reaction to his touch. Her gasp when his thumb brushed her wrist had felt like a triumph. When she'd leaned into him, all he could think about was leaning down, tasting her lips. The flavor of her rising desire in her scent so delicious he wanted to lap it up with a spoon. He wanted to lap her up, tasting her everywhere, hunting for that flavor.

Letting her hand slip through his had taken an act of will. He craved another touch, more contact. More her. And getting her somewhere private seemed more important that getting high ground to hunt for the other shifters.

Later, he promised himself. They still had plenty of time, likely another long night of stargazing ahead. He just wanted to make sure the tigers weren't an issue. Then he could concentrate fully on Cat—a focus he relished.

The line for the hot air balloons wasn't as long as he'd have expected, their timing must have been good since everywhere else had long lines. By the time they reached the boarding platform, Dylan was edgier than he'd been over lunch. He caught the scent of the tigers again, but still they kept out of sight. If they weren't going to acknowledge him, why did they keep coming in so close?

He kept trying to convince his animal instincts it was all just coincidence. They were here at the event, enjoying the festival. Neither the campgrounds nor the fairgrounds were large enough for them to avoid each other completely. Of course he'd catch their scents occasionally.

But... His animal side kept reminding him that if it was all just coincidence, the tigers wouldn't be working so hard to avoid being spotted.

And it did seem like they were working at it.

As the person taking money and shuffling people into the basket of the balloon smiled at them, Dylan realized he wasn't the only edgy one. Cat stared up at the huge rainbow-colored bulb of nylon overhead, her foot tapping a rapid rhythm. She studied the central propane burner, mostly banked now, the sturdy wicker basket, the space inside the basket, the thick ropes holding everything down, the various flaps and the vent at the top of the balloon. Her mouth pursed as her gaze moved over everything, even the pilot.

"You okay with this still?" he asked.

She blinked. "Hmm? Oh, yes. I'm good. I'm just…fascinated. I've never been this close to a hot air balloon. Feels a lot bigger up close. Which is good. Need the square footage to get us off the ground, right? Just, they seem so…airy when up in the air." She made a face, her cheeks flushing pink. "Told you I wasn't good with words."

He chuckled. "It'll be fine."

"I know. I'm not worried about the flight. Amy would hate this, though."

They stepped through the open door into the baskets, finding a spot against the railing near some of the ropes anchoring the balloon and a small stack of sandbag ballast. "Your sister's been up in one of these before?"

"Not that I know of. But she hates Ferris Wheels and being able to see between her feet when she's up high. Seeing straight down like this would terrify her."

"How about you?" The small confines of the basket meant he had to stand very close to her. At least, that was his excuse for leaning in enough to almost touch her while still avoiding the contact that would make him forget himself. "This going to scare you?"

She grinned. "I love Ferris Wheels. And I love being able to see between my feet from a height. Feels like space, with no real up or down."

"Except, gravity here," he reminded her.

"I can pretend."

A few more people filled in the basket, the door closed, and the fire overhead whooshed to life. Ropes dropped, and the basket gave a little wobbling jerk as it moved off the platform, rising and drifting to one side at the same time. Dylan's stomach dropped as the basket lifted. Cat gasped, her grin growing as she looked over the side, watching the ground slowly recede.

Seeing her hang over the basket without fear had a funny duel effect on Dylan. He loved her joy and amusement, happy this adventure brought her pleasure. He couldn't help wondering if the sense of adventure carried into all parts of her life, and that lead him to thoughts of exploring her adventurous spirit in bed.

But he also very much wanted to wrap an arm around her waist so she didn't accidently tip out of the basket. His leopard wasn't so sure about this being in the air with only a thin layer of wicker between him and the ground—though it hadn't occurred to Dylan he might be bothered. He liked Ferris Wheels, too. His leopard, apparently, had different ideas and his animal instincts rose fast to start his heartbeat pounding. He had to flex his hands into fists to keep from reaching for Cat and pulling her away from the basket's edge, especially when she leaned farther out without fear, staring straight down.

He forced himself to look away so he didn't do something embarrassing, like jerk her against his side. He'd suggested the idea. His reaction to seeing her hanging off the balloon—that duel combination of amusement and terror—surprised the hell out of him. Enough that it took him several minutes of staring out over the landscape before he really *saw* their surroundings.

The fairgrounds stretched out below them in a patchwork of roads, farmland, and the buildings and tents inside the grounds. A second balloon had just landed on its own platform below, people who looked tiny from this height disembarking. The sky was bright, the day warm, giving them a spectacular view of their surroundings. When he stopped worrying, he realized just how fun this all was.

He grabbed the railing and faced outward, taking it all in while keeping Cat in his peripheral vision. To his leopard's relief, she pulled back from her position hanging over the rail, to look up at the balloon, and the burner heating the air. A little flap near the top of the balloon opened and closed a few times, releasing the hot air and giving the pilot control of their altitude.

Cat's eyes were wide, the wonder on her face captivating. She seemed to be studying everything, watching the pilot's actions, then jumping her gaze to the balloon to see the results. Her fascination with the process of it all made him grin.

"Enjoying yourself?" he asked.

"This is so cool," she muttered without looking at him. "Or I should say warm. So the flap opens, cool air, hot air, adjusted..." She continued to murmur under breath, dissecting the process, her full attention on that while the other passengers in the basket were busy oohing and aahing over the scenery.

For long moments, Dylan just watched Cat, as fascinated by her as she was by the balloon's mechanics. He had to shake himself when he remembered he'd had an ulterior motive for this ride. Forcing his gaze back to the fairgrounds, he hunted the crowds. While he was no eagle, his still had excellent vision, and even at this distance, he could pick out individuals from the mass of humanity shuffling around the site below. He obviously couldn't scent the tigers from up here—all he smelled at the moment were propane, fire, and if he leaned close enough, Cat—but he hoped something would stand out, some indication of who these other shifters were.

He looked for trios of people, especially trios of men. He was sure, based on their scents, that all three shifters were men, so that seemed the easiest way to spot them without being able to verify their scent signatures. Unfortunately, there were several groups of men in the crowds, a few in twos and threes. One group, with one particularly tall individual, caught his attention. They seemed to walk through the crowd without actually looking at the booths they passed. One of them hunted the surrounding people, but the other two just stared ahead, cutting a direct path toward the parking lot.

Dylan narrowed his gaze a little as his leopard growled in his head. Were those the tigers? If so, they seemed to be on their way out of the fairgrounds, which was a relief.

Something about the way they moved...as if they had no interest in what was going on around them. That struck him as odd. Why come to the festival if you weren't interested in enjoying the sights?

But then, he could just be imagining things. Hunting for telltale signs of danger where there were none. Picking out three men in the crowd who might well just be humans who'd seen everything already and were heading out.

Still, he watched the men closely. His every instinct honed in on them even when he knew he should keep searching the crowds for other possibilities.

Something about the way they moved…

He turned as the balloon turned to keep the men in sight and didn't stop staring at them until they reached an SUV in the parking area. He might have continued to watch them until they'd driven away but Cat's light touch on his arm startled him back into his surroundings.

"Hey, you okay?" she asked, staring up at him, her eyes narrowed in concern.

"Sure. Yeah. Why?"

"You just…growled."

"I did?" He had? Hell, he hadn't even noticed. He shrugged and tried to brush off the moment with a smile. "Guess I'm not as comfortable up here as I thought I'd be."

She studied him as closely as she'd been studying the mechanics of the balloon, and Dylan had to fight not to look away from her penetrating gaze. He had a feeling she saw more of him than he was entirely comfortable revealing.

Yet.

He blinked. Yet? That thought surprised him as much as the fact he'd let out an audible growl on accident. Did he want Cat to know so much about him? See him in ways other people didn't? Because his leopard side seemed to be welcoming that idea even as his human half balked.

What the hell was happening to him?

9

C at let Dylan's explanation go but she kept flicking glances at him from the corner of her eye as she pretended to stare out over the landscape below. She'd been having a great time studying the inner workings of the balloon. She kept calculating various parts of the process—balloon area to mass ratios, air flow, temperature, propane adjustments. She'd even asked the pilot a few questions, which he'd been happy to answer.

It had taken her half the ride to realize Dylan seemed… She wasn't sure. Kind of like he wasn't there, but also hyper focused. He'd been watching the ground, or maybe someone on the ground, with so much intensity she'd swear his jaw was going to crack under the strain.

And then the growl.

The sound was quiet enough she was pretty sure no one else in the basket had heard. They might have been pressed against the sides of the basket in terror if they had. It had been a very low, deep, menacing growl. The kind that made the hairs on your neck stand up. Not in a good way either. Not the kind of growl she'd been fantasizing about pulling out of him in bed. No, this was a dangerous sound. A sound of warming.

An animal sound.

And it reminded her so very much of the tiger shifters she had to work not to scurry to the opposite end of the basket herself.

But he wasn't a tiger shifter. She'd know if he was. Well, not the way her sister could tell when a tiger shifter was around. But still, she was sure she'd know. None of them had had any qualms about revealing who they were to her before this. They all just came right out and demanded her time because of who they were.

She'd been living under the assumption that all of them would do that, announce themselves and their intentions. She'd assumed they *had* to.

But… Did they? Was that one of the rules? Or had the tigers she'd been dealing with just been exceptionally arrogant? Because it occurred to her as she watched Dylan from the corner of her eye that one of them deciding to take a more subtle route, coming to her on more human terms and doing all the normal things humans did when they were attracted to each other—flirting, dating, talking, getting to know each other—that a tiger smart enough to take that approach might just breach her defenses.

And Dylan was a very smart man.

Her heartbeat thumped harder as she considered the possibility. She couldn't ignore it. She couldn't afford to. There was too much at stake. She had purposefully avoided getting romantically involved with a tiger shifter—not that any had succeeded in endearing themselves to her anyway; too many demanded her attention, none of them tried to win her in a more palatable way. She loved Ethan, and Amy was happy with her choice of husbands, but there was too damned much baggage associated with having a tiger shifter partner. Too much emphasis on reproduction. She just didn't want any of that. She wanted to stay as far away from it as possible because she wanted to live her life on *her* terms.

If Dylan wasn't just another grad student, an ordinary human here to enjoy the eclipse, she needed to know. Because she was falling hard for him, quickly. Too quickly really. And that had been scary enough. If he was part of the shifter world… That changed everything. Comfort or no, lust or no, she couldn't allow herself to be seduced into that world. She had plans. And they didn't include turning her life upside down for the tigers.

A sneaky and irritating part of her mind reminded her that she hadn't settled on her future plans yet. That she'd been waffling and considering another stint in grad school until she could decide.

That she had a job offer in California very close to where Dylan currently lived.

She shook her head. No. She wouldn't think that way. Not now. She had to know first if he was just an ordinary man, or if he was tied to the tigers. She could be imagining all this because she was so hyper conscious of the shifters. She could be making up excuses to dismiss her feelings for Dylan and run away.

She could be right to worry and need to get out, now, before she got any deeper in.

The balloon caught a stronger breeze and lurched gently to one side, enough of a jolt to pull her back to the present. She grabbed the rail and looked down. Hey, they were returning to the platform already. She hadn't realized so much time had passed.

"Shame it's over already," Dylan said, smiling down at her.

Her thighs actually clenched at that smile. Heat spread into her veins, bubbling with desire. Damn but he was handsome. If she had to walk away from him because he was a tiger shifter, she was going to be so pissed.

The balloon set down on the platform with a few gentle bumps and was immediate surrounded by people getting it anchored back to the ground. The pilot banked the flame and thanked everyone as they stepped back out of the basket. Cat took an extra moment to thank him for answering her questions. Then she and Dylan moved back onto solid ground.

She laughed a little when her knees wobbled. "That was fun. Thanks for suggesting it. Almost as good as a Ferris Wheel."

His answering grin left her breathless. And had the unfortunate side effect of drawing her attention to his mouth. His extremely kissable mouth.

No. She had to get a few answers before she indulged in those sexy fantasies again. She couldn't afford to take chances. She was likely imagining things, making excuses. He probably had nothing to do with the shifter world. And if she brought up shapeshifters directly, he'd probably think she was one of those scientists whose mental health had cracked and they now had only one foot in reality. She had to be more subtle.

But how did one find out if the person they were lusting after was actually a tiger shifter if said source of lust was pretending to be human? Amy hadn't had a clue until Ethan had outright told her. Neither she nor Amy had had any idea such things existed to even ask the questions. If Dylan was a normal human, he wouldn't have any idea either, and so if she didn't handle this right, she risked driving him away.

Which, given how much she wanted him, how much she didn't want to let him go already, might actually be for the best.

She pushed that thought aside. First things first. Find out if he was a tiger shifter.

Then she could worry about her feelings for him.

They wove through the crowds, heading back toward the pavilion for the next NASA talk without having to discuss where they were going next. That kind of synchronous thinking confirmed Cat was in trouble, one way or the other.

She gave herself a little internal shake. They'd discussed going to the talk earlier. She needed to stop making more of this attraction than was there. Especially since there was still a lot she didn't know about him. As they took seats near the back of the pavilion to await the start of the talk, she considered options for uncovering if he was a shifter or not, but no actual clever conversational tricks arose. Which wasn't surprising since clever conversational tricks were not her forte.

But when getting to know someone, she could ask about things like family, right? That might help. Maybe there'd be some hints in his family history.

"You have siblings?" she asked. She had to hide a slight frown. It was an out of nowhere question, not really related to anything prior, and felt as awkward as she did in that moment. But it was personal conversation. It might not help with the shifter issue, but she had to try.

He smiled, not showing any signs of being confused by the non sequitur. "I have a lot of siblings. My parents didn't know when to call it quits."

Her eyes widened. "How many is a lot?"

"I have six sisters, including a twin, and eight brothers." He held her gaze, and his lips twitched.

She imagined her expression was the thing amusing him. "You have fourteen siblings? Fourteen. As in…fourteen?"

"Yes, math genius. Fourteen."

"And a twin?"

"Julia. She doesn't love astronomy the way I do."

"Fair enough," she murmured. Fourteen siblings. Who had fourteen kids these days? That was the kind of thing her grandparents did. And even then…fourteen? How could his parents afford that? "Are you… Where do you fall in the birth order?"

"Youngest." He chuckled and shrugged. "But in a family that size, it's good to be the baby."

"Sure." She'd been the family baby too, the youngest. But there was her and Amy. Her parents hadn't felt the need for… "Fourteen kids. Wow. That's…"

"A lot? Yeah, it is. Believe it or not, we all get along, too. Most of the time. No one has officially been disowned anyway. At least not in the last few years." He laughed so she assumed this was a family joke.

"Not to be too personal but how do your parents afford so many kids? If I didn't get scholarships and things, I'd be up to my eyeballs in student loans by now. Did some of your siblings not go to college?" She knew not everyone went to college. She wasn't that naïve about everyone else's desire for a higher degree and academic pursuits. But if even a few of that many kids went to college, that could cost a fortune. And that was outside the usual costs of just raising so many kids.

She gave herself a little mental shake. Dylan was a grown man in graduate school, and if he was the youngest, that meant his siblings were all grown too. One way or the other, his parents had managed it.

"My mom…had some money when she moved to this country."

"Where's she from?"

"Guyana. She worked her way up through Central America and then did quite well here when she settled in the US. My dad had accumulated a few resources too by the time they met. They managed. Plus, the family business does well enough for us."

"Family business?"

"The Joneses run animal rescue shelters around the country. We specialize in exotics."

"Really? Your family's business is rescuing animals?" At his nod, she blinked a few times. "That's really cool! Amy and I have a dog… or, well, she lives with Amy right now. Her name's Spike. She's a poodle."

He grinned. "Spike, huh? Sounds vicious."

"She's a badass alright." His grin was infectious. "Do you like animals?" Just because it was his family's business, didn't mean he was an animal lover.

"Love them. I'm particular fond of dogs." His mouth twitched and his blue eyes sparkled. There was more to that look than she could interpret.

"Then why didn't you go to work in your family's business?" She realized the moment she asked that the answer was obvious. Because he'd loved astronomy more.

But he surprised her when he said, "I did for a few years. We all work in the business in one way or another, even if it's not our primary job. Lot of fundraisers and stuff."

"How did you fit all that in?"

He shrugged. "Just managed. Took a little longer to get my degrees, but the extra money helped pay for everything. Kept me out of debt."

"Useful." A lot of the grad students she knew hadn't been so lucky. "Amy worked even after going back to finish her degree, too. She didn't want debt either and someone had to pay the rent. She insisted I not work while in college."

"How come?"

She rolled her eyes and glanced toward the front of the pavilion where a man in a NASA t-shirt and shorts was coming up to the small stage. "I'm…not great at focusing on a lot of things at once. I mean. Sometimes I'm not great at focusing period. But when I am focused, I don't do very well with distractions. My multi-tasking skills are what my sister would politely call weak."

He laughed. The sound brought her gaze back to him. He looked so damned gorgeous when he laughed. How was that possible? She'd never really noticed that with other men before. Even hot guys. Was it just him? Or was it her fascination with him that made watching him laugh the sexiest thing she'd ever seen?

"Focus is good," he said, lowering his voice as the speaker at the front of the room got started.

His gaze dropped briefly to her mouth, and when he met her gaze again, his expression had gone from amused to intent. Her stomach did a flip dance and her pulse started pounding harder. And just like that, she went from wanting to make him laugh again, to wanting to strip him naked and crawl onto his lap. He'd done that to her with a glance.

What would he do to her if they were naked?

The idea was enough to warm her cheeks, her body flashing hot as the possibilities rose to entice her, fantasies that had nothing to do with where they were and what they were doing. Thoughts entirely inappropriate to the talk that had started. For a few long moments, she wasn't even sure what the NASA guy was saying.

She just wanted to get Dylan alone.

Her earlier worry seemed silly now. She was seeing tiger shifters were there weren't any. He was an ordinary man. Well, maybe not ordinary. No one that gorgeous and sexy and smart could be called *ordinary*. But he was a human, like her, and there was no reason to be suspicious of him. The tigers had made her paranoid. She was determined that they wouldn't drive her life, but they had been, whether she liked it or not. And if she wasn't careful, she'd push Dylan away for no good reason.

She dragged her gaze from his, turning her attention to the talk, because if she didn't, she was going to lean in and kiss him. And she had a feeling that would be very dangerous in such a public space. Although, kissing him in private would be very dangerous, too.

She felt him watching her for a beat longer before he faced the speaker as well, and his attention left a tingling of awareness in its wake, like a physical caress across her cheek.

The talk was probably interesting. She was sure at any other point in time, she'd have found it fun. But in that moment, multitasking wasn't an option.

Her entire focus was on Dylan.

By the time they got back to camp, Dylan noticed Cat's occasional yawns had increased from more-than-occasional to she-was-likely-to-break-her-jaw-if-she-didn't-get-some-sleep.

"You want to do more stargazing tonight, you need to sleep," he warned.

"What about you? You don't seem tired."

"I am," he lied. Well, not entirely a lie. He was a little tired. But he could stay up for days if needs be and be fine. He needed less sleep to manage and function than the average human did.

While Cat might not be average, she was definitely human. She needed sleep.

And he needed a little time away from her—even though his leopard rebelled at the very thought. His leopard wanted to curl up next to her while she slept so he could guard her and just be near her. Dylan needed to examine that instinct, because it wasn't anything he'd felt for anyone before. He had to get some space and privacy so he could think through what was happening, study and analyze the "why"s of his leopard's reaction to Cat. But he couldn't do that while they were together. His brain short circuited while they were together, and all he wanted to do was drag her into her tent for activities that would only later lead to sleep.

"But I'm also a little restless," he finished. "All the excitement. I'm going for a run and then I'll nap too."

"Fair enough." She shrugged and covered up yet another yawn.

He chuckled. "You're going to hurt yourself doing that if you're not careful. Go sleep."

There were plenty of people around the camp, the late afternoon buzzing with activity, but the quiet kind that happened at this time of day when people were a little tired, the air was a little hotter, and everyone was settling in before dinner. Tom was sitting outside his tent with a drink in one hand and an astronomy magazine in the other. He'd greeted them when they'd arrived back and they'd talked for a few minutes about the festival, but even he'd noticed Cat's exhaustion.

For reasons Dylan couldn't precisely pinpoint, he felt safer leaving Cat while the older man was at his site. He wasn't sure why. He liked Tom well enough and got a good feeling from his scent and presence, but he was also still mostly a stranger. Still, it was another instinctive response that Dylan could analyze when he was alone.

"Enjoy your run," Cat said. "Don't let me sleep through dinner."

"Never," he said, very seriously. They were both very serious about their food.

She grinned, hesitating a moment longer. Without meaning to, Dylan's gaze drop to her mouth again, to the curve of her lush lips. His more noble instincts wavered. He had to stuff his hands into his pockets to keep from brushing his fingers along her cheek, just to see how soft her skin was. If he did that, he'd just want to touch her more. Kiss her. And if he kissed her, he'd be lost, no hope of logical thought after that.

"Sleep well," he said, telling himself he had to step back. He didn't move. He couldn't seem to drag himself away.

Fortunately for them both, she was a lot stronger than him. Or maybe just more sleepy. She gave him a little nod and ducked into her tent, zipping the flap closed.

He hesitated another few moments as he listened for her to settle, his gaze traveling the surroundings as he scented the air. No threats that he could pick up.

No tiger shifters either. At least not downwind where he might catch their scents.

When the shuffling movements inside her tent finally stopped and Dylan was comfortable she was safe, he ducked into his own tent to change into running shorts and shoes. He'd have preferred a four-legged run. He needed to stretch more than a human run would allow. But in the middle of the day, this would have to do.

He took to the fields next to the campsite, with the dual purpose of also scouting out a good place to set up for the eclipse.

Running over the uneven ground kept his attention focused on what he was doing, helped him push his body and shut off his mind for a bit. He had to carefully balance speed against his need to appear human on the run, which also kept him focused and concentrated. When he finally stopped a few miles from the campsite to look around, his body felt the kind of contentment that came with a short burst of physical release. Sweat dripped down his cheeks and back, cooled in a soft breeze. And while he wasn't breathing very hard because he'd had to stick to human speeds, his lungs still felt pushed and full. It wasn't the same as a flat out, long run in his leopard form, but it helped.

The fields he'd ended up in were too far away for what he wanted for the eclipse, but he had a new perspective from out here. A new view of his surroundings that opened up the area for him. The afternoon heat shimmered in the air over the dry grasses. He'd kept to fallow fields so he didn't disturb crops, but the scent of nearby alfalfa hay and wheat fields, the freshness of growing things against the dry grass and heated air settled some of his inner turmoil. In the distance, he could just see the white tent of the concessions area at the campsite. Behind him the majestic grandeur of a still snow-capped Mount Jefferson. The wide open space closer to the site would make for great eclipse viewing even if the area filled with people.

He let his arms hang at his sides as he scanned the landscape, his brain slowly starting to work again. Work in a way it hadn't seemed to do for the last twenty-four hours. This far from Cat, he could finally think.

Sort of.

Because his leopard kept insisting he hurry back to her. Like being away was actually physically difficult. The strain of it surprised him. He hadn't known her very long, and yes, he liked spending as much time with her as possible because they only had a few days before they ended up on opposite sides of the country again. That didn't explain the difficulty he felt just standing here, though. The way his animal side kept pacing and growling in his head like something was wrong. Like he needed to be next to her. Now. Or else.

But there was no real reason for the "or else" in those thoughts. She was safe and surrounded by other humans. If needs be, he could reach her in five minutes—if he were willing to race back at shifter speeds and chance being caught. And he hadn't sensed the tigers anywhere near their sites. He'd even run at the edge of the campsite scenting for them before taking to the fields. Whoever they were, they weren't in the camp when he left. So why such an insistent need to return to her side? Why did he feel like his animal was ready to burst out the longer he stood out here and kept his distance from her?

If he didn't know better…

No. She was definitely human. She wasn't a leopard. And while this might have happened to his oldest brother, there was no way it happened again, to him. The coincidence would be too weird, the probability too low. He knew low probability things happened. And because it had happened to Deacon, of course it was possible. But it was so unlikely, so rare. In the history of leopard shifters, the number of times this had happened could be counted on two hands.

He shook himself, an all over body shake, as if he could release the thought with the physical act. The chances, the coincidences, were just so unbelievable. His logical half couldn't buy it. No, there had to be another explanation. Another reason he felt antsy the longer he stood here. Another explanation for the way his pulse had started to pound and his adrenaline rose because he *wasn't* running back toward the camp. He lifted his head and breathed in the air, taking a measure of his surroundings. There wasn't any danger nearby to explain the adrenaline. But sometimes his other senses picked up things even when his nose didn't. Maybe the tigers were near and that's why he was starting to feel his leopard rise too close to the surface, why he almost couldn't resist the call to reach Cat in the next few minutes.

Because it just couldn't be… He couldn't have found…

No. Leopard shifters only mated with other leopard shifters. At least most of the time. He absolutely had not found his mate in a human woman. He would have known, in her scent, he would have realized.

Wouldn't he?

He faced the camp, almost without thought turning in the direction of his and Cat's sites. His leopard rose closer, and that part of him that was all instinct and action growled, *Mine*.

Dylan shivered, no longer a conscious act. This time with just a touch of…not exactly fear but a close cousin of the emotion. Because if his leopard wasn't just fucking with him, if his instincts were right…

He was in big, big trouble.

11

Dylan had very nearly talked himself out of the idea by the time
he reached the camp again. Ignoring the fact that the closer he
got, the more relaxed his leopard got, he logiced himself out of the idea
of Cat Donovan being his mate despite being human. It was a silly
idea. A nonsensical one. He liked her. And he wanted her ferociously.
He hadn't wanted a woman this badly in ages.

But that didn't make her his mate. It was just attraction. Plan and
simple. That was possible and logical. She was beautiful and smart and
fun and sexy. Of course he was attracted to her. Of course he wanted to
spend time with her while he could. Of course he wouldn't mind at all
spending the next two nights fucking her like the world was going to
end. That was just logical given his instant attraction to her and how
much he'd grown to *like* her in the last day. But this other thing…

No. Couldn't be. Wasn't possible. His instincts had just confused
the issue. Probably because his oldest brother had found his mate in a
human woman. The thought was there in his head. And he was
conflating a great deal of attraction and lust with the idea that a human
mate was possible for a leopard. That was all. Nothing real, just his
imagination getting the best of him.

He grabbed a towel, change of clothes, and a kit with his shower supplies in it, and headed to the shower trailers. And yes, he did pause and listen to make sure Cat was okay, but again, that was logical. He filtered out the other sounds of the active camp, ensured she was breathing deeply, sound asleep inside her tent, and felt his muscles relax once he knew she was safe. But that didn't *mean* anything.

Tom gave him a wave as he passed. "Enjoy the run?" he asked without rising from his seat, the magazine still open in his lap.

"Great," Dylan grunted.

"I don't know how you kids do it. Wouldn't catch me running in this heat to save my life." He lifted his beer and took a swig. "This is the way you deal with the heat."

Dylan laughed. "I'll move on to that next," he said.

The shower trailer had a line so he had to wait for something to open up. Inside, there were stalls for privacy, the set up small and cramped but not unlike a series of gym showers. The water wasn't very hot but it wasn't cold. And given his mood, and the run, the cooler water felt refreshing instead of irritating. When he was done with the shower, he took a few minutes at one of the sinks to shave away twenty-four-hour's worth of itchy stubble from his cheeks.

By the time he returned to his tent, showered, shaved, and significantly cooler, he felt refreshed and clear-headed. Well, almost clear-headed. He still found himself acutely aware of Cat in her tent, of the very quiet sounds of her breathing. Sounds he almost didn't have to focus on to hear, despite the noise around him. As the evening approached, activity around the camp picked up, people heading toward the concessions tent for dinner, or pulling out their grills. The scents of cooking meat and grilling vegetables perfumed the air and made his stomach growl. Between the run and the emotional gut punch of his earlier thoughts, he was starving.

And it wasn't just an excuse to wake Cat, to hear her voice and see her face again.

He ignored his own anticipation as he gently tapped at her tent. "You ready for dinner yet, or would you like to sleep more?" he called.

Her shuffling movements within set his whole body on alert, the anticipation no longer something he could ignore. He tensed with the waiting, the hoping she'd step out and join him again. Relieve him of this weird discomfort at being away from her.

"Be out in a minute," she said. "Wait for me. I'm starving."

His pulse started to pound at the sound of her voice, his mood rose, and his skin tingled. "Take your time," he called. Then, "Well, don't take too long. I'm starved, too."

Her low chuckle made his body heat in a way that had nothing to do with the weather.

He stepped all the way back to his truck to wait on her because it seemed safest, sanest. He hoped that space, small though it was, would allow him room to breathe and think. It didn't. His entire body remained focused on her tent and the sounds of her inside, getting ready. He nearly pounced when he heard the zip on her tent flap. Shoving his hands into his jeans pockets, he pushed away from the truck, but didn't dare get too close as she immerged.

She'd pulled her colorful hair up into a high bun, the style high-lighting her high cheekbones and the lovely line of her neck. Little wisps had escaped to frame her pixie face. The lowering evening light caught her skin, giving it a pink glow that seemed almost ethereal. His breath caught. She literally took his breath away. He'd always assumed that was hyperbole, until he found himself gasping in a gulp of air when his lungs protested.

He gave himself a little shake, attempting to drag himself out of his stunned silence. "Ready?" He had to clear his throat. "The concessions tent is busy. We'll probably get stuck in another line."

"That's fine so long as there's food at the end of that line." She smiled.

And everything in him tightened into a coil of need. He kept his hands carefully in his pockets as she joined him. Her smile turned to a funny little frown. "You okay? You seem tense."

"Fine." He forced his own smile even though what he really wanted to do was bury his fingers in her hair, loosen that bun, and taste her perfect mouth. He wasn't going to do that just then. But suddenly food seemed a lot less important than kissing Cat. "Just hungry."

"How was your run?" she asked, then before he could answer. "You showered? How are the showers? I need one later."

"There was a line, but the water was nice." He couldn't think of her in the shower. He couldn't think of her in the shower.

He was thinking of her in the shower. Naked. Wet.

His head was going to explode.

"You shaved," she said with a little grin. "I liked the scruff but this is nice, too."

She blinked and her cheeks slowly turned the most delightful shade of pink he'd ever seen.

He swallowed his growl, afraid she'd misinterpret it. But he did manage, "I'm glad you approve." He'd been going for light and teasing, but his voice came out a lot deeper and more intense than he'd intended.

She sucked in a sharp breath that drew his gaze down, from her mouth to her breasts, the increasing rise and fall as her breathing subtly sped. Lust, sharp and sweet, filled her scent, tasting better than any food. He met her gaze again. Her brown eyes were wide, and this close, he could see little streaks of gold inside the brown, fascinating patterns of sparkling light against the darker depths. Luminous. It was the only word he could think of. She was luminous.

Without meaning to, he leaned a little closer to her, pulling in a deep breath, letting her scent fill his head. His leopard's insistent growl, the push to claim, nearly overwhelmed him. Again, his instinctive half murmured, *Mine*. And for a second, Dylan didn't even want to question that instinct. He didn't care about the implications or consequences. He just wanted to pull Cat close, and kiss her until they were both weak-kneed and breathless.

He blinked first. She pulled back first. And only when she did, did he realize she'd leaned into him as well.

"Shall we go forage for some food," she said, too brightly, her voice a little high. She blinked rapidly, her gaze jumping around as she refused to look directly at him.

He looked away from her too, although the effort was a lot more wrenching than it should have been, and motioned her toward the concessions tent, letting her walk just in front of him so he could take a moment to rein himself in.

Lust was one thing. What he felt for Cat…this was a lot more powerful and intense than simple lust. Overwhelming. Like he was drowning, out at sea, and she was the land he needed to reach to survive. That, all by itself, should have been shocking enough to pull him back from the brink, give him pause, force him to reconsider spending any more time with her. He could step away now, break any bond forming before it had time to solidify. They'd only known each other twenty-four hours. He could walk away now and not let things go too far.

He contemplated the tendrils of hair against her long neck, the way her skin flushed in the evening warmth. She waved to Tom on the way past and Tom gave her a solute with his beer. Her chuckled caught Dylan in the gut, spiking that hot slide of desire in his blood.

And he knew he wasn't going to walk away. He wasn't sure he really could even if he had wanted to. But the truth was, he didn't want to.

He only wanted her.

12

Cat had never felt quite so awkward as she did in that short trip to the concession tent. Her movements were self-conscious and jerky. Everything in her was aware of Dylan at her back and that awareness made it increasingly difficult to focus on the simple act of walking.

She was a little embarrassed by her reaction back at his truck, the way she'd very nearly kissed him just because he looked so yummy and hot and delicious, but she was also a little desperate to follow through with that impulse to pull his face down to hers and kiss him like the world was ending. His hair was still wet from his shower, and her fingers had itched—literally itched!—to reach up and tunnel through that thick mass, see if his skin was cool or warm from his shower. His cheeks were a little darker after his run, the flush of his exertion making her consider how they might exert themselves in other ways that would make them both flush.

He wore a t-shirt and jeans and honestly, she was pretty sure that should be illegal because he looked so absolutely, perfectly, deliciously hot in a t-shirt, his thick muscles straining the poor cotton material until she thought she should really rescue the shirt by removing it. But the thought of his naked chest on full display made her brain short circuit.

It was almost enough to make her forget how hungry she was. In fact, if she had given in to the impulse to kiss him, she was certain she'd have completely forgotten about food for the next few hours because the only thing she'd want in her mouth was him.

She tripped on…probably nothing, she wasn't even sure. Dylan caught her elbow, keeping her from falling. But the touch of his warm, roughened fingers against her bare skin overwhelmed her already sensitive nerves. She came so close to melting back into him it was embarrassing.

She forced out a little laugh and thanked him, but she couldn't meet his gaze. If she looked into those dark blue eyes again, she'd be lost. The knowledge was more than a little disconcerting.

The concessions tent was overflowing with people at this time of the evening and with the campsite now nearly full. The beer tent was doing a good trade, and there were lines outside all the food venders. She sighed a little. She hated waiting. But it was this or leave the campsite to find a restaurant or drive thru or something, and given the sheer number of people here for this event, they probably wouldn't have any better luck out in the little town.

They shuffled through the crowd, and without having to discuss it, got into the shortest line they could find, which was still too long but was not as long as the hamburger line. And this one moved fast, which was a relief. She'd have to gnaw on a bone soon if she didn't eat.

Except then Dylan set a hand to the small of her back as a gentle guide when some people pushed passed, and that got her thinking about a completely different kind of bone. And sucking, not gnawing. Was it hot in here? She was pretty sure the tent was too hot.

In all honesty, it was pretty warm between the food and the crowds. A good excuse for her warm cheeks. She hoped. She still couldn't look directly at Dylan though. Since waking up and seeing him leaning against his truck looking all stunning and delicious, she wasn't having much luck keeping her thoughts off sex. This wasn't her usual line of obsessive thinking, so she wasn't entirely sure what to do with herself.

"You okay?" he asked, leaning in so she could hear him over the noise under the tent.

"Yeah. Sure. Why?" Shit. Her voice squeaked!

"You're fidgeting and you seem a little tense," he said. "I shouldn't have woken you."

"No!" She swallowed. "No. I'm good. Hungry." She forced a smile that didn't feel very natural and then turned her back to him again as her cheeks warmed.

This was ridiculous. What the hell was wrong with her? She'd spent the entire day with him, most of last night. They'd been able to carry on perfectly ordinary conversations even when she'd spent too much time picturing him naked. Why could she *not* seem to get it together this evening? It was like suddenly seeing him flushed and fresh from the shower had flipped a switch in her brain and now she couldn't just return to the ease she'd felt with him earlier in the day.

To be fair, she'd wanted to strip him and kiss all of him then too. She hadn't *not* wanted him for even a moment since meeting him. She'd been jitterier with him from the start because of her lust. But something felt… She wasn't sure. She didn't have the words for it. And there was absolutely no math that could frame this feeling into an understandable context. Everything just felt more somehow. More intense, more desperate, more imperative, more…wanting.

What the hell kind of sleep did she just have? Was she even awake?

As she thought about it, she realized that while she had slept and slept hard because she was tired, the sleep had also been restless, with a sense of something missing. Like her dreams were searches for something, except nothing that clear cut or obvious, just the sensation that she needed to find something. And when his voice woke her, and then she'd walked out and seen him standing there waiting for her, it had felt almost like she'd finally found the thing she'd been missing.

Except none of that made any sense! She hated when things didn't make sense. Things should make sense. There was math for that. Math made sense. At least to her. And it formed the framework, the field on which to ensure other things made sense. But there was no math for her current predicament. No way to explain this…overwhelming draw to Dylan.

Maybe she was just punchy from not enough sleep and an eventful few days. She'd gone up in a hot air balloon for the first time today. That had been an adrenaline rush. And she really hadn't slept much since leaving New York, even the night in the hotel in Portland, because she'd been too excited. The eclipse was only a day and a half away. And there was a lot of activity and excitement around her at the festival. All of these weird feelings could just be a side effect of her exhaustion.

And hunger. She really was very very hungry.

She looked at the sign for the food stall they were waiting in line at and realized it was Mexican food and all worry about her reactions to Dylan went out the window. "Tacos! And empanadas." She leaned around the crowd a little, delighted to see burritos as well. It didn't matter that she'd had tacos for lunch. There was no such thing as too many tacos in a person's life.

Dylan's low chuckle danced along her skin, distracting her from the food, but only just barely this time.

"I take it we chose well," he said. "Even if it was just because the line was shortest."

"How is this the shortest line? Mexican food is the best. Second only to cake."

"I don't think the line's short because the food isn't popular. I think it's short because these people can move. They're turning over orders fast."

"Well, I've just found my favorite vendors then," she said. Very seriously. Not only was this a favorite food category, but she was all for food that reached her as quickly as possible.

"I don't think we've got a hope of getting a seat in here," he said, leaning in a little close again as a noisy family walked past, the kids screeching about something. "Can you wait long enough to get the food back to our tents?"

"Maybe. I might have to eat and walk." And if she got a few empanadas to go with the tacos she intended to order, she could eat and walk no problem. "But I'll manage. It'll be quieter back at the tents anyway."

The noise level under the canopy was pretty epic now. But the atmosphere was still happy and energetic—except for the occasional screeching kid—so she didn't really mind. She liked all the excitement in the air.

Once they reached the head of the line, they ordered and received their food in minutes, which thrilled Cat and, true to her threat, she did start eating on the walk back to their tents. The cheesy interior and the fried dough were so delicious she hummed in contentment.

"Didn't you eat enough for lunch?" Dylan asked, his lips quirked as he watched her finish off an empanada in three bites.

"I did," she said, after swallowing. "I thought so anyway." She shrugged. "Maybe I threw my body off staying up most of the night and now it can't tell what time of day it is."

The sun was dipping low in the horizon now, the evening slowly fading to a deep blue purple. Stars were already starting to pop out overhead. Around them, camp activity continued and a lot of cooking smells permeated the air, mostly things grilling which, to Cat, was a really nice smell.

She started on a second empanada, this one stuffed with cheese and deliciously spicy chicken. "I usually only eat like this when I've been forced to sit still for too long," she said with a shrug. "Amy used to keep our favorite pizza place on speed dial for times like this." She dipped her head to one side. "Or when I got focused on something and forgot to eat for a bit."

"How long was a bit?" Dylan said, waving to Tom as they reached their tents.

"Depended on what I was thinking about."

Dylan held her food while she set up her folding chair and she did the same for him while he got his chair out of his truck. He did that one handed snap open thing again and she had to hide her expression in her food because she wasn't sure if he was showing off when he did that, but it did show off the muscles in his arms and staring at his arm muscles flexing was becoming a real obsession for her.

"How long was the longest 'bit'?" he asked as he took his food back.

She considered that. "I think the longest was probably…two days. Before she came into my room and made me eat something. I had gone down a rabbit hole of contemplating black hole evaporation and the information paradox, and I sort of lost track of time."

Dylan stared at her, his expression unreadable. "You forgot to eat for two days?"

She shrugged. "I was thinking."

He let out a sound that might have been a chuckle if she were being generous. "Why did your sister let you go two days without eating?"

"Hey, she was busy. She had things to do." She got a little defensive and protective of her big sister at times like these. It wasn't Amy's fault. She'd done her best in a really tough situation. And Cat refused to let anyone say otherwise. She did admit, though, "After that, she didn't let me get away with not eating for so long. At least while we still lived together."

"Did you move out for college?"

"No. Well, at least not for my undergraduate degree. I moved out when she and Ethan got together so they could have some privacy. But not far."

"You're very close with your sister," he said.

"It was just the two of us for a long time. So yeah, I guess we are pretty tight."

"Was it hard moving out?"

"Not as hard as I would have expected." She chuckled. "I was still in the same building, just a few floors up. And I got Spike."

"Amy was okay with that?"

"Not at first, to be honest." They'd had some pretty serious debates about who should be in charge of Spike most of the time. "I only won custody—" she grinned at the word, "—because I was living alone and I had a more flexible schedule so was home for the daily walks more often than she or Ethan were." She finished off one of her three beef tacos before admitting. "I think Amy agreed more, though, because without her there to remind me, she assumed I'd remember my surroundings and remember to eat if I had to walk Spike every day."

"Did that work?"

He started in on his second burrito and she realized she hadn't noticed him finish off the first. He was obviously as hungry as she was. Which made sense after he'd gone for a run. She'd just taken a nap.

"Well, the first time it didn't," she said, "and I missed a walk, Spike left me a very clear and messy message outside my bedroom door that this was unacceptable, so I never forgot again. Forcing myself out of my head a couple times a day did mean I remembered to eat, though. Most of the time. So yeah, no more two day fasts after that."

At least not when she was taking care of Spike. On the days Amy took Spike for an extended visit, Cat had to admit she'd fallen into the thinking rabbit hole once or twice. But she'd ensured she had the pizza place keyed up on her phone, so no harm.

"How about you?" she asked, because she didn't want to talk about herself anymore. She was insanely curious about him. She felt like she knew him already and yet she didn't. She wanted more details. "You're close with your family. Was it hard moving all the way to California?"

"A bit," he said admitted. "The space was nice. And a few of my siblings live in other parts of the country, so it wasn't like I was the first to leave or anything. My oldest sister lives on the east coast. But not having Julia around every day was an adjustment."

"You and your twin are very close, then?"

"Sure. We don't do that twin psychic communication or anything." He grinned at her chuckle.

The grin momentarily distracted Cat from her tacos.

"But we were the youngest by a few years and spent a lot of time plotting against our older siblings together. That sort of conspiratorial planning really helps solidify bonds."

She laughed. Trying to imagine Dylan as a kid playing tricks on his older brothers and sisters. She wondered what he looked like as a kid. "Do you and Julia look a lot alike?"

"Similar enough, but she's got our mother's darker eyes." He pointed at his own. "Got these from our dad. And she likes to dye her hair so there's no telling what hair color she'll have at any point."

Cat fingered one of her blue streaks. "I'm pretty fond of colors, too."

"She did do that all over purple gray color not too long ago," he said. "But that didn't last long. At least, between that visit home and the next she'd gone from purple gray to a more somber white."

"I think I'd like your sister."

"I'm sure she'll like you, too. Although, fair warning, she doesn't like astronomy and actively hates conversations about physics, so you'll probably have to stick to talking about hair color and dogs."

The way he said that, like obviously she'd meet his sister one day, made her pulse pound harder. Had he realized he'd done that? He paused with his burrito halfway to his mouth, the hesitance lasting only a moment, but it was enough. He hadn't realized the implications of his comment until after he'd spoken.

Was he sorry he'd said it? Would he take it back?

He continued eating, not saying anything about the assumption one way or the other, and Cat let out a very slow breath.

Because she was glad he didn't take it back. Glad he'd made the assumption in the first place. The fact that it had implied they'd stay in touch, that this—whatever it was—wouldn't end on Monday afternoon, that he assumed, whether on accident or on purpose, that they'd see each other again was...

A relief.

1 3

After dinner, Cat went to shower off the sweat and heat of the day. She needed the cooler water to clear her mind, too. She wasn't sure how to deal with the way she felt about Dylan and she needed a few minutes alone to process everything.

Just a few hours ago, she'd been worrying about him being a tiger shifter trying to trick her into a relationship, and now she was giddy at the thought he might want to keep in touch after the end of the eclipse. Her emotions were jumping around so much and so erratically she didn't even feel like herself. She was used to thinking things through. Logic didn't have to make sense in the real world—quantum field theory didn't make obvious, common-knowledge, intuitive sense—but she was still used to logic making sense of some kind. And her logic centers seemed to have short circuited the minute she met Dylan Jones.

Maybe she shouldn't try to stay in touch after the eclipse. If she was this messed up after just a day, how was she going to feel trying to maintain a long distance relationship with a man she barely knew.

Oh, but she wanted to know him more. Everything. Every little detail. The glimpses she'd gotten already only made the draw worse.

By the time she got out of the shower, she was no closer to resolving her chaotic feelings. She was itchy to get back to him for reasons she didn't understand, restless being away from him. A sensation that bothered her on multiple levels.

As if to prove to herself that she could stay away from him for longer than a half hour, she took her time returning to her tent. With her towel over her shoulder and her shower kit in hand, she wandered the campsite, stopping to watch one of the hot air balloons at their site returning with its last passengers of the day, swinging past the beer tent to listen to conversations, wandering down neat rows of campsites in parts of the site she hadn't been before. She even stopped to talk to one of the people with a larger ten inch telescope out, discussing what filters he would be using on Monday and if he'd gotten any good sun spot pictures that day.

The sky overhead had turned black and star speckled by the time she wandered back to her site. She'd managed to delay her return by a whole extra half hour. She'd have called that progress if she hadn't picked up her pace the closer she got to her own tent. The closer she got to Dylan.

Her cheeks heated as she turned down the path for her site, embarrassed at how eager she was to get back. She felt like a teenager with her first crush, skipping to school just so she could see the boy from halfway across the cafeteria. Ridiculous. Amy would never let her live this down.

To be fair, she'd teased Amy pretty mercilessly about Ethan. She'd probably earned some ribbing from her sister in return.

She waved to Tom as she passed. He was setting up his scope for the night. "Another late night?" she stopped to ask.

"Wouldn't miss it for the world," he said with a gentle smile. "Not every day I get to stay up past my bedtime so many nights in a row." He waggled his eyebrows and she laughed. "You keeping me company tonight again or hitting the sack early? You young ones had a busy day."

"I took an absurdly long nap," she said, even though it hadn't been long enough to shake some of her tiredness. "I wouldn't miss another night under the stars for anything."

"Good. Good." He leaned a little on his scope. "You been enjoying the event? No problems or hassles?"

It was a strange question. She frowned a little. "I've been having a great time. Outside of the long lines for the showers and food."

He snorted. "That's why I stick to beer. No line for my cooler."

"Don't you forget to eat," she told him very seriously. "I do that and it's bad. You need protein to keep your brain working."

"I thought I was the teacher here." He grinned as his gaze flicked past her. But the smile dropped a moment later, and he frowned at something behind her.

She glanced over her shoulder. She couldn't see anything out of the ordinary. Dylan stood at his truck, his shoulders stiff as he stared in vaguely the same direction as Tom. She looked out over the rows of mobile homes, camper vans, and tents. Was there a fire? Smoke?

But she couldn't see what had drawn both men's attention. "What's wrong?" she asked, turning back to Tom. Maybe she was missing something.

He gave himself a little shake, blinked a few times, and faced her, smiling again, though the expression seemed forced. "Nothing. Nothing at all. Just thinking about food."

"Uh huh. Well, you let me know if you need anything tonight. I owe you for last night's beer. If you want, I can go stand in a line and bring you back dinner."

"You're a sweet girl." He waved off her offer. "But I've got some sandwiches packed in that cooler alongside the beer. I'll be good."

"Fair enough. Still, let me know if you do need anything, okay?"

"I will. You too." He nodded in Dylan's direction. "Now, I think that young man is waiting for you. He's been a little restless while you were gone. It's good for him, though." He winked, then returned to his scope.

Her cheeks heating, she faced Dylan again. He still had his back to her, so she had a chance to study him. Which maybe wasn't so good because his shoulders stretched his t-shirt in a way that made her want to drag his t-shirt off. He had one hand on the side of his truck's flatbed and one hand fisted at his side. The fist did things to his forearms.

Flexing, yummy type things. But she had to wonder what he was thinking that made him bunch his hand up like that. As she neared, she realized his entire body was tensed, coiled, practically vibrating with… readiness. Again, she looked past him, but she couldn't tell what he was staring at.

A sound like a growl escaped him, raising the hairs on the back of her neck.

She stepped up close, but didn't touch him because he hadn't seemed to notice her yet and she didn't want to startle him. "Hey," she said. "You okay?"

He jerked, and gave himself a whole body shake, before facing her. She frowned a little. The light from the nearby mobile home caught in his eyes, making them look like they glowed a little golden. He blinked and they were the normal blue color again, with just a hint of that reflected light at the edges.

"You okay?" she asked again. Without thinking, she reached to touch his arm, but stopped herself mid-motion, letting her hand fall back to her side. "You look a little…upset."

"No. No." He smiled, though it looked a little strained at the edges. "Sorry. Deep in thought. Didn't hear you come back. How was the shower?"

"Great. Line was too long and the water's a little cool now, but it felt good." She frowned. "You sure you're okay?"

"Fine. Fine," he said, not sounding fine. He looked around. "Must have been a long line. You've been gone awhile."

She didn't want to admit she'd stayed away longer on purpose, because then she might have to admit to her weird, conflicting emotions, so she just said, "Yeah. Lot of people here now."

He nodded. Then he seemed to shake himself again and fully return to the moment. "Sorry about that…" He made a gesture she assumed meant the last few minutes. "I got a text about some family stuff and was thinking."

"Bad?"

"Just business stuff. I might not be actively working for the business at the moment, but Julia keeps me in the loop."

She nodded, but she got a funny feeling he wasn't telling her the truth. She couldn't say why. He sounded perfectly honest. And there was no real reason to lie about a text from his twin. Still. She could tell he was keeping something from her.

But did she have the right to dig? If he didn't want to tell her something, he didn't have to. Twenty-four hours of knowing him hadn't given her the right to all his secrets. She didn't even have any right to be upset that he wasn't telling her the truth.

She forced a smile. "Glad it isn't bad." She gestured to her tent. "Need to put my stuff up. You setting up your scope tonight or…"

"Of course. You are too, right?"

The eagerness and hesitance in his voice relaxed her worry a little. He sounded like himself again. But as she returned her shower things to her car and got her scope out, she realized she didn't know him well enough to say he "sounded like himself" more at any given moment. Despite all the time they'd spent together, she had to stop thinking she knew him better than she did.

There had been something wild in his expression when he'd first faced her, something that reminded her of that moment in the hot air balloon, when he'd growled and her thoughts had jumped to the tiger shifters. She glanced his way as he hefted his scope up onto the tripod. There was more to Dylan Jones than she knew. And that part of himself he was keeping back…

It felt dangerous.

So why the hell wasn't she afraid?

14

D ylan forced himself to relax in his seat, but his every instinct was to hunt the damned tigers down and confront them. They were back. Circling his section of the camp while still remaining out of view. Hanging closer this time, but still not approaching or confronting him. He knew they weren't just at their own campsite, or moving around the site like others here were. Their movements were too deliberate, and the focus was on Dylan's site, not some other nearby location within the camp.

He kept trying to convince himself he was imagining all this. That he was edgy because of Cat, because his leopard was hanging out too near the surface. He felt little slips in his control of his animal nature that he hadn't experienced in years. His senses heightened. His awareness of sounds and smells more intense than usual. All that got worse while Cat was at the showers.

He'd only just kept his leopard down when it urged him to follow her, guard her, and protect her from threats. That made no sense. She was perfectly safe. And she'd think he was stalking her if he followed her to the *showers* for fuck sake. That logic, and the social conventions of humans, meant very little to his leopard half. But he could usually control his animal's instinctive drives easily.

Tonight, that control kept slipping.

The tigers weren't making things any easier. Their presence, at the periphery of his awareness, continually circling his site, only made his edginess worse.

What the hell were they doing? *Why* were they doing this? It made no sense. Dylan hated when things didn't make sense. It irritated the hell out of him. And he was used to a world that ordinary humans would disregard as fantasy. Most of that world still made sense. And when it didn't, even then an eventual reason emerged. There was always an explanation, even when the answers were strange.

But damned if he could figure out the reason for the tigers' behavior. Why court a conflict with a random leopard shifter they didn't even know?

And he was positive he didn't know these tigers. They'd been close enough, frequently enough, to give him a good measure of their scents, enough he'd be able to tell if he'd ever met them before. He hadn't. Which just made all of this more mysterious.

He'd have been tempted to say they were circling someone else, one of the humans camped near him. Except why? The one thing he did know for sure about tiger shifters was that they had a law expressly forbidding them from killing or harming humans. Most shifters tried to adhere to that rule, whether it was codified by a governing body or not, because killing humans drew too much the attention from humans. Especially in modern times with modern forensic science to tease out weird injuries. While shifters might all be stronger and faster than humans, humans outnumbered shifters by a significant margin, even with all the shifter species combined. By the numbers, it just didn't make sense to draw human attention to shapeshifters.

So he was pretty certain this didn't have to do with one of the humans camped near him. But he couldn't be positive.

Cat made a slight movement next to him, adjusting her eyepiece as she hunted the eastern part of the sky. The distraction brought him back to his surroundings. To her. And to his ever growing and complicated feelings.

He watched her from the corner of his eye. If he wasn't careful, he found himself just staring at her, studying the curve of her jaw, the way her eyes sparkled when she spoke about something she found fascinating, the way every conversation was filled with big hand gestures and animation. She was so rarely still. He'd only seen her go truly still when she stopped to think intently about something. Those were the hardest moments not to stare.

It was after midnight. They had less than two days before the festival ended and they went their separate ways. Every part of him objected loudly to this idea of not seeing her again. Impossible. Not seeing her again felt impossible.

He couldn't even console himself with the time left anymore. Every moment that passed felt like a moment closer to losing her. But, in reality, he didn't *have* her. Hell, they hadn't even kissed—though that had been a near constant preoccupation for him. A part of him knew a kiss would make the leaving harder. Anything more than a kiss… And he was back to impossible. Leaving would be impossible. But she had a life back in New York, and he had a life on this coast and a degree to finish. He couldn't just up and move to follow a woman he'd only just met.

Could he?

No. Of course not. Talk about stalking. He had no idea what Cat wanted, if she even wanted to stay in touch after the event was over. Their whole time together had been relatively platonic and friendly. He could scent her desire. He wasn't the only one lusting here. But beyond that… He kept making these leaps as if there were more of a relationship between them. Moving? Following her back to New York? Absurd. Ridiculous. Strange and too too serious.

And yet he'd had that thought more than once tonight.

"You're brooding."

Her quiet comment startled him into looking more directly at her. She was still looking through her scope, not at him, but her lips were curved in a faint smile.

"What?"

"You're brooding," she said again. "What's wrong? You haven't looked into your scope for a while."

He hadn't? Damn. He hadn't even noticed. Although the fact that she had was, for some reason, extremely satisfying.

"Thinking I guess," he said.

"About? Anything you want to talk about?"

Yes. No. Maybe… He couldn't tell her about the tigers, of course. And he didn't dare bring up his thoughts about her and their future—that would likely terrify her more than knowing tiger shifters existed. What could he say? He actually did want to tell her…well, everything. But he couldn't. So…

"Just thinking over my thesis," he said, then winced. Outside of considering how to finish it from New York, his thesis hadn't crossed his mind all that much since meeting her.

"I've been thinking I might get a third Ph.D.," she said suddenly. Then made a face and finally looked at him. "I'm not sure why I just told you that."

"Why get another degree?" he asked, ignoring the rush of delight that she'd confided something in him she hadn't meant to.

"I'm… You know I have a few job offers."

He nodded. "Don't any of them appeal to you?"

"It's not that. It's… It's the finality of picking a focus, I guess." She winced again. "I'm just not sure *which* topic to focus my research on. And in a job, I'll be expected to commit to something, right? But what if it's the wrong thing and I don't make any progress or significant discoveries? Okay, yes, I know that might happen. I could be happy with a focus, spend my whole career on one path, and turns out it was the wrong path all along. Any number of scientists have had this happen to them. Going down one path only to have someone else disprove all their work. It happens. But…"

"But you don't want to be that scientist," he guessed.

"Yes!" She slapped her leg and then gestured at him. "I want to answer questions, not follow false leads and wrong theories."

"But we only learn theories are wrong because people study them and try to disprove them. Without the people pursuing those wrong ideas, poking holes in them and analyzing them, we don't learn which ideas are more correct."

She stilled, one of the rare moments of stillness, and then her smile slowly spread. "I guess that's true." The smile dropped into a rueful expression and her gaze jumped away from his, though, when she said, "I just don't want that to be *my* career." She rolled her eyes. "I want the Nobel," she admitted. "I want the cutting edge. Not just a life of quietly working away at the data with no breakthroughs."

As someone who was happy just to work away at the data, he should probably take offense at that statement. But he wasn't a genius. He was a good scientist, but he'd never assumed he'd make huge strides in his field. Just contribute more to their overall understanding over time. Cat had likely been told most of her life she'd do more than that. Geniuses were expected to live up to that genius by making big discoveries.

"There's nothing stopping you from doing great things, Cat," he said quietly. "Even if you pick the wrong focus to start, you can always change tack."

"I know," she said on a sigh. "I'm just..." She glanced down at her lap, then out over the camp, then at the ground. "I'm scared, I guess." She shrugged. "And I'm not sure why I got onto this topic out of nowhere."

"Obviously, you've been thinking about it."

"Amy would kill me."

"For thinking about your future?"

She chuckled. "No. For turning down the job offers and staying in college for yet another degree. She'd say I was stalling on making a commitment."

"You are," he said.

She tried to scowl, but the expression dissolved into a laugh. He loved that sound so much he took a moment to bask in it.

"Fine," she said. "I am. I might have a problem with commitment." Her gaze jumped to his and her cheeks flushed. "I mean, with science. I have a commitment problem with science."

Between the blush and her hurry to correct her statement, Dylan wanted very much to read something more into her comment. But he didn't dare. "I'm sure whatever you decide, it'll be the right decision for you. If you aren't ready to take on a job, if you want to study more, you should."

"Thank you for enabling my stalling," she said with a slight smile. "But I am just giving in to my worries and fear."

"Does that mean you will take one of the jobs?"

"I don't know." She fluttered her hands. "I figure I've got another two months to waffle before I have to commit." She straightened and her gaze jumped to his again. "But this started because you said you were brooding over your thesis. We should be talking about that, not my fear of failure. I didn't meant to send the conversation off track."

"You didn't." Mostly because he hadn't been thinking about his own thesis at all and had been happy to talk about something that didn't have to do with tiger shifters or whether he and Cat had a future.

"Oh, good. I do that sometimes, get sidetracked. I don't mean to."

"I like the way your mind jumps around. Keeps me on my toes."

He could live in the light of her answering smile. Who needed sunshine?

She opened her mouth to say something but then snapped it shut and her entire expression changed. The smile dissolved into a frown so fierce and angry he actually blinked. Her gaze had zeroed in on something behind him.

And with a start, Dylan realized the scent of the tigers had gotten stronger while he'd been distracted by Cat. He followed her gaze, turning with deliberate slowness…

To face the three shifters.

15

Dylan scowled at the three men slowly walking toward them, standing to place himself between them and Cat without thinking. He couldn't fathom why they choose now for this confrontation. It was after midnight, and outside of Tom, a lot of the other humans had gone into their campers or tents. Less human witnesses, he supposed.

Fewer people he'd likely have to protect.

Though, he realized he had no idea why he thought he'd have to protect anyone from the tigers. They'd been here for days, not causing any kind of trouble. Blending in with the humans, same as he'd been doing. Why were his hackles up?

Because they'd been circling him for almost two days, purposefully staying out of sight. If they'd been harmless, they wouldn't have gone so far out of their way to remain hidden and yet let him know they were there.

Now that he could finally see them, he knew these were the same three men who'd caught his attention at the festival, when he and Cat had been in the hot air balloon. And he was positive he'd never seen them before that. He had no idea who they were.

The one leading was about six foot, a little shorter than he was but not by much, and outwardly looked strong even if he hadn't been a shifter. Dark blond hair, no sign of his tiger rising in his brown eyes. Jeans and t-shirt. Hiking boots. No backpack. Nothing obvious in his pockets that could be a weapon. Not that tiger shifters needed weapons. But that didn't mean he wouldn't have one.

One of the men flanking the leader was easily a half foot taller than Dylan and thick through the shoulders. His black hair was slicked against his head. He didn't have any packs or obvious weapons either. His eyes barely glowed in the darkness, but the hints of his animal side rising were there. He was so large, if Dylan didn't know better, it would be easy to assume he'd also be slow.

The third man was the shortest, and the palest, with white blond hair and eyes gone almost entirely yellow with the presence of his tiger. He was jittery, moving constantly, little twitches that didn't still as they approached. His gaze darted around the campsite as if watching for an attack. That one looked unpredictable, and unpredictable was dangerous.

But the leader was the one Dylan focused on. They approached slowly, their movements gauged to appear human. Yet with the jittery one's eyes gone so yellow, Dylan wasn't sure even a human would be fooled.

Cat rose to her feet, coming to stand next to him. He glance down at her, ready to suggest she might want to go into her tent, then noticed her expression. Her scowl was fierce. The angriest he'd seen her in their short acquaintance. She was very nearly snarling.

At the three tigers.

Did she know them?

He faced the approaching shifters again. And realized they weren't focused on him. Their attention was entirely on Cat. Intently zeroed in…on Cat. Stalking toward *her* with purpose.

They'd been circling *her*. Not him. This wasn't about him at all.

They were here for Cat.

She didn't look away from the men as they approached, but she did take a step closer to him. He wondered if she realized she'd done that.

"What the hell are you doing here?" she said as soon as the men were close enough she could speak quietly. "I've told you before, I'm not interested. Go away."

"You know them?" Dylan asked.

"Two of them."

"Friends?" He knew they weren't. Even if her tone hadn't said otherwise, her scent was full of annoyance. Not fear—which he supposed was good. But she was angry. Very angry. What had they done to her to earn that reaction?

His leopard growled.

"No," she said firmly in answer to his question and put her hands on her hips. "Leave me alone," she said to the tigers. "How many ways do I have to say that?"

Dylan's head spun, trying to catch up to this radically different situation. Why the hell were tiger shifters bothering Cat? And apparently had been for long enough that their attentions angered her? She wasn't a tiger shifter. She wasn't a shifter at all. What did the men want with a *human* woman?

Dylan's leopard growled again, deep in his head. Without thinking, he moved a little closer to her, and she leaned in to him, her back brushing up against his arm. And a deep part of him he didn't recognize again whispered, *Mine*.

He ignored his reaction and focused on the men. He would worry about his possessiveness later.

"Hello, Catalina," the leader said. "You haven't returned my calls."

"Take a hint," she said.

His gaze flicked to Dylan. "Who's this?"

To Dylan's surprise, she moved further in front of him, like she was blocking him from the tigers.

"No one you need to worry about. Why are you here?"

"You wouldn't return my calls," he said with a shrug. "I wanted to see you."

"So you followed me across the country? Do you know how *wrong* that is?" She sighed, long and loud. "I've explained this. A lot. And if you aren't careful, I'm going to call the police and have you arrested for stalking. Your...people won't like that."

"We can handle the human cops."

She hissed in a breath and nodded across the road to where Tom still stood at his telescope, though his gaze kept darting their way. "Shut up. There are people here."

Dylan resisted the urge to glance down at her, but her reaction startled him. Because she hadn't questioned the tiger's use of the word "human" to describe the cops.

The larger man behind the leader narrowed his eyes at Dylan. "You're out of your territory," he said.

"So are you," Dylan answered back. "Don't see a telescope on you anywhere."

"I could take yours," the large man said.

"You could try."

The man lifted his lip in a snarl. Dylan smiled, slowly. Bullies hated that. And he hated bullies.

"You should stay out of this," the large man said.

"No," Dylan said.

While in their animal forms, the tigers might be larger than Dylan's leopard, Dylan's mother was the queen of their people in the Pacific Northwest. He'd grown up learning how to fight other shifters, from one of the toughest fighters on the west coast—his mom.

"She's one of ours," the leader said, without taking his gaze off Cat.

"She seems to think differently," Dylan said.

Although why the hell the tigers were claiming a human woman as one of their people was beyond him. Unless she was mated to a tiger. Dylan carefully kept his reaction to that thought to himself, though his leopard objected loudly in his head. He didn't want the tigers to realize he was upset by the idea.

Given the time they'd been spending together, and the obvious chemistry sparking between them, he was certain Cat would already have mentioned being in a relationship. She didn't seem the type to hide that kind of thing. He was also pretty sure if she was in a relationship with a tiger, he would have picked that up in her scent on their first meeting. Maybe.

Whether she was mated to a tiger or not, though, it didn't explain why these guys were harassing her. He could tell she wasn't even a little attracted to any of them. Her scent was all anger and frustration.

And a hint of something else... Maybe desperation? He wasn't sure. It was coated in too much of her anger. Whatever that extra emotion was, it made his leopard want to whisk her away to safety. Also rip out the throats of the men making her so angry. He wasn't going to do that—and potentially start a war with the tiger shifters—at least not so long as they didn't hurt her. But his every instinct demanded he protect her from the threat. He just couldn't decide exactly what the threat was.

"She can also speak for herself," Cat said, sounding annoyed.

Dylan tried not to grin, but it was hard. She definitely wasn't scared of the tigers. Which went a long way toward calming his animal side down. The spike of her annoyance, the taste of it like an extra hit of lemon in her scent, tugged at his grin.

But, he noticed, the jittery tiger took a hesitant step back and his nose wrinkled.

"And I am not anyone's anything," Cat finished. "I've said this to your...people, I'll say it to you. I'm not playing this game. I have things to do. You can go find other...interested parties."

She was hesitating over her word choice a lot, Dylan noted. Speaking more carefully than she had since they met. His suspicions grew, but he kept them to himself.

"And if you guys disrupt this event for me and jeopardize me seeing the eclipse," she said, "I'm going to sic Ethan on you. Or worse, my sister." She leaned closer when she said the last, her voice low and ominous.

The jittery tiger sucked in a breath and took another step back. Dylan pressed his lips together to contain his smile. He couldn't wait to meet Amy.

When the leader leaned in toward Cat, Dylan growled softly. He hadn't meant to do that out loud, the reaction was instinctive. But if that man's face got any closer to Cat, he was going to smash it.

The leader flicked him a smirk before focusing on her again. "They want you to choose one of us."

"They can all go to hell," Cat answered. She wasn't flinching away from the man or showing any fear.

Her lack of concern for her own physical harm was the one thing that kept Dylan's leopard from ripping the leader away from her. If she wasn't worried these men would hurt her, he could resist the call to attack. His control over that urge was slipping, though, and that worried him as much as the tigers. Because he usually had complete control over his leopard's more violent instincts. Until meeting Cat, he'd never experienced this before, like he was hanging on by his fingernails to the greased up rope of his control, and he didn't like it.

"You're one of ours," the leader said quietly. "You need to pick one of us."

"I don't need to do anything but breathe and one day die," Cat said. "And even breathing is optional if I don't care about the timing of the dying. I've made myself clear on this. The stalking isn't helping your cause. I don't want any of you. You can go to hell."

"We'll let you take your littler pictures," the leader said.

Dylan felt his lips lift in a snarl at the condescension. He heard Cat growl softly at it too.

"But then we'll be back," leader said, ignoring their reactions. "We still have things to discuss."

"No. We don't."

"Don't waste any more time on this guy," the leader said, flicking his hand in Dylan's direction without looking at him. "You have better choices with us. We're your only choice. You need to learn that now."

Dylan felt another growl rising in his throat. The leader was begging for a broken nose. And from Cat's scent, it was a tossup which one of them was going to deliver the blow.

"If you assholes don't leave me alone—" she leaned in even closer, putting her nose right into the leader's, "—I'm gonna tell Elizaveta."

The jittery tiger actually jumped back, a full two feet, and panic filled his scent with an acrid tang. The larger man, who'd been smirking at Dylan, dropped his smile to flick a worried glance at the leader.

Interesting. Whoever Elizaveta was, she was a serious threat to these assholes.

Dylan liked her immediately.

The lead tiger eased away from Cat, moving slowly as if to prove he wasn't worried. But that pulse of panic in his scent proved Cat's threat hit home.

"You're distracted right now," he said. "We'll talk later. After the eclipse on Monday. I'm sure I can convince you to make the right decision." He glanced at Dylan, holding his gaze. "Why pick a leopard when you can have a tiger?"

Dylan didn't growl or hiss or do any of the things his leopard wanted him to do at the man for having said those things aloud, for curious humans to hear—even if the only humans awake were Tom and Cat. It was reckless and stupid. But if Dylan reacted, he'd make it worse.

For the first time in his life, he envied his oldest brother's iron control. Deacon wouldn't have had to hide a reaction to the tiger. He wouldn't have reacted at all. Dylan, on the other hand, would happily *react* with his fists all over the tiger's smug face.

"Enjoy the rest of the festival," the leader said, waving a hand vaguely to encompass the campsite. He held Cat's gaze. "We'll see you after."

"No," she said.

But all three men had turned and walked away.

He and Cat both watched until the tigers had disappeared into the darkness at the far end of the dirt road, heading out into the fallow fields beyond. And Dylan kept his eyes on the spot they'd last been, letting his sense of smell track them farther, until they were far enough away, their scents didn't reach him on the breeze anymore.

Silence followed. For a long moment, Cat stood still with her back to him, hands on her hips. He realized he was still standing close enough to brush against her back and took a few steps away so he wouldn't crowd her. After that run in, he didn't want to make her feel any more uncomfortable.

She turned toward him slowly, her beautiful brown eyes narrowed to slits as she frowned up at him.

Then very quietly, so only he could have heard, she said, "What did he mean…leopard?"

16

Cat's brain had jumped to a conclusion she didn't want to believe, didn't want to acknowledge. After her worry today that Dylan was a tiger and had been lying to her, then her dismissal and conviction that he couldn't be, that he had to be human…

The idea that maybe he wasn't after all, that she had almost been right and he still wasn't what she'd thought…

The night around them hadn't changed in the last minute, but she felt like it should have. The world should have shifted on its axis because her stomach was churning and her entire body felt disorientation and flipped upside down. But no, everything was the same. Still a cool breeze fluttering the edges of Dylan's hair, black star-speckled skies overhead, sleeping people in the surrounding sites. Tom at his telescope across the road. She could just see him from the corner of her eye and knew he had made a show of going back to looking through his own scope, but she was also acutely aware that he was there and if they weren't careful, he'd overhear their conversation.

A conversation she didn't want to have. She wanted to ignore Lenny's innuendo and pretend she hadn't heard, didn't suspect. She wanted to go back to daydreaming about pulling Dylan into her tent and worrying about what would happen on Monday after the eclipse. Ordinary things. The things humans worried about when they were falling for a new person and were concerned about those new and nebulous feelings. She wanted to return to *only* worrying about whether he'd want to stay in touch, and what that might mean to her, and whatever this was that was between them.

But she couldn't. She couldn't ignore what Lenny had said. Couldn't pretend it hadn't happened. Much as she wanted to. She couldn't let this go. Not after the last four years of dealing with the damned tigers.

Dylan held her gaze, a crease between his brows, his mouth set in a line. She couldn't read is expression, wasn't sure if he'd answer her question or not. The waiting stretched her nerves to breaking. The stillness of the moment snapped her.

"Well?" she finally said into the silence. She shifted from one foot to the other, then shoved her hands into her pockets. That only irritated her more, so she pulled them out again and tried to hold still. Her foot started tapping in the next moment.

"You…" He paused again, still frowning. "How long have you known those guys? The two you did know?" His voice was so quiet she had to strain to hear him. Probably good since Tom was still within earshot.

"You first," she said.

"I'm trying to decide if you understand what you're asking me."

"I do."

"You think you do," he said, but quietly enough this time she got the impression he was talking to himself and he hadn't meant for her to hear.

"What does that mean?"

He gave himself a little shake. "Nothing." He glanced around, his gaze landing on Tom briefly before returning to her. "This isn't a good place to have this conversation, even with most…people asleep. The… man just now said things that shouldn't be discussed out loud in front of others."

And there it was. He knew what Lenny and his goons were. She could hear it in the way he hesitated over "man" and "people," like he wanted to use other words. Words like "tiger" and "humans."

"You know what they are?" she said, her voice low.

He tapped his nose. "I have a very good sense of smell."

She dragged in a long breath.

Because she'd asked and studied and learned, she knew that the world was full of things she used to think were impossible. Meeting Ethan and her sister's biological father, learning about tiger shifters, all that had broken the universe open for her in a way that, for a little while, scrambled her perception of science and reality. She'd had to have some pretty long conversations with tiger scientists, and study their genetics research, to settle that upending.

But it turned out the macro world was just as strange as the subatomic world. The quantum world wasn't the only bizzaro thing that was still, nevertheless, natural.

Lenny had called him a leopard.

"You aren't one of their…people," she said for lack of a better word. "Are you?"

"No. My people are different."

"Leopard," she whispered, so quietly it was barely sound on the breeze. If he was what he'd just implied he was, he'd hear her just fine.

His nod proved he had.

Then without another word, he returned to his telescope, leaving her blinking at his back.

He'd answered her question. But it was the most unsatisfactory answer she'd ever gotten to a question. It wasn't *enough*. She wanted more answers. More explanation. Why was he here? What did he have to do with the tigers? Was this all some sort of weird plot to drive her to the tigers? Or was it just coincidence she was spending so much time with another species of shifter?

He'd questioned whether she understood who and what the tigers were. Which made her think he hadn't known she was anything other than an ordinary human woman with no idea the shifter world existed. And, to be fair, that's how she tried to live. But she didn't want to ignore this, to just leave it at that. She wanted…

She paused mid-mental-whine when he lifted his telescope off the tripod and proceeded to return it to his truck. She blinked a few times. Was he… Was he done for the night? Just… Going to sleep now, after all that?

Or had he decided he didn't want to spend any more time with her, now that he knew she had ties to the tiger shifters? Had he believed what Lenny said, that she belonged to the tigers? He hadn't seemed like he had, but maybe she'd misread him. She obviously didn't know him as well as she thought she did. And thinking she knew him at all after only two days had already seemed ridiculous.

Still, it bothered her to her bones that he might assume she somehow "belonged" to the tigers and so was therefore off limits. In fact, that didn't just bother her. It enraged her. The fucking tigers interfering with her life. Again! If Dylan didn't want to see her again, or any more, or whatever, it should be because of how he felt about her, not because of some fucking territorial dispute between shifter species. She was Not. Territory.

She marched up to him as he returned to close his tripod, intent on demanding an explanation. She was confused and hated that feeling. And she was angry. The anger built the closer she got to him.

"Hey," she hissed. "So that's it? You're just going to put your toys away and go to sleep?"

"Put your scope up," he said quietly, without looking at her. "We can't talk out here. Even if only Tom is still awake. We can either go for a walk in the fields, or if you'd feel safer, we can sit in one of our cars and talk. It'll be too easy for someone to overhear us if we just go into one of the tents."

All said in a voice that couldn't have carried farther than her. He folded his tripod and walked back to his truck again, leaving her—once again—blinking at his back. She followed him to his truck.

"One question," she whispered.

He faced her, waiting patiently.

She realized she'd asked more than one so far. But this one was important. "Do you mean me any harm?"

His patient expression dissolved into a scowl. "Of course not." Said with enough hiss and intensity she believed him.

"Not going to kill me because I know your secret then?"

"Is that what you think? You think I'm that kind of person?"

"No. Just making sure. We'll go for a walk in the fields. I intend to see you shift."

He rocked back a little, as if she'd hit him. "Why?"

Why? That was the question. She believed him because she'd seen Ethan shift. And any number of tigers since then. She didn't *have* to see him in his animal form to believe he wasn't human. So why did she want to see him shift?

"Because I want to see your leopard," she said. It was the most honest answer she could give. She wanted to see him shift because she *wanted* to. Because her curiosity insisted. Because she wanted to see him in his other form and *know* that in her bones. "You can say no. I'm only familiar with tiger shifters, and they don't seem to be shy about showing their animal sides, but I don't know enough about…others to know if it's taboo, so if it is—"

He cut her off with a raised hand. "I'll show you."

He flicked a glance around the camp. They'd kept their voices very low. Too low to be overheard, she was certain. But as she also kept saying the words shift and animal side, she suspected he was leery even their quiet conversation might be overheard.

"You feel safe enough walking out into the fields with me?" he asked, his gaze still flickering over their surroundings.

"From you? Yes."

"I'll keep you safe from the tigers, too. If they follow."

He still wasn't looking at her when he said that, so he missed her surprise—thankfully because she was sure her entire face showed her reaction to his comment. Surprise and…pleasure. She wasn't sure what the pleasure meant. She wasn't his to protect. Still… She couldn't quite squash the little heart leap of happiness. She did, however, wipe it from her expression.

"There won't be a need," she murmured. "They won't hurt me. They aren't allowed."

His gaze finally returned to her, his eyes narrowing. And now, now that she knew, she no longer wrote off that very faint glow in his eyes as a trick of the light. The little hint of gold glowing at the edges of the blue. Now she knew, that was his shifter side, his animal side just below the surface.

That should have been a lot more upsetting than it was.

No. No. She was still upset. She was still angry.

"We have a lot to discuss," Dylan murmured. She couldn't tell if he'd intended her to hear or not. "Put your scope away. Lock up."

Because she wanted answers pretty desperately, she hurried to do as he said, returning her scope and tripod to her car's trunk. Folding up her camping chair and sticking it in the trunk too.

She met him at the front of his tent and they turned without a word toward the fields. Tom waved at them as they passed. "Done for the night?" he asked, his voice low but loud enough to carry.

"Just a little walk before calling it a night," Dylan said, his tone cheerful even if his shoulders were stiff and tight.

The fact that she noticed the contrast between his body language and his voice startled her. She'd been paying too much attention to his body language.

Tom chuckled. "You kids." He waved. "Have a good night."

Cat smiled and waved back, her smile feeling forced. But when she looked at Tom, she realized his body language didn't match his tone either. He was leaning against his scope, his eyes narrowed, his mouth pinched. And she felt his gaze following them until they'd turned off the dirt path, moving out of his direct line of sight.

She considered that. All three of them forcing a polite, casual conversation when none of them seemed to feel particularly casual.

She pushed her worry about Tom's reaction to the back of her mind. Right now, she wanted answers from Dylan, since he seemed willing to give them.

He'd succeeded in upending her world, from the minute she laid eyes on him.

And she'd hate to try righting her world without first understanding why she shouldn't just leave it all upside down.

17

Dylan kept silent as he and Cat walked farther into the fields, though explanations and questions bubbled up in his chest, struggling to spill out. He wanted them far enough away from the camp they wouldn't be overheard. But close enough, she'd feel safe, like she could scream and someone would come running.

Not that he intended to hurt her, but she'd just discovered he wasn't human. Her continuing to feel safe around him seemed…important.

She wanted to see him shift.

For some reason that surprised him. It shouldn't. This was Cat, with her infinite curiosity and quick, questioning mind. Of course she'd want proof. She obviously didn't need it. If she knew what tiger shifters were, she knew shifters existed. Might have even see one of the tigers shift before. But maybe she needed confirmation. That he wasn't trying to trick or deceive her. The peppery sharp lemon scent of her suspicion and anger was strong enough to make him sneeze. Beyond those emotions, though, he couldn't parse out the rest of what she was feeling. The mix was complex and changing, too fast and chaotically for him to fully understand. But the churn of emotion was enough to leave him hesitant.

Hesitant to do the wrong thing. To scare her. To send her away.

His leopard side objected loudly to the thought of sending her away.

He stopped close enough to see the lights of the campsite, far enough away no human would overhear, in a dark enough patch of field no human would likely see them. Given all the telescopes and binoculars at this site, they might still be spotted out here, but it was a risk he had to take.

Cat stopped a few feet away and shoved her hands into the single pocket on the front of her NYU sweatshirt. The high desert temperatures had fallen into the chilly forties this late at night, and while he barely noticed thanks to his metabolism, the cool breeze had forced Cat into warmer clothes earlier in the evening.

She looked a little swamped by the sweatshirt, like it was several sizes too big for her pixie frame, but she also looked huggable and soft. The fact that his first thoughts were to pull her close for a hug and not strip the sweatshirt off so he could fuck her were another interesting shift in his feelings. He'd have to examine that reaction later.

Not that his lust had banked. But there was something…more there now. Something growing between them. And he was a little afraid it had to do with his earlier thoughts, while he'd been out in these same fields trying to run away from the idea that there was more between them.

That "something more" faced a pretty big test just then, though. And he wasn't sure it would survive the cold bite of reality.

"Well," she said after a moment.

"You want me to shift first and then we'll talk?" he said, just to be sure they were on the same page.

"If you're willing."

"Have you seen anyone shift? You know tiger shifters are…a thing. Have you watched one of them shift before?"

She nodded, without providing more details.

"You know it's not always pretty?" He couldn't change in a blink the way his oldest brother could, the way his mother could. He was an ordinary shifter, with a birth order that didn't imbue him with any great advantages. That mattered in leopards, the birth order, but he'd never begrudged his. His life could be a little more ordinary without the supposed advantages his brother and mother had to deal with.

"I know. I know you'll have to strip."

"And you're okay with that, too?" he asked, because he had to make sure.

"My brother-in-law is a life model. My sister is an artist. I don't have issues with nudity."

"Fair enough." He didn't normally either. Most shifters didn't view nudity the same way humans did. They had to strip to shift. And often did so easily around others of their kind. But humans weren't always so sanguine about those kinds of things.

And, if he were being honest with himself, stripping with Cat wasn't going to be the usual experience for him either. There was a lot more between them and none of it had to do with shifting.

"Will you be cold out here?" she asked quietly.

The slight worry in her voice made him smile despite himself. "No. I'm good. Look away if you're bothered by any of this."

"I won't need to."

"You know I'll still be me?"

"Get on with it. You're stalling."

"Checking on your comfort," he said. "I shift all the time."

"And I've seen it enough not to freak out."

"Well, then…" He pulled his shirt off and toed out of his boots.

He didn't miss her sharp inhale. He was too attuned to her scent to mistake that sound for anything but lust. The curl of desire in her lemony scent made him want to purr. Which meant he'd better get this shift done fast, or he wouldn't be able to stop from getting hard the minute he pulled his jeans off.

Making an effort not to think too much—which was never easy for him—he stripped off the last of his clothing and set everything to one side. Then he let his leopard out.

His animal side emerged faster than usual, thanks to the confrontation with the tigers and his awareness of Cat. His adrenaline hummed in his veins, and he hadn't spent enough time in animal form lately. His leopard was eager and antsy and ready to be turned free.

When the change finished, he gave himself a full body shake, letting his senses adjust to his new position in the world—closer to the ground, night vision sharp and clear, sense of smell heightened, muscles bunched, the feel of *himself* in this different form. He flicked his tail and stretched, enjoying the pull of his muscles, opening his mouth in a wide yawn—a move he regretted a moment later because it revealed his very sharp teeth.

But when he returned his focus to Cat, prepared to make himself look less threatening, he realized she didn't look threatened. Or scared. Or disturbed. She looked…fascinated.

"Visually close. A little lager." She murmured under her breath, her brow creased with a slight frown of concentration. "Yellow glow in the eyes similar. More mass displacement than tigers…" She trailed off but he could tell by the way her lips moved, she was still thinking hard and assessing what she'd just seen.

A smile in this form flashed his teeth in a way that could be considered a threat, so he held back, but inside he was grinning. Of course Cat wasn't bothered. She was analyzing the process the same way she would any scientific phenomenon.

"Your vision, hearing, sense of smell…all heightened now?" she asked.

He nodded. A little sound like a purr rumbled in his throat. Relief. Pleasure. He wasn't sure which dominated. Just that he felt better now, watching her analyze all this without freaking out. Scenting her curiosity, the fading anger, the complete lack of fear. Knowing a thing existed, and witnessing it were two different things. Her reaction to all this left him dizzy with the relief.

And it meant there was one less barrier to overcome later, when they discussed—if they discussed—other things.

Like his leopard's current conviction she was his mate.

That conviction increased in this form, when his animal side dominated his thinking and senses. Her scent wrapped around him tight and his leopard, at least, had no doubts at all. It didn't matter that she was human. That this was so rare the fact that it had happened in a single family should have been impossible. Deacon's mate was a human woman. She wasn't an ordinary human woman—or at least, they didn't think she was. Exactly *what* she was was still something of a mystery to everyone. Except maybe his mother. He got the feeling his mother understood what Cary was.

But Catalina Donovan wasn't anything more than human. She was a stunning, fun, genius human woman, but ordinary human all the same. And leopards almost always found their mates in other leopards. Or they didn't find their mates at all.

He'd have to save the probability analysis for his human form, though, because his leopard didn't give two flying fucks about probability or possibility. To his animal side, this was a fact of the world. Cat was his mate.

And that changed…everything.

But first they had to deal with this current revelation.

He also wanted to talk about the tigers and why they considered her one of theirs. To have these conversations, he needed to be in human form, though.

She raised a hand to stop him when he stood. "Wait. Don't change back yet. Just…" She stepped closer, her hand out, palm up, as if approaching a strange dog.

He snorted in response and narrowed his eyes, batting gently at her hand, his claws safely retracted.

She had the grace to blush, a creep of darker color in her pale skin that took on different dimensions in the dark, with his animal's night vision.

"Sorry," she muttered. "But, can I… Can I touch you like this?"

He nodded.

The gentle brush of her fingers across the top of his head ruffled his fur in a pleasant way. Another gentle brush over his ears brought a little shiver. He didn't even notice his rumbling purr until she chuckled.

"If you're going to scold me for treating you like an oversized pet cat, maybe you shouldn't purr when I scratch behind your ears."

He shrugged and leaned into her hand. Having her touch him, no matter his form, was a pleasure he wasn't about to reject. The contact satisfied a restlessness in him he hadn't recognized earlier. Settled something deep in his chest. He felt more in control with that physical contact between them. As if he could think more clearly again.

Shit. That probably wasn't a good thing.

He stepped back from her touch, despite his leopard's objections, forcing himself to put enough space between them so that he could shift. But he couldn't help the jolt of pleasure at her reluctance to break contact, the little sigh she let out as she slowly dropped her hand.

He decided not to think about his reactions too closely yet. First back to human form. For this, for the conversation they had to have, his human side needed to be in charge. Or at least as in charge as it ever was.

The return to his human form went a little more slowly than the change to leopard because his adrenaline had slowed. But not so much he thought she might notice. When done, he faced her, adapting once again to his new perspective.

Her gaze danced away from his, and to his surprise, she turned her back to him.

"What's wrong?" he asked.

"Nothing. Nothing. You're going to get cold. You should get dressed."

Her scent drifted to him and he realized… Ah, that scent of desire curling through her natural flavor. He could live in that scent.

Scooping up his jeans, he had to work not to grin at her back. But he couldn't help teasing, "I thought you didn't have an issue with nudity?"

Her shoulders hunched and she groaned, low enough he probably wasn't supposed to hear it. "You can scent my feelings, can't you?" she muttered, sounding resigned.

"Yes," he said as he stepped into his boots.

"From the beginning." She wasn't asking a question.

"From the beginning," he agreed.

Her response, for reasons he couldn't entirely explain, made him want to burst out laughing.

She shook her head, put her hands on her hips and huffed out a breath. "Well, shit."

1 8

Cat hung her head. She should have considered this the minute he admitted to being a shapeshifter. He could smell everything she was feeling. All the lusty need. Since she'd first set eyes on him.

Damn it.

To be fair, she hadn't exactly been doing a good job at hiding her desire. She was pretty sure even a human would have figured it out. But that wasn't the same as having a shifter *know* because she was pumping out pheromones. She'd always wondered how Amy dealt with that, having Ethan know how she was feeling at any given point just because it was there in her scent. Was it suffocating in a partner?

Cat hadn't worried too much about it from her perspective. She didn't care if Ethan or his family knew what she was feeling. And she *wanted* the stupid tiger males stalking her to know she was angry and absolutely not happy with their attentions.

But with Dylan…

She heard him make a sound like a strangled sort of cough and she realized he might well be laughing, but until he was dressed, she just couldn't turn around and face him again. She'd meant what she said earlier about not having an issue with nudity. It was natural, and normal, and she rejected all puritanical ideas that the naked human body was something to be ashamed of.

She just hadn't realized how much Dylan's nudity in particular would affect her.

The man had the body of a fucking sex god, and she wasn't okay just then. He was magnificent. All thick and hard. And that was just his chest and arms. She'd turned her back before the temptation to look lower got the better of her. He wasn't an object. He'd stripped and shifted because she'd asked, and ogling him afterward seemed rude.

Still… Dylan, naked, was probably the most delicious thing she'd ever seen. His skin fairly glowed in the darkness, paler than he seemed in the light, his chest covered with dark hair that arrowed down his abdomen. His shoulders were wide and rounded with muscles. His arms, without the admittedly inadequate cover of his t-shirt, were glorious, all bulging, flexing muscles. She wanted to wrap herself around him, explore every ridge and dip, first with her fingers, then her tongue. She wanted to sink against him and feel all that glorious heat, bath in the way he smelled, watch him fall apart for her.

She sucked in a breath and silently snapped at her thoughts, demanding they get back to the situation at hand. They weren't out here so she could jump his bones. They had some important things to talk about and those things were not how quickly they could both get naked.

She attempted to focus on what he'd looked like in his animal form, to go back to analyzing his shift, because that wasn't even a little sexy. The change from one form to another wasn't a pretty process. But it was fascinating. One of the phenomenon that had upended her world and perceptions of what could be real when she'd first seen it.

Watching Dylan move from human shape to leopard shape, a species of shifter she'd never encountered before, her analytical brain had glommed onto the differences. There weren't a lot in the actual change. It was a little scary and messy looking, fur racing over skin, body parts seeming to break and adjust and reform. There wasn't blood. Nothing turned inside out. But the way things like tails appeared while fur covered skin, the lengthening and shortening of various body parts as they took on the new form, was a fascinating study in the weirder ways physics could assert itself in the real world.

In leopard form, he'd been a little larger than a mundane leopard but not so much that a casual observer would notice. The tigers were the same, able to blend in with their mundane counterparts when in animal form. She understood not all shifters were like that. Were-wolves in particular could never be confused for an ordinary wolf.

Dylan's leopard was a light tawny brown with deep black spots in a pattern that made him seem to flicker in and out of her visual awareness in the dark. Like if he sat still enough, she'd have a hard time seeing him. His eyes had glowed yellow, the way tiger eyes did in animal form, a very clear sign of shifter instead of mundane animal. His fur had been soft to the touch, and for reasons she couldn't explain, she'd felt...settled when she had her hand on him. Comforted and comfortable. As if touching him answered some question she didn't know she was asking.

Which had been such a disorienting response she'd been distracted enough to forget that when he shifted back to human he'd still be naked. Seeing him before the shift like that had been bad enough. The minute he was back in human form and she was confronted with his glorious body again, she'd... Well, she might have panicked.

And he'd picked up the whole thing. In her scent.

"Don't worry about me being able to scent what you're feeling," he said, as if he knew the precise moment to comment to increase her mortification. "It's nice knowing when your feelings are returned."

That got her full attention and she turned to stare at him. Blinked once because he hadn't put his shirt back on and that was very very distracting. She had to blink again before what he'd said forced itself back into her consciousness.

"Returned?" she managed over a dry throat.

"You haven't realized?" He stepped closer but slowly and still leaving plenty of room between them.

Not that she wanted the space. She wanted to plaster herself against him and devour him. But she appreciated the care and caution.

"Realized?" she repeated and mentally gave herself a smack in the back of the head. Why was she repeating his words like a parrot? She could speak. She had more words than this.

"That I want you too," he murmured, his gaze dropping to her lips.

Cat felt the look like an actual touch and shivered.

"Are you cold?"

"Not even a little bit," she said. He could tell what she was feeling. No point in trying to hide with words what her scent would give away.

He nodded, his breathing increasing enough she noticed the rise and fall of his chest. "There are things we need to discuss before…" He swallowed. "Before we can talk about…other things."

She smiled a little. "Words are tough right now, huh?"

He ran a hand through his hair and chuckled.

Her body actually pulsed in reaction to the lust that flooded her. She took a step closer to him without meaning to. Damn. She stopped herself. He was right. They had to have an actual conversation right now. And not about their mutual desire. Which would distract from the main point. Although, it might just *be* the main point a part of her whispered. Since that part was between her legs and not supposed to be in charge of her thinking, she hushed those musings to try and focus.

"Your scent is distracting," he admitted. "But that's also part of what I need to discuss with you first."

She liked that he was as distracted as she was in that moment. And she couldn't help teasing, "First, huh? Getting a little presumptuous there."

He raised his brows, giving her a look, and she rolled her eyes as her cheeks heated. Kind of hard to hide the fact that yes, yes, she did want to strip his jeans back off and ride his cock until the sun came up. But following through on that lust wasn't a foregone conclusion when there were still unknowns between them.

"Don't get cocky," she said. "As you say, still have some things to discuss. First."

He nodded, but his smile faded and his jaw set in a hard line as he stared off to a spot past her shoulder, his gaze turned inward, his expression pensive.

"Will you tell me why the tigers think you're one of theirs?"

The request was made quietly, and it was a request. Not a demand. Given how damned much time she spent fending off tiger demands, it was a nice change of pace from a shifter.

"I'll explain that, what I can of that, if you'll tell me more about… you. Your people. I've known intellectually that there were other shifters. But I haven't met any outside of the tigers." She rolled her eyes. "And my experiences with them have been a mixed bag."

He huffed out a sound that was almost a laugh. "I'll tell you anything you want to know about the leopards. I'm not sure where to start, what you want to know…"

"How many of you are there?" she asked the first thing that came to mind. Numbers and population size were a huge deal to the tigers because they were so close to extinction. They literally knew the number of female tigers in the different countries exactly. Most tigers in a given country even knew all the names of the females in that country because there were so few to know.

He frowned a little and let out a breath. "I'm not sure worldwide. I'd have to ask my mother. But on the west coast, there are probably a few thousand of us scattered around."

"So many?"

"We're pretty good at disguising our natures. And even a few thousand is nothing compared to the number of humans we're surrounded by."

That was one of the tiger worries, too. Being so outnumbered by such an unpredictable species like humans. "Are there…a lot of different kinds of shifters? I mean, I know there are. I've read what I can. But, I guess I mean here. Or…" She trailed off. "Let's keep this more contained. How many different shifter species live on this coast?"

"Dozens. There are even some tiger shifter territories here. Last I heard, there was one living in Portland, but no one has had any contact with that tiger in years, so it's possible they've moved on. Tigers are pretty self-contained and don't interact with the rest of us much."

She'd learned that too, but it was interesting hearing it confirmed by another type of shifter. "Is territory a thing?"

"Depends on the species. Most of the time we can cross territories with other species, or have some overlap to accommodate everyone. Sometimes…that gets a little trickier." He frowned. "My people have some trouble with the cougars in this part of the country. Territorial disputes that have gone back decades. I suppose it's good there aren't any cougars here. That could have gotten complicated."

"It's complicated enough with the tigers."

"Are you ready to tell me why they think you're one of theirs?"

"There's only so much I'm allowed to tell," she admitted. "The tigers are extremely private, and they have a reason for it."

"Got that impression."

"It's…" How to tell him without betraying any trusts? What to tell him? "Let's just say that reproduction for the tigers is a really big deal. The whole thing, mating, having babies, it's grown into a huge part of their social and political system."

Because of their near-extinction. Because so very few female tigers were born. For two centuries they'd been struggling against this march to extinction, trying to hold their people together even as the number of female tiger shifters dwindled. She had some sympathy for their situation. A lot actually. But she really really hated the way they dealt with it.

"I think Ethan won't mind me saying that he's a tiger shifter," she continued. "He was the first one I saw shift, because he had to convince my sister he wasn't crazy." She smiled a little at the memory. They'd been fully prepared to call the cops on him.

It was on the tip of her tongue to say, *When you meet him, you'll be able to scent each other anyway.* But she bit her tongue before the words escaped. Talk about presumptuousness. They weren't anywhere near those discussions yet.

Instead, she said, "They met in an art class, and at the time, my sister and I had no idea anything like shifters existed."

"Most humans don't."

"Thing is, my sister isn't…entirely human. I mean, she is. She can't shift. But, her biological father was a tiger shifter. We just didn't know until after she met Ethan."

"Your father?"

"Was human. I'm fully human. We have the same mother." She swallowed the old grief. It had been a long time since they'd lost their parents. But she still felt the loss and the hollow ache.

"I didn't think tiger shifters could have children with humans." His brow creased with his frown.

She had to resist the urge to smooth out those creases, and then she had to wonder why she had that urge in the first place.

"They aren't supposed to be able to," she said. "That's the reason Amy's father didn't actually stick around. He thought it was impossible that the baby our mother was carrying could be his. That just pissed mom off, as you might guess. But she ended up just fine." She'd fallen in love with and married her best friend in the end. And they'd had a very loving family. "We did meet him finally a few years ago, when Ethan came into our lives. Amy's biological father, I mean. He's a nice man. They've managed to…have a friendship since meeting."

"Your mother was human?"

"Fully human, yes. My sister not being human was a shock to us all."

"I bet."

"And because of that, she can have children with tiger shifters, too. They've found more hybrids since discovering they were possible. Some have had children with shifter partners. That ability…is important to the tigers."

Even necessary. Many of them felt the hybrids were the answer to their extinction problem. Unfortunately, there were also a lot who thought the hybrids would be the tigers' downfall eventually. Diluting their bloodlines until all those with the ability to shift were gone. But again, this was information she couldn't pass on to Dylan. The tigers trusted her with their secrets—although, they sort of had to given Amy and Ethan's relationship—and she didn't want to betray them.

"Leopards can have kids with humans," Dylan said, "but it's really rare. Not all bonded mates where one partner is human have children."

Something in the way he said "bonded mates" caught her attention, but she filed her questions about that away for later. "Do the kids end up being shifters or human?" she asked instead.

With tigers, they'd had both shifter and non-shifter offspring with humans. The chance of a shifter offspring went up when the human partner was a hybrid, though. Still, even with one fully human partner, some of the kids born had been shifters.

"When it happens, the kids are usually leopards," he said. "If it happens."

"It goes both ways with the tigers. The hybrids can be shifters or human. The chances of a shifter baby increase when one partner is a hybrid and the other is a tiger. The human-tiger matings have closer to a thirty percent chance of producing a shifter."

"Is Amy's status as a half tiger the reason the tigers seem to think you're one of theirs, even though your parents were both human?"

"That. And the fact that we have the same mother and our mother had a baby with a tiger shifter."

He narrowed his eyes. "I'm missing some reason for that being important, aren't I?"

She sighed. "They think I can probably have babies with a shifter."

"Do you want kids?"

The fact that he asked made her want to hug him. "Thank you!" She flicked her hands up at the sky. "Not everyone even *wants* to have kids. I haven't decided yet, and I'm not going to be pressured into it just because—" She cut off the rest of that sentence because that was information she wasn't free to share.

But it was hard not to share with Dylan, she realized. She wanted to tell him everything. All of it. And she had no idea why. She'd never had so much trouble keeping this secret before. Although, to be fair, she'd never spent so much time with a shifter who wasn't a tiger before. Maybe that was it. Maybe knowing he *knew* shifters existed made her less reticent.

She was going to believe that for now.

Because considering any other possibility terrified her.

19

The breeze shifted, lifting the fine hairs on Cat's forehead as she
and Dylan stared at each other. The fields were quiet, the stars
overhead bright in the darkness. The crisp air cooled her warm cheeks
and filled her lungs with the earthy scent of grass and dirt. If not for the
faint lights from the campsite and road behind them, she could almost
feel like she and Dylan were alone in the world.

If they had been, she supposed that would make all this a lot less
complicated.

"The tigers are pressuring you to have kids?" he asked quietly, his
voice even. "With a tiger?"

She sighed. Of course he hadn't missed her conversational slip.
And she couldn't read his scent to tell what he was feeling. Which
made their current situation very lopsided. She was tempted to call it
unfair, but she studied the universe. Fair rarely had anything to do with
anything. Things just were. Still, it was annoying that she couldn't read
his mood the way he could read hers.

"Sort of," she said with huff. "They're…strongly encouraging me
to pick a tiger mate." She sneered involuntarily when she said this last.
She couldn't help it. Their insistence that she needed to choose a mate
made her want to pull her hair out.

"What if…" He frowned. "What if you find a…partner who's not a tiger?"

"Not that I've had a lot of time to date," she said with a little smile, trying to lighten a topic that left her mostly too angry for humor, "but as far as I'm concerned, they'd just have to deal with that." She gave a little shrug. "Amy and I have been… It's hard to explain without talking about things I'm not allowed to talk about," she admitted. If he understood there were things she couldn't say, she hoped he'd be able to accept what explanations she could give.

"You don't owe me more than you want to tell me," he said. "I'd like to understand, because the tigers here seem to be…a problem."

She groaned. "Argh. They are. They're not supposed to be following me around. But Lenny—the one who did most of the talking—and the big guy, Rick, they've been pressing their attentions a little too insistently." She shook her head. "I'm going to talk to someone about them soon. This is getting ridiculous."

"Are they dangerous? To you?"

"Not technically. Just a pain in my ass. They aren't allowed, by law, to hurt me."

"By law?"

"Tiger laws. Very strict. And my sister and I are covered under those laws. But that also gives the sonofabitches this idea that I'm supposed to follow other laws that I refuse to participate in." She sighed. "Anyway. It's complicated, but yeah, they've been pestering me, and yeah, they think I should be settling down with a tiger shifter husband, and *no*, I have no intention of doing anything like that any time in the near future."

"Settling down with a tiger or settling down period?"

She opened her mouth to answer quickly that she wasn't settling down period yet, and then…couldn't. The words didn't come out as fast or as sharp as they usually did. That was strange. She actually choked up on that declaration.

She frowned a little and said, "I'm not interested in any of the tigers I've met."

Which was an honest answer. She supposed it would have made

everyone happy if she had just happened to fall for a tiger. Despite their best efforts though, she'd never even had a twinge of attraction to any of the ones who'd been following her around the last few months.

Not anything like what she felt for Dylan.

That realization was sobering.

"Tigers don't…bond," Dylan said slowly. "As far as I know. They don't form permanent mate bonds."

"No. Just regular relationships like humans. Fall in love. It works or it doesn't. Do other shifters do things differently?" Because suddenly that seemed very very important.

"Some," he said.

"Leopards?" No point dancing around the topic.

He ran a hand through his hair, a gesture which drew her attention to his flexing arms, and the fact that he was still only half dressed. And that he looked magnificent without a shirt on. And looked even better without any clothes on. And she still wanted to get him back to being naked, but with more privacy. In her tent.

"Aren't you cold?" she snapped before she could stop herself. It was really hard to concentrate when he kept flexing and distracting her with all those glorious muscles.

His expression softened into a smile that made her toes curl in her tennis shoes.

"No," he said. "Fast metabolism. Keeps me warm."

She rolled her eyes and looked away, mostly out of self-preservation. They wouldn't finish this conversation if they got caught up in lust and hormones and all the things she'd rather be caught up in at the moment.

He moved closer. She could feel his heat pumping off him even with a few feet still between them.

"Are you cold? We could go back," he said, his voice deep and low.

The sound glided over her skin like a caress. Damn him. She shivered but said, "I'm not cold."

"You just shivered."

"And you can tell why, and that it had nothing to do with me being cold," she snapped. How did Amy do this? Knowing Dylan could scent her lust was… Well, it made keeping focused a lot more difficult. As someone who'd never had trouble focusing before, that was wholly disconcerting.

He didn't touch her, but he stopped close enough that leaning into him would have been so very easy. Close enough, all she'd have to do was turn and wrap her arms around his neck, pull him in for a kiss she was desperate for. Her lips actually tingled with the wanting, a wanting that rose fast and hard and with so much power it stole her breath.

"Cat." His voice had roughened and the rumble was another caress over her nerves.

"Stop," she said, sounding more breathy than assertive. "We still have to… Have to finish this…" She swallowed. "This conversation. Before…"

"Before?"

"Before anything else," she forced out. Before I strip you naked and push you back into the grass and devour you, she thought.

"You're right," he said.

But he didn't step back. And this close his scent wrapped around her along with his heat and she was a moth to the flame. Dancing just beyond the heat, flying too close for safety, flittering headlong into disaster.

"You asked if leopard relationships were the same as humans and tigers."

His voice was even deeper now, quiet, and it took her a long moment to decipher the words because she was so caught up in the sound of his voice. She couldn't really speak so she just nodded.

"Some…yes. If they never find their mate. But leopards do form mate bonds, bonds that link two individuals together."

The haze of lust cleared enough for her to ask, "Permanently?"

While she'd made an effort to learn a little about other shifters—mostly that they existed—she'd focused on relationships and reproduction among tigers because that directly impacted her life. And her sister's life. She hadn't bothered researching other shifters and how they did relationships.

He nodded. "Pretty much permanent. If…if the couple don't get along despite the chemistry drawing them together, it's possible to break the bond. But it's not easy on anyone involved."

"Does that happen often?"

"No. Usually the chemistry wins out. The bond…solidifies, and the couple are together for life."

Wow. "Just couples? Are there any polyamorous mating bonds?"

His lips lifted in a slightly amused smile. "There can be, yes. It's not unheard of."

She nodded but mostly to show she'd heard him as her brain went down the rabbit hole of thinking. Mating bonds. Mostly permanent. "Is it a reproductive thing? Do the mates have to be capable of creating babies together? Or is it less biological than that?"

The tigers were so obsessed with reproduction, and most animals—shifter and non-shifter alike—developed mating behaviors and strategies to enable reproduction at a biological level. There'd have to be some of that in the leopard's mate bond, wouldn't there? Or was it just strictly a romantic thing? That didn't seem right from a biological point of view. Though, she supposed it would be nice if the people involved in the bond also had romantic feelings—it would strengthen things, make the reproduction part easier."

"Since there are same-sex mates, the bond isn't strictly a reproductive thing," he said, still sounding a little bemused. "It's easier for mates to have babies together, or through other methods—in modern times sperm donation and artificial insemination are easy enough. The bonding seems to enable easier conception even when the individuals involved aren't biologically able to combine their own gametes."

The technical, scientific phrasing made her brain happy and she continued down the rabbit hole. "So for example, you have two cis-gendered male leopards mate bonded," she said, then paused. "Wait, do you get trans-gendered shifters?"

She'd never considered that with tigers before. A strange oversight. She'd have to look into it. But since they could shapeshift, wouldn't someone who got the wrong biological body just…shift it to the right one? Or maybe they couldn't. Maybe they were locked into the biology they were born with one way or the other and surgical intervention was required to change that if necessary. Although, she knew for a fact surgery with tiger shifters was complicated. And were both animal form and human form…did they have the same gender at all times or where they sometimes different genders? Male animal body, female human body for example? That was an interesting possibility.

She blinked when Dylan waved a hand in her face. "Sorry," she said in a knee-jerk reaction. "Thinking."

"I noticed," he said, smiling. "Obviously, there's a lot here to discuss. For the record, there can be trans-gendered shifters, and it's as complicated an issue with shifters as it is with humans, with a wide spectrum of experiences. It's rarer in shifters than humans. And each species has different approaches to trans-gendered individuals in their populations. There are also non-binary shifters and gender fluidity. In fact, with some types of shifters there's more gender fluidity than strict binary gendering."

"Really? Which species?"

"A lot of the aquatic species. Dragon shifters have a lot of gender range and fluidity."

Aquatic species? She hadn't really learned about any of those yet. She had a lot to learn. And her brain did a giddy dance at the idea.

"But…" Dylan said, breaking into her spiral of thought. "If you don't mind, most of this is something we can talk about later."

"Oh! Oh, right. Sure. Yes." She'd gotten really far off track here, hadn't she? She frowned. What had they been talking about? Mate bonding! "Leopards and mate bonding," she said aloud.

"That," Dylan said.

She met his gaze as her cheeks heated. "It's all pretty fascinating, though, you have to admit."

"Even for a physicist?"

"Yeah," she said as if that should be obvious.

"I love the way your brain works," he murmured, though so quietly, she wasn't sure he meant for her to hear.

They were still standing very close, so close she was a little surprised she'd gotten distracted, because now that she was aware of it again, she caught herself leaning even closer, gravitating toward his heat. She stopped herself with a little mental shake.

He took another step closer, which was much too close now. She tipped her head back to look up at him and hear heartbeat started hammering so fast she couldn't tell what emotion had her pulse rushing around. There was something intent in his gaze that caught at her breath.

"Mate bonding in leopards is…serious," he murmured. "And almost always happens between two leopards."

"Not with other shifters?"

"Or with humans. Usually."

"Usually?" Was that fear rushing through her blood now? It felt like maybe a little fear.

"Sometimes the mate bond happens between a leopard and a human. It happened that way for my oldest brother. But it's very rare."

"Okay," she said because it felt like the place to comment. But she wasn't sure why he seemed so intent on this topic. Unless… "Do you have a leopard mate? Is that what you're trying to tell me?"

Because if that was the case, she needed to step back now.

"No. No, I don't. I wouldn't…" He swallowed visibly. "I wouldn't want anyone else if I had a mate already. Once we're bonded, that's it for us."

Her eyes widened. He'd said mostly permanent. "Forever?" That sounded like…a lot. "Dylan, why are we discussing this?" It suddenly seemed very important that he answer that particular question.

"Rare," he murmured. "But not impossible."

She narrowed her eyes at him, his implication sinking in. "You don't think…"

He held her gaze, but he frowned deeply. "I didn't at first. I'm still hesitant to believe. Having this kind of thing happen twice in one family… It's improbable."

"Improbable but not impossible?"

He nodded.

"You're not positive, though."

Something passed through his eyes, something she couldn't read.

"The thing is…" He finally glanced away for a moment, before meeting her gaze again. "The thing is, in the early stages, the bond is tenuous and can be broken. Leopards tend to…lose a lot of the control they have over their animal instincts during the initial phase. They need the bond to solidify for the control to return. Or they can break the bond and go their separate ways. A few weeks of discomfort and strict distance between each other ensures the bond doesn't reform."

"How do you solidify the bond?"

His lips quirk, a brief break in his serious expression. "Sex."

She blinked. "Sex?"

"Lots of it."

"Oh. Wow. Okay." But then she realized one more implication of this conversation, and her stomach did a flip. "Wait, after…after sex, can the bond still be broken?"

"With leopards? No."

His jaw muscles tensed. She was close enough to practically feel the vibration of tension in his muscles. She should probably step back. They needed space between them for this. Especially if she was reading his implications right. She wasn't sure why she couldn't force herself back. It would be smart. Prudent even. But her legs weren't obeying the command.

"With humans?"

He'd said it was rare but not impossible. That it had happened with his brother. Rare. But not impossible. Those words kept repeating in her head. He had to be mistaken about all this. She was sure he was. But for some reason, his answer to this question still felt important.

"It's still extremely difficult. Not as permanent as between two leopards. But…"

"But no longer easy."

"It's never easy," he said.

"You sure?" she murmured. And was glad when he didn't misunderstand her question.

"Pretty sure." He tapped his nose. "Took me some time to figure it out, but the scent of someone's mate is really hard to miss."

"Did you try to talk yourself out of it?" she asked.

A short laugh leapt from him, and from his expression, he was as startled by the sudden sound and reaction as she was. "I did actually. There are a lot of very valid reasons why this shouldn't be happening."

"Couldn't logic it away?"

"Couldn't logic it away."

"What if we're talking about something different right now? You haven't actually said…out loud."

"I'm waiting for you to run away."

"You think I will?"

"I think this isn't something you'll take lightly."

"No. I don't."

"And if you want to leave, if you don't want this to happen, it's important we get far away from each other."

"I'm not leaving before the eclipse," she said, very seriously.

"I'll stay away from you. I can…" He shrugged. "I'll figure it out."

"You won't miss the eclipse either."

"No. But I can manage between now and then."

"So long as we don't…" So long as they didn't have sex. Probably shouldn't even kiss him if she didn't want this. And she definitely shouldn't reach out and brush her fingers against his cheek.

She pulled in a deep breath. This was a lot more serious than a fling with a hot guy during the festival. This was even a lot more serious than she'd already worried about, given her developing feelings for that hot guy.

And still, he hadn't said the words out loud.

"Say it," she said. "Out loud. No prevarication."

"Despite the improbability," he said, "Cat Donovan, you're my mate."

2 O

Dylan's heart hammered hard against his ribs in a rhythm he couldn't seem to calm. He fisted his hands at his sides to keep from reaching for her, even though his every instinct screamed to close the last foot of distance between them and claim her.

This was too serious a moment to let his animal overwhelm his logic and sense.

A cold breeze ruffled the hairs on her forehead and lifted some of the soft blue and purple tendrils. She'd left her hair down but for a clip holding back a few strand from her face. In the darkness, she looked luminous, her skin glowing faintly. She wet her lips with a brief flick of her tongue and his muscles tightened in response.

He wanted her so much his body burned with the need.

But he couldn't follow through on that need, not now, when the implications were so huge. This wouldn't…couldn't be just a fling.

He'd been of at college when Deacon first met his mate, and had only seen them together after they'd been with each other for a couple of months. Even then, his brother had been…edgy. Less controlled than usual. And when Deacon had thought Cary was in trouble, he'd lost his fucking mind. He'd lost control completely. Dylan had never, not once, seen his oldest brother in that state. So out of control. So dangerous.

It had taken longer for Deacon to settle with his mate, to regain some of his control, than it usually did. Because she was human.

If Dylan didn't stop things with Cat now, if they let this go any farther, they risked that… That for the next few months, he'd be… dangerous. And they lived on opposite coasts. They had plans for their futures. Important to both of them. They couldn't just drop what they were doing, either of them, without it costing something.

This would change everything. *If* they let things go any farther.

He was no more certain he wanted that change than she was. His leopard was certain. His leopard wanted her and that was that. But logically, Dylan knew it wasn't that simple. As he watched Cat considering, thinking hard about what all this meant, he wondered if other mates confronted this same issue. Of course they did, in one form or another. But did they seriously consider saying no to the mate bond?

Finding a mate wasn't a guarantee. Most leopards would consider it ridiculous to turn this bond down. At least, he'd always thought so. He'd never honestly considered what he'd do when he found his mate, if he found one. He sort of assumed since he hadn't among the west coast leopards, it might not be in the cards for him. And he'd been okay with that. He'd been so focused on his studies, the idea of finding his mate really hadn't occurred to him. His sister never talked about finding hers. She seemed as disinclined to go looking for a mate as he was. But once found, would she—would any leopard—seriously consider turning down the chance at that future, full of love and companionship, family, maybe children?

He probably should have asked these questions, at least considered them, well before actually meeting is own mate. Especially since she, improbably, turned out to be a human.

A human with ties to tiger shifters.

Tiger shifters who considered her one of theirs.

That complicated things even further. He didn't want to start an entire battle with yet another group of shifters. They had enough issues with the cougars in the area. The last thing his mother needed to worry about was a war with the tigers as well.

"You've been quiet for a long time," Cat said softly, breaking into his thoughts.

"So have you."

"Thinking."

"Yeah."

"This is…big, huh?"

"Big. And complicated."

"Very," she said with feeling. "The tigers are going to lose their shit."

He almost laughed. "I was just thinking the same thing."

"You have no idea. They're really desperate these days." She frowned a little. "I can trust you with a secret, can't I? I mean, with this mate thing and all?"

Since they technically weren't bonded yet, not too tightly anyway, he wasn't sure her trust should be absolute based on that. But he did want her to trust him. "I'll keep your secret."

"Even from your family?"

"Yes." And he meant it.

"The tigers are on the brink of extinction. They have been for a while now." The words poured out of her like she'd opened a faucet valve and released a deluge. "They don't have enough female tigers. The numbers are so low, they actually know them all by name. They know the exact number in each part of the world. And so few female babies are born, the extinction issue isn't getting better. When they discovered hybrids, many thought that would solve the problem, but a lot of tigers hate the hybrids too. It's caused significant conflict over the years since the discovery. But the ones who see the hybrids—and by extension humans who could conceive with a tiger to produce a hybrid—as species saviors, they want all the women hybrids and humans to pick tiger partners. And they get very very jealous and angry when the human woman or hybrid doesn't. It's an issue. The male tigers… Okay not all of them, but a lot of them, have lost their minds when it comes to this shit, and they are so aggressive it's a pain in the ass."

He remembered her mentioning on that very first day—was that just yesterday? Shit.—something about men being a pain her ass. She'd been referring to her colleagues, but he wondered if the tigers hadn't figured into her assessment.

"And I'm not supposed to have told you about the extinction," she said. "They worry that will get out. That other shifters will discover they're so close to extinction and drive them all the way out of existence. So the fact that you're a shifter and I've just told you all this would be considered very bad. But probably not as bad as the fact that if I… If we… Then I won't be available to have tiger babies—which *I'm* good with by the way—and so in short, if…if we don't break this bond, there will be trouble with the tigers," she finished on a huge exhale.

He had to work not to grin. This wasn't a grinning moment. But damn she was adorable. And he was in a lot deeper than he should have let himself get.

"My people don't need another war with yet another shifter group," he said, carefully, "but they would absolutely back us against the tigers without hesitance. No questions at all. So don't let that part… That doesn't need to be part of this decision."

"It'll complicate things, though," she said.

"Things are already complicated. What's one more factor?"

She huffed out a sound that might have been a laugh. At least, he hoped it was. He liked when she laughed.

"I'm not sure what to do about this or how to feel about it," she said, meeting his gaze. Then she winced, "Is it rude to say that I'm kind of glad I'll be able to send the tigers packing?"

"Maybe a little rough on my ego if that's the only benefit you see here. But understandable."

"Well, not the only benefit," she said with an eye roll. "More of a value-added bonus."

His lips twitched. "You aren't running away," he said, because he was a little surprised.

"No. But I'm also not agreeing to anything." She frowned up at him. "How do you feel about all this?"

"Conflicted," he said honestly. "We both have goals, plans, things we're right in the middle of, on opposite coasts. If we allow the bond to form—" more than it already had, but he didn't think she needed to hear that part, "—I won't be able to be away from you for a while. Maybe months. My leopard will insist I stay close to you, or else."

"Or else?" Her eyes widened.

"I won't have as much control over my animal side until our bond is solidified. Which means I'll be dangerous and edgy. I'll need to be around you to keep my leopard settled in the meantime. It happens with all mate bonds. But usually the people involved understand the process and make allowances for it."

She frowned, her gaze turning inward as she considered these details. Finally, she said, "Do you want this? Honestly, the timing of it all sucks. But if not for that... Is this something you'd want? Even knowing it comes with a probable conflict with the tiger shifters?"

"I would," he admitted, to her and to himself. Only when he'd said the words out loud did he realize how true they were. He was worried about the circumstances, how they'd navigate the next few months, how they'd deal with the tigers. But when it came right down to it, he didn't want to let her get away.

He couldn't have imagined a more perfect mate for himself. And he didn't want to risk losing her.

"I could..." She glanced away as a flush crept up her cheeks.

The blush fascinated him, and it was all he could do not to cup her cheek, to see if he could feel the heat.

"I could always ask for allowances to finish my Ph.D. remotely. It happens. People take jobs and work on finishing their thesis in different parts of the country. There's nothing tying me to New York, necessarily."

"Except your family," he murmured. Because his leopard was leaping around in enthusiastic agreement with her plan, and he wanted to put the brakes on that sense of hope before he got carried away.

"There are airplanes. And video calls. It's not like I'd be on a different planet." She shrugged and met his gaze again. "Most of my job offers would have required I move anyway. I only had one near New York, at Princeton. But the only reason I was considering that one was to stay closer to Amy. And she wouldn't want me to make my decision that way."

"Would she want you to make your choice just to be closer to a man?"

"Not an ordinary one, no," she said. And he had to appreciate her honesty. "But you wouldn't be just an ordinary man. I wouldn't just be running off at a whim to follow an uncertain future."

He had to suppress a growl of satisfaction when she said he wasn't just any ordinary man to her. The hope in his chest was growing with each moment and it was getting harder to remain logical in the face of his leopard's triumph.

She let out a long breath. "I've been stalling, on getting on with my future," she said. "I haven't wanted to commit to anything. To be honest, the Cal Tech job was always my top choice. But I was…afraid to take it." She held her hands up, a little helpless gesture that made him want to pull her close. "I wouldn't be giving up my future to move to this coast. I'd finally be pursuing it. Because even if things between us didn't…work, I'd still be working in my field, pursuing my dreams. I wouldn't be sacrificing anything there."

She took one step closer to him and his muscles all tightened in anticipation. The closer she was, the more her scent overwhelmed him, creeping into his very soul, twisting tendrils of longing and need around him until she was his everything. And if she stayed this close, kept saying things that gave him so much hope, he wasn't going to be able to resist her much longer.

His leopard approved of that crumbling resistance.

She held his gaze. "I don't know what will happen between us. And, honestly, this is a little scary. But it's not nearly as scary as it should be. I'll have to think about that later. There must be a reason."

His lips twitched. "It's chemistry. Are you sure you want to go down the chemistry rabbit hole?"

"I have a working knowledge on the subject. I can manage," she said primly.

And his smile broke free.

Her own grin left him more than a little breathless.

"There's definitely something here," she said. "I haven't felt anything like this before. Certainly not with any of the tigers trying to convince me I need a shifter for a partner. I like this. I like you." She shrugged. "I'd like to see where this goes. At the least, it'll be an interesting study."

He laughed. He couldn't help it. "Most men would be offended at that, you know?"

"I wouldn't be making this decision in the same way with most men."

"I'm glad to hear it. For the record, I'd be disappointed if you didn't *also* want to study the mate bond."

"Also?"

"Well, I assume study isn't the only thing you want here." He finally lifted his hands to touch her, a gentle caress up her arms. The thick material of her sweatshirt kept him from her skin. Which was probably for the best. He was too on edge and this was too delicate a moment. Touching the softness of her skin, too quickly, would open up something in him, and he wasn't sure either of them was ready for that yet.

But soon. Very very soon.

She shivered and leaned into him, so he could feel her breath against his chest. His heart pounded loud enough he thought she might be able to hear it even with her human hearing. Her scent overwhelmed most of his logic now. She made up his entire world in that moment.

And she was as stunning as any star.

"How do we deal with the tigers?" she murmured.

"We'll talk to my mother. She'll know someone who can help."

"Oh, I can talk to Elizaveta, too. She'll be able to do…something."

"Elizaveta?"

"Chernikova. She's one of the tiger elders. Their governing body. She's an advocate. She'll help."

"Will she be upset you didn't end up with a tiger shifter?"

"Probably. But technically, she's…sort of family now, though marriages. Ethan's sister is married to one of Elizaveta's grandsons. So she has to be nice to me."

"Family doesn't always have to be nice to you, you know."

"Is your family all nice to you?"

"Well, yes. But I'm the baby. They have to be."

She laughed and drew her a little closer. He slid his hands farther up her arms, cupping her shoulders. He brushed his thumb near the edge of the material next to her collarbone, barely resisting the soft warmth of her skin.

"This isn't going to be simple," she said.

"No. But worth it, I think." Without really making a conscious decision, he lowered his head to hers, bringing their mouths closer.

She set her hands gently on his waist, as she drifted ever closer, and the contact of her touching his bare skin made him groan. His nerves were sensitive after the shift, and his awareness of her was almost more than he could take. The feel of such a simple touch did him in, broke open that thing inside he'd been trying to contain. She was warm and her touch felt so incredibly right he didn't want her to stop touching him. Ever.

"This is happening fast," she murmured.

"That's how things go with mates." His voice sounded rough and deep even to him.

"It's weird, though. Because it feels like I've known you for ages. Like a lot of time has passed since we met. It's been less than two full days. And I still feel like I *know* you. How is that possible?"

"Time paradox caused by the mate bond," he said firmly, though his voice was still gravel rough and coherent thought was getting more and more difficult by the second.

"Fair enough," she said. "I accept your hypothesis."

He started to smile, but the gesture froze as she reached up and pressed her lips to his.

And Dylan's world exploded around him.

21

C at had kissed men before. More than one, since the age of fourteen when she'd had her very first kiss during an otherwise disappointing game of truth-or-dare with a group of high school friends she'd lost track of in the years since. She liked kissing.

But nothing had prepared her for how she'd feel with her lips on Dylan's.

The jolt of shocking desire, the pulse of heat, the absolute sense of…perfection. Especially when he groaned, when he angled his head to deepen the kiss, when she parted her lips and his tongue swept into her mouth and she tasted him fully for the first time. Her fingers flexed on his waist, the heat of his skin seeping into her, warming her to her bones. The taste of him, the pressure of their mouths together, still gentle and exploring, still learning… The intensity of the moment quieted her mind in a way she rarely experienced. She was all sensation and *this* moment.

His scent filled her awareness, heat and male and that scent of nature like woods and earth and grass. She wasn't sure how much of that was him and how much was their surroundings in the field, but she didn't care. Because this scent would always be indelibly tied to this moment in her mind, to this man.

She pressed into him, finally satisfying a craving she'd had since meeting him, to feel the length of him against her, all of him. Without his shirt in the way, she gloried at the feel of hard muscles, soft chest hair, the way his grip on her shoulders tightened. She sighed into his mouth and deepened her kiss, wanting to fill herself up with him.

He pulled her closer, wrapping one arm around her waist, cradling the back of her head in his other. His hands felt so large and strong and something in her belly sang at the sheer masculinity of him. His kiss changed with his grip, taking on an intensity, a hunger she answered without hesitance.

If this was what it was like just kissing him, she could only imagine what might happen when they finally got naked together. And while good kisses, and good sex, were no guarantee of a good relationship, they sure as hell helped.

She rubbed against him, unable to resist, wanting to strip her shirt and sweatshirt off so she could just luxuriate in his heat and hardness. His hands flexed on her, his groan filled her. The press of his hardening cock against her lower abdomen set her on fire. She wanted more. All. And she wanted it now.

So when he jerked back, just a little, and pulled in a deep lungful of air, she huffed out a breath that she'd have called a pout if she were being honest with herself and tried to pull him back to her. Instead of kissing her, though, he set his forehead against hers, very gently.

"I have to stop now. We do. This won't be… Sex with mates is…"

"Intense? Lovely? Hot as hell?" she offered when he seemed lost for words.

His chuckle came out strained and choked. "I mean, once mates have sex, it starts to tighten the mate bond. Making it impossible to break. You need at least a night to sleep on this."

"I'd rather sleep on you," she interrupted.

"You're trying to kill me, right?"

"Well, okay, I wasn't planning on sleeping while on you. If that helps at all."

He groaned. "Yes. Trying to kill me. You're a little more sadistic than I would have guessed."

She laughed. Then cupped his cheeks with her hands. "I understand. I'd rather drag you into my tent and spend the night fucking you." His arms tightened around her. "But you're right. This is a more serious step than a fling. And I appreciate you thinking about how it affects me and giving me time. I might not like taking the time, but I need to. So do you. So thank you. Very noble of you."

"I need to take you back now, if I have any hope of following through with my noble urge."

"Okay." She went to take a step away from him, but he didn't loosen his hold. "We're not going to get anywhere like this," she said with a little chuckle. She wasn't objecting. She'd rather stay right here in his arms all night. Or, well, really she'd rather stay in his arms inside her tent. Or his tent. She wasn't picky.

"It'll be faster if I carry you," he said.

"Carry me?" She'd seen the speeds shifters could move. It was terrifying but also…intriguing. "So you can run fast?"

"Will that bother you?"

"The being in your arms or the running part? Because neither will bother me."

His grip flexed again, before he relaxed enough to adjust his hold on her, swinging her up with an arm under her knees and one wrapped around her back. The move lifted her high enough she was face to face with him without him having to lean over. She liked that a lot. To her wonder, she realized his eyes were glowing, just faintly, with that shifter glittering yellow gold. The blue almost entirely subsumed under his otherworldly nature.

She touched his cheek. "Animal is close to the surface, huh?"

"Very. And he's not nearly as noble about giving you time to think as I am."

She grinned.

But before she could comment, he said, "Hold on."

She had just enough time to wrap her arms around his neck and then he moved.

Her stomach jumped and dropped all at once, like being on a roller coaster. The world around her blurred into shadows with brief flashes of muted colors. The distance back to the camp wasn't all that far, so the journey only took a minute, maybe. But it was long enough for her thrill to overwhelm her ability to analyze the sensations. She blinked in surprised wonder when he stopped moving and they were just outside her tent.

"That was fun," she said. "We need to do that again. A longer run so I can see how it all works."

He shook his head, looking a little bemused by her comment. "Not nauseous or anything?" he asked, studying her face.

"Nope. Does that happen?"

"There's usually some motion sickness with humans after a run at shifter speeds."

"Run around with a lot of humans in your arms, do you?" She waggled her eyebrows.

He frowned a little. "Actually, no. This might be a first for me."

"Well, now I'm flatter."

He let her legs drop to the ground, and she savored sliding down his body, the tremble in his muscles she was certain had nothing to do with the run here. She leaned into him, unable to resist. And because he made a rough sound that felt like a delicious caress along her nerves, she rose onto her toes to kiss him again. He gripped her sweat-shirt hard. A part of her recognized the cotton wasn't going to hold up under that strain for much longer. She wasn't worried about it, though. A torn sweatshirt was a valid price for the pleasure of feeling Dylan's control slip a little.

She was surprised by her reaction to all this. The lack of fear. She would have thought somewhere in all this she'd be terrified. She'd been afraid of commitment before. He was talking about a lifetime of commitment. Of months where he'd need to be near her or risk losing control of his leopard half. She should have felt, at the very least, stifled by that thought. *She* should be the one pulling back, asking for time to think and consider, to make sure before they fell into bed—or in this case a sleeping bag—together.

Instead, she felt…free and happy and wonderfully eager. Was that her or the mate bond chemistry? She'd never felt like this around any of the human men she'd dated. Or any of the tiger shifters trying to convince her she should take them as a partner. She'd never even imagined this feeling was possible.

A part of her mind was quite happy analyzing her reactions, too. Cataloguing and labeling and trying to trace the source and find the answers. But a surprising amount of her brain was just as happy *not* to analyze all this. To simply savor the feel of Dylan's mouth on hers, to enjoy the slide of his tongue against hers and the rough flex of his muscles around her. To sink into feelings and sensations like there was nothing else to do.

The whole of it was a delicious contrast she'd never imagined possible. The thinking and the not thinking all at once in a way that left her breathless and eager for more, deeper, harder, faster…

And for a very long time.

If this was the mate bond, then she liked it. The thrill, the slight terror but a fun sort of terror, again like a roller coaster. Like floating in the hot air balloon above the fields, knowing her life was in someone else's hand and at the whims of physics.

She could live this way.

She pressed harder into him, forgetting that she wasn't supposed to drag him into her tent, forgetting that he wanted to be noble and give her a night to think. She'd already thought. And analyzed. And come to a decision. But she wanted to respect the decision enough to give him time, too.

Sort of. The lusty part of her just wanted to strip him naked and spend the rest of the night learning what made him groan.

Apparently breaking off their kiss was one of the things that made him groan, although that groan sounded more pained than pleasured. "We need to…" He swallowed. "I'm going to let you go inside your tent now. Alone. And then I'm going to lock myself in my truck."

"That seems a little extreme," she said, amused and delighted by his reluctance to let her go.

"Necessary," he assured. "Very necessary."

"If you're sure," she said, pressing a little tighter to him, loving the feel of his hard cock against her. She was tingling everywhere, wet and ready and eager. And sleeping alone wasn't going to be nearly as much fun as taking him to bed with her would be. She wasn't actually consciously trying to tempt his control. She just didn't want to let him go.

"I'm not sure even a little bit," he said, his voice deep and rough. "Except for the part about having to lock myself in the truck."

She hummed under her breath, a sound of both pleasure with a touch of reluctance and disappointment. She cupped his face in her hands, his jaw muscles tight under her fingers. "I'd rather have you with me, but I understand taking at least the night," she said. His eyes glittered as he looked down at her, the intensity making her insides melt. She grinned. "Ah, Dylan. We're going to have so much fun."

Then she ducked into her tent before either of them could change their minds and zipped up the flap—not to keep him out, but to keep herself in.

Dylan took an involuntary step toward the tent the instant Cat disappeared inside. He wasn't even aware of making the move toward her, but when he did realize what he was doing, he muttered a curse.

Before his better instincts could be buried under his lust, he swung back to his truck, and true to his word, locked himself in. He moved his telescope equipment to the front seat, then folded up the narrow back seat so he could lay on the floor of the cab. A less comfortable night sleeping stretched out in the truck seemed safer than his tent—which didn't have a lock on the door. And it wasn't like he'd be comfortable tonight anyway. Or that he'd get much sleep.

We're going to have so much fun.

Her words echoed in his mind as he settled on his back on the hard cab floor, staring up at the dark roof. Her smile danced in his mind alongside the words, making his leopard purr in frustrated contentment. He'd anticipated a lot of resistance to the mate bond, that she'd need a lot of time to adjust and accept all this. He'd been prepared for the wait because he wanted to do this right. Mate bonds were supposed to be forever. The last thing he wanted to do was start out that future on the wrong foot.

Her acceptance, her eagerness actually left him dizzy. And a lot of that reaction was relief. He was disoriented by having found his mate, and he knew her being human would come with some complications. Her being tied to the tiger shifters carried some of its own complications.

But all of that seemed minor compared to her acceptance of the bond. Of him.

We're going to have so much fun.

He smiled up at the black roof, despite the unanswered lust thrumming through his veins.

Yeah. They were definitely going to have fun.

22

Sunday passed in lusty looks and deliberate touches and a lot of building tension all while the party around them grew. Dylan brought out his big telescope and took some early pictures of the sun, testing his filters to make sure nothing would go wrong the next morning. Cat did the same, her scope set right next to his. They chatted with Tom, bemoaned the showers flooding and being shut down, ate more delicious food from the concessions tent, and in general had such a great day, Dylan couldn't remember ever enjoying a single day more.

He felt a weird kind of hope he hadn't really experienced before, and hadn't thought he was missing until Cat. But he liked it. The fact that she hadn't run the opposite way when he'd explained the mate bond still astounded him. Given her experience with shifters trying to control her life, the last thing he expected was for her to accept the bond and the way it would control her life.

Growing up, knowing if he found his mate, that bond would affect everything, he'd accepted but hadn't really considered the implications. He'd seen many mates in happy relationships—including one of his sisters who had been with her mate for years now and had kids and everything. Outside of Brigit though, most of his siblings had remained mateless until Deacon met Cary last year. And it had occurred to Dylan more than once that a mate bond might not be in the cards for him. But he was young for a shifter, he had a long life expectancy, he hadn't really worried about finding a mate.

And maybe that was why Cat could accept their bond so easily? Because he hadn't pushed it or tried to force it on her the way the tigers kept trying to force her into…whatever the hell they kept trying to force her into?

She revealed more about her time with the tiger shifters whenever they were alone and could speak without the surrounding humans over-hearing. The moments were rare, but he'd gotten a glimpse of what modern tiger society was like and he wasn't sure how to feel about it. He had a lot of sympathy for their extinction issue. He'd seen species driven to extremes in the face of annihilation. And it sounded like they'd reached a compromise that had managed to keep them from imploding for the last two centuries. But the edges of that compromise were fraying. After what Cat told him, he was a little surprised they'd managed any stability for as long as they had. He wasn't sure they'd be able to maintain that balance much longer.

But he wasn't a tiger. He didn't even know any personally. It was hard to judge from the outside, if not impossible.

The way so many of the male tigers had been harassing Cat, on the other hand, was something he could judge. And he had a very dim opinion of it. She swore she wasn't in danger. They weren't allowed, by law, to harm a human and she was, without question, a human. She wasn't afraid of them—despite the fact that they were stronger, faster, and more deadly than she could possibly be. But they wanted her to pick a tiger male and start having kids immediately. And the pressure they exerted to convince her this was a good idea was… Creepy was the only way he could think of it.

"It's creepy," she said aloud, quietly, as she adjusted her scope.

He tried not to smile that her words echoed his thoughts.

The late afternoon sun continued to warm the site, the heat cut by a breeze that brushed erratically through the neatly lined tents and campers. Activity had lessened in the last hour as people took to the shade, or the beer tent, to stave off the afternoon heat. Shadows lengthened down the dirt road separating his lot from Tom's—who'd gone for a walk about fifteen minutes earlier. And someone nearby was cooking something with a lot of delicious smelling spices in it. Stretched, wispy clouds blew through the bright sky, but didn't disrupt his sun pictures. With luck, they'd have very few of those clouds tomorrow to interfere with the big event.

"Look," she murmured, after scanning their surroundings one more time, ensuring no one was close enough to overhear, "I know a lot of tigers at this stage, and almost everyone I've met is nice—except for that hot assassin guy—and normal, and not creepily obsessed with reproduction. On an individual basis. It's just that their society as a whole *is* obsessed with reproduction, and that's driven some of the males to be…well, creepy."

"Hot assassin guy?" he asked, because he got caught on both the assassin part and the fact that she'd called him hot. His leopard didn't approve.

She waved that away. "That was a few years ago. Right after Amy and Ethan met. He turned out to be okay. I mean, he didn't kill us, so that was good, right? He is pretty scary."

"And hot?" Was he growling? That was a growl in his voice. She'd just said she'd known this guy years ago. Why the hell was he growling? He mentally swatted at his leopard half for acting like a jealous idiot. He wasn't normally a jealous person. That was weird.

She grinned at him, obviously not as thrown off by his jealousy as he was. "Objectively speaking, there was no denying he was hot. Gorgeous *and* smart. Well, I mean not me smart, but still smart enough to keep up."

Dylan officially hated the man.

And the fact that he did, left him confused enough he didn't know what to say for a long moment.

Finally, he managed, "See him much? An assassin doesn't sound like safe company."

Wow, his voice sounded weird. Deep. Gravely. Shit, where his eyes glowing? His leopard felt very near the surface. He hid his face in his scope so none of the passing people would notice and tried to rein in the weird surge of jealousy. Damn. His mother had warned him about this, warned them all. And he'd seen some of it first hand with other mates. But he hadn't realized the suddenness of it, or the…power. Chemistry at its worst.

He cleared his throat. "Sorry about the questions on this," he muttered. "I… Turns out the mate bond sparks a lot of jealousy and, uh, I don't seem to have a very good handle on controlling it just now."

She stepped close and pressed into his arm. The move settled him almost instantly. And left him breathless.

She kissed his cheek. "We should talk about something else, because your eyes are glowing. Thank you for recognizing the jealousy was an over-the-top reaction. Especially considering I haven't seen Zhong in a couple of years, and also he did try to kill my sister at one point. Even epic levels of hotness can't make up for that."

"It's really weird that I'm relieved to hear that," he said. "I shouldn't be relieved that he tried to kill your sister."

She chuckled, but then turned more serious when she said, "This is the bond? This is how it works?"

"'Fraid so. My mother warned me. I saw my sister and my brother go through this. I just didn't realize…how fast it would hit."

"Your mother warned you?" She smiled. "That's sweet."

"It is?" He turned to face her, finally feeling like his leopard had settled enough he didn't risk revealing himself to a casual passerby. She remained close enough that they were still touching and the touching did wonderful, settling things for him. Although, a different kind of edginess crept in when his gaze dropped to her mouth. But he'd been controlling the urge to drag her into a tent and fuck her until they were both exhausted since meeting her, so he had more practice with that reaction.

He wasn't any better at controlling it. But it was less dangerous.

"You're close with your family," she said. "You talk with your mother about things like relationships." She shrugged. "It's nice." Her gaze turned a little wistful. "My parents, Amy and I, were all really close. It's been years, eleven years since they died, and I still miss that closeness sometimes. That family bond. Amy and I are still close, and she did her best to be a mother when I needed one, but it's not the same. It shouldn't be the same." She smiled, but there was a little dip of tightness at the corners, and the scent of melancholy flavored her emotions. "I miss my mom," she said. "And it's…nice, knowing you get along with yours."

He wanted desperately to wipe the sadness from her gaze. "We all get along, as much as any family," he said, "but I should warn you, my mother is scary. Like, scary scary to most people who don't know her. You might be a little less sentimental about her after meeting her."

A real grin brightened her expression. The look made his heart do a funny flipping thing in his chest.

"I've met plenty of scary matriarchs at this stage. Really really scary ones. Turns out their mostly wonderful people. I like a good scary matriarch."

"Then you'll love my mom," he said, with as much seriousness as he could manage in the face of her grin.

"This was a good topic change," she said.

He dipped his head closer, focused again on her mouth and the way her lips looked very plump and kissable at the moment. "Absolutely. Can't even remember what we were talking about." Which wasn't hyperbole. He'd completely forgotten what they'd been discussing. He leaned closer and brushed his mouth over hers, a quick taste, testing her reactions.

She pulled in a sharp breath that made him smile, so he brushed her lips with his again, gently, quickly, just enough to tease them both. She rose a little on her toes, following him as he retreated, and he couldn't resist the invitation, kissing her more fully this time, wrapping his arms around her waist to pull her flush to him. Her tongue teased at his as she leaned into him, tangling her fingers in his hair. Her scent filled with that spicy lemon scent of lust. Her body warmed and softened against him. And his head spun with how much he wanted her.

This could easily get out of hand. Quickly. He was already getting hard and losing any awareness that they weren't alone, that there were people all over the campsite. He needed to step back. Stop now.

He didn't. He didn't even want to.

So when a throat clearing and the sharp scent of angry tigers interrupted the kiss, the shock to his system was abrupt, unwelcome, and dragged a vicious hissing growl from him before he could suppress the sound.

He snarled at the three tigers standing only a few feet away, even as he pulled Cat closer—a reaction he wasn't entirely in control of. It took a concerted effort for him to force some logical thought through the haze of angry instincts. Humans everywhere. Couldn't go full shifter at the moment. That would be bad.

But, oh, how he wanted to.

23

Music from a nearby campsite was the only sound for a long moment after the tigers appeared. Dylan cursed himself for not noticing them sooner. But he realized they'd kept themselves downwind, purposefully hiding their approach. They'd meant to sneak up on him and Cat, to prove a point.

Dylan snarled again.

The leader, Lenny Cat had called him, returned Dylan's snarl. The big guy behind him, Rick, answered his growl with one of his own. And the jittery guy, who Cat didn't know, his eye twitched as he stared hard at Dylan.

"Thought we'd seen the last of you guys until after the eclipse," Dylan said. His voice back to deep and gravely.

"You're poaching on our territory, leopard," Lenny said. "That can't stand."

"Oh, you did not just say that," Cat said, her snarl vicious enough to match any of the shifters present. "I am not *territory*, you asshole."

Dylan's lip twitched as anger and outrage suffused her scent. Without thought, he pulled her a little closer and she leaned in to him, which he found embarrassingly satisfying.

"All three of you can fuck off. Now." Cat stared them down. "I'm officially off the market. Taken. Committed."

The committed part made Dylan look down at the top of her head and his heart did that funny flipping thing again. He knew most of what she was saying was just to send the tigers packing. But her words filled him with a lot of…relief. Hope.

Possibilities.

They needed a lot more time together. Nothing was completely settled. But he found himself thanking the universe that she was so willing to give them a shot that she'd just announced as much to the tigers. Without any hesitance.

Lenny's gaze narrowed on them. "A fling is allowed, Cat. But nothing permanent. You know that."

"You sonofabitch. I know no such thing. How dare you? How *dare* you! You do not own me. Your people do no own me."

"If you don't pick a tiger mate, you lose our protection."

"Fuck. You," she said.

"She'll have ours," Dylan said at the same time. "And none of your people want to fuck with my mother."

"Who the fuck is your mother?" Rick said with a condescending snarl.

"Maria Jones."

The jittery guy's twitch increased even as his eyes widened. He looked between his two companions as the smell of panic filled his scent.

Dylan smiled at him. "I see one of you has some sense. From this coast, are you?" he asked the jittery guy.

The man gave him a single chin raise nod but that was his only response.

Lenny's mouth tightened. "You know the rules, Catalina. You refuse a tiger mate, you lose any status you have under our laws."

"Actually, that's not the law, Leonard," she said. "My status and protections are not dependent on me choosing a tiger mate. And never have been. You don't want to believe that, you can take it up with Elizaveta."

The jittery guy's whole body twitched. Rick glanced down at Lenny, his expression fixed into unreadable lines, but his scent carried that punch of wariness he'd had the last time Cat mentioned Elizaveta to them. Now Dylan better understood why.

"And even without my status—" she snarled the word, "—I'm human and still safe from you. So you can officially fuck off now. My mate and I were in the middle of something."

Dylan's entire body, every nerve, muscle, cell, every particle, hell every quark that made up every particle stilled. She'd called him her mate. She'd acknowledged him as her mate to other shifters who would understand what that meant.

In the instant after the stillness, everything in him exploded with light and energy and a fierce satisfaction that shocked him. He'd pull out that reaction later and examine it. But in that moment, he didn't even try to hide his joy. And he was very happy to reveal his satisfaction to the three tigers.

"He's not your mate," Lenny said. "Leopards only mate bond with other leopards."

"Apparently not," Cat said, shrugging.

"He's lying to you to get in your pants."

She laughed. "He wouldn't have had to. I wanted to fuck him well before the whole mate thing came up."

Well, he was glad to hear that.

"And more to the point, he knew that." She tapped her nose. "I wasn't exactly able to hide my lust. So there was no point in lying about being my mate."

"He's still lying to you," Lenny said.

"About what?" she asked, sounding genuinely interested.

Dylan frowned down at the top of her head. Did *she* think he'd lied about something? She didn't have doubt or misgivings in her scent anywhere. He took an extra moment to analyze what he could of her scent and...no, nothing like doubt in her lemony and lightning spice. Just curiosity.

"He told you the bond was permanent. That you had no choice." Lenny sounded arrogantly sure of that.

"Nope. Told me how to break the thing as soon as he told me about it. Gave me a choice immediately in which direction I wanted to go with all this." She waited a beat before saying, "Is that all you have for me? Guesses and assumptions? Because you're assumptions are wrong and leading you to draw spurious conclusions. He's not you."

Lenny blinked slowly. Dylan recognized that controlled reaction for what it was. Very tightly leashed anger about to erupt. He angled himself just a little, curving slightly in front of Cat, readying to move if the shifter attacked.

"You aren't bound to him yet," Lenny said.

"More guesses?"

"Leopard bonds take time to solidify." Lenny raised his brows. "Did he tell you that? That you're not bound yet?"

"Yes." She said it so matter-of-factly, Lenny blinked again.

"You belong to the tigers," he said quietly.

"No. I belong to me. No one else."

"Not even your supposed mate," Rick said around a snarl, making the word "mate" sound like a disease.

"To *no one but me*," she said. "I choose who I'm with."

"You've always had a choice with us," Lenny said. A comment which made her snort. "But only a choice of which *tiger* you'll pick. Others…" He moved his gaze to Dylan's, his eyes glowing obviously yellow even though it was the middle of the afternoon and any human could see him. "Are not welcome," he finished.

Cat let out a long, loud, exasperated sigh. "No tigers. Not now. Not ever as it turns out. And that's that. It's Dylan or no one. That's *my* choice."

He had to squelch the rapid leap of joy her words sparked because the situation was already tense and he didn't want to give the tigers any ammunition. But when the threat was gone, he was going to relive what she'd just said and savor it.

"You're not allowed to make that choice," Lenny said.

"All right." She put her hands on her hips. "That's about as much of that as I can take. That is so much bullshit, my brain hurts. *My* brain. Hurts. From. The. Bullshit. So I will no longer tolerate it. I know you're thick-headed and all, but hear this very clearly. I'm done with tigers I'm not related to. Done. All finished. No more. I'm contacting Elizaveta tonight. There will be no more of this stalking, no more of these threats, no more of this weird and twisted sense of entitlement you think you have over my relationship decisions. You are *not* entitled to me. I am *not* yours. And I will have no more of this. If you try it again, I swear you will pay for it."

Rick actually raised his brows at her and the jittery guy's gaze jumped around, as if he wanted an escape.

Lenny narrowed his still very yellow eyes. "You're a human. You can't threaten us."

She leaned in, putting her face in Lenny's. "Try me, asshole. I know how to fuck you up. And I will destroy you if you do not stop stalking me."

"You're saying this because the leopard has twisted your thinking."

Lenny sounded calm but the anger and rage in his scent nearly choked Dylan. Thick and heavy and full of so much resentment, Dylan wasn't sure he'd ever smelled anything so acrid and bitter coming from a single being.

"Your duty is to the tigers, and you know it."

"I swear to the universe and all that is stringy, if you call having babies my duty again, I will punch you in the throat."

Dylan pressed his lips together. A laugh right now would be inappropriate—and hard to explain. Especially since he believed her threat. She would absolutely punch Lenny in the throat if he didn't back off. Still... He had a very hard time hiding just how delighted he was by her.

"When the leopard is gone," Lenny said, his voice very low, "you'll remember what's right."

Dylan heard the threat as clearly as if Lenny had said it outright. A low, almost impossible for humans to hear, hiss escaped him before he could swallow it. Lenny didn't move his gaze from Cat's but his lip twitched. He'd heard Dylan answer the threat.

Cat pulled her cellphone out of the back pocket of her jeans and showed Lenny the screen as she pulled up a number. "I'm calling Elizaveta now. You wanna talk to her?"

She hit a button and the phone started to ring. Even without the speaker on, every shifter there heard the call connect clearly.

The jittery guy gave Dylan one last, wide-eyed look and then took off, too fast, almost full shifter speed. In the middle of the damned day. Dylan shook his head. Idiot. Dangerous idiot.

The big guy studied his surroundings and then turned and walked away. "Come on, Len. Let's go."

Lenny remained where he was for a long moment, his gaze locked with Cat's. Dylan's fingers flexed into fists, but he held still, half his attention on Lenny's littlest movement, the other on the ringing call. A click and an answer broke the tense standoff.

"Hello?" A woman's voice, with a distinct Russian accent. "Is this you, Catalina? Is there a problem?"

At the last sentence a hard note filled the voice and Dylan watched Lenny's pulse jump in his throat. He spared Dylan a snarl and then hurried after Rick, moving at a more human pace as they walked away.

But Lenny's eyes were still glowing yellow.

Dylan watched the tigers disappear down the road as Cat put the phone to her ear.

"Hi Elizavata. Thanks for taking my call."

"Is there a problem, kotik?" the woman with the Russian accent said.

Dylan stepped closer to Cat while he watched to make sure the tigers had really left, keeping his senses open and alert to his surroundings this time. Later, he'd kick himself for having let them sneak up on him and Cat in the first place. He didn't intend to let that happen again. Although, given their reactions to the voice on the phone, he assumed they'd stay away now. At least for a little while.

"Yes," Cat said. "Lenny and Rick have been here. With some little guy they haven't seen fit to introduce."

"I am sorry they've been bothering you," the woman said. "I will speak with them."

Cat's smile looked absolutely feral. It was a side of her Dylan hadn't seen before. He found he liked it, which probably said things about him that weren't particularly flattering, but he didn't feel the need to look at that too closely.

But the satisfaction in her smile dropped when she looked up at him and said into the phone, "There's more. I'll probably have to meet with the elders soon. And they aren't going to like what I have to say."

"Tell me," the woman said.

"I have a mate."

"But that's wonderful. We did hope—"

"No," Cat cut in. "He's not a tiger."

There was a long silence on the other end of the phone. Then, "Human?"

"No." She mouthed to Dylan, *Can I tell her?*

He got the impression she would have to, one way or the other, so he nodded.

"He's a leopard," Cat said, very quietly, holding his gaze as she did.

Another silence. "He tells you you're his mate?"

"Yes."

"You believe him?"

"Yes."

"You understand this is…different for leopards. The mate bond. He's explained this?"

"Yes."

"And that it is very unusual for a human to bond with a leopard?"

"He's explained everything."

"I see." Another pause, then, "You're right. The other elders will hate this. But… It is what it is, isn't it."

Cat's lip's twitched but she didn't smile. "It is."

"Do you accept him?"

"Yes." She said this while still holding his gaze.

Without the threat of the tigers, Dylan finally allowed himself to smile, watching her smile in return.

"Then it is done," the woman said firmly. "At least, I assume you two have…"

The pointed pause and the innuendo wasn't lost on Dylan.

Or Cat apparently. She smirked at the phone. "I'm not giving you details of my sex life, Elizaveta, but if you could see him, you wouldn't be asking that question."

Dylan chuckled silently. She hadn't answered the elder's question, but her implications were clear enough—even if still not entirely true. A very adept way to lie to a shifter without actually lying. Even though Elizaveta wasn't here to scent the fib in Cat's scent, she'd obviously gotten used to avoiding direct answers with comments that weren't lies that shifters could smell.

As if he hadn't already known she was a genius.

"Do I get to know this young man's name?" Elizaveta asked, sounding like a scolding mother.

"Dylan Jones."

Another long pause. "Is his mother Maria Jones?"

Cat raised her eyebrows at Dylan in question. He'd mentioned his mother's name during the standoff with the tigers, but he wasn't sure she'd picked up on that. She could also be asking if he wanted her to tell the elder who his mother was. Either way, he nodded. If the tiger had heard of his mother, it was best they understood upfront the politics of this situation.

And he knew it was going to turn, at least a little, political before all was said and done.

"That's his mother, yes," Cat said.

"Well."

Elizaveta's word didn't reveal anything and without the woman here, Dylan couldn't read her scent any more than she could read theirs. Still, he got the impression that single word meant a lot. He just wasn't sure what.

"I will take care of Leonard and Richard," Elizaveta said after a few moments. "And smooth the way with the other elders. They'll want to *discuss* this, of course."

Cat groaned. "Do they ever, ever stop arguing?"

"No," Elizaveta said. "They are all old and querulous. Well, most of them. It gives their lives meaning to argue."

Cat let out a little laugh. "I'm not sure when I can get to them."

"I'll arrange matters. Do no worry." Another pause and then, "I will admit to my disappointment, kotik. But are you happy with this turn of events?"

"I am," Cat said quietly.

"Then I am happy for you. Have you told your sister yet?"

Cat let out another groan. "No. I haven't had a chance. Don't you tell her before I can. This should come from me."

"Tell her soon, then. Word will spread fast. We're all a terrible bunch of gossips."

The line disconnected abruptly and Cat shook her head as she put her phone away. When she looked up at him, she said, "They are. Terrible gossips. She's right, this will spread fast. I need to warn Amy."

He nodded, but he was thinking and missed her expression until she put a hand to his cheek and turned him to face her.

"What's wrong?" she asked.

"It's just… Telling the tigers, telling your sister, this all feels like… Like we're doing what Lenny accused me of doing. Rushing you. Forcing your hand. The mate bond isn't just a regular relationship. It's not something, once it's settled, that can be broken. At least not easily. We haven't fully bonded yet. So telling your sister, confronting the elders, could be premature. Starting trouble you don't need to start. There's time for you to decide you don't want this."

"Is that what you want? To stop this before it gets started?"

The worry and hurt in her scent made his chest tightened. "No. Not even a little. I'm… I'm in. I don't want to break our bond. But I don't want you to feel forced, pressured into it. And…"

He swallowed hard, just now realizing how important this part was. She'd made a joke about this last night, but he'd been too wrapped up in making sure she understood what the bond was to take the joke seriously or even really think about it. Now, he needed her to seriously consider this.

"I don't want you accepting the bond just to get away from the tigers," he said. "I don't want this thing between us to be your excuse, your justification for avoiding them. That wouldn't be fair to either of us."

She pulled in a deep breath and straightened her shoulders but her gaze turned inward and she nodded a little as she thought.

Waiting, attempting to patiently stand there while she considered her real motivations was torturous. A part of him wanted to take back what he'd said. Tell her to forget it. He'd take her no matter what, even if she was just using him and the mate bond to avoid the tigers. He'd still have her, and he was sure they could make a relationship work, he was sure they'd be good together.

But a part of him would always doubt, wonder, if she'd chosen him as the lesser of two evils. He'd never be settled in the strength of their bond and that meant his leopard would remain edgy and dangerous, well past the period when he should settle. So he couldn't avoid this discussion. He couldn't pretend it wasn't important that she choose to be with him because she wanted this future, not just an escape from an uncomfortable situation. It mattered to all parts of him. Not knowing would end up creating far worse consequences than knowing and risking losing her.

But waiting for her to think through what he'd said was still torture.

After what felt like years but was probably only a few minutes given how fast her mind worked, Cat looked up at him, frowning slightly.

"I'm very glad you brought this up," she said after a moment. "I really don't want to use you. That wouldn't be good. Or right."

He found himself holding his breath and had to consciously drag in some air, let it out slowly. His gut churned and his chest felt tight, but he held silent, waiting.

"I don't want to use you to escape them," she said. "It is, however, a side…benefit for me to the bond. I can't deny that. Like… I don't know, like icing on cake. Cake is always good. Even without icing. But the icing pushes it over the top into epic deliciousness. And to be honest, that's what getting rid of the tigers feels like —icing." She held up a hand as if to stop him from saying anything even though he hadn't moved to speak. "But, I would take the cake no matter what. I'd still want the cake, even if I were denied the icing."

He considered that for a moment before he had to ask, "Does this mean that even if the tigers keep insisting you should…be a part of their world, if the mate bond makes no difference to your status with them, you'll still want…want me?"

"Yes," she said.

The simplicity of her answer, the sincerity and honesty he got from her scent, made him blink. He'd been expecting a lot more hesitance and worry. Her easy acceptance, and her saying exactly what he needed to hear, left him strangely disoriented.

"How about you?" she asked quietly. "After seeing that…" She gestured vaguely in the direction the three tigers had gone. "After hearing what Elizaveta said, knowing you'll end up in the middle of all that mess for a little while… Do *you* still want this?"

He pulled her close, suddenly and with just an edge of panic shooting into his blood. He couldn't say where the panic came from. But the thought that she might think he didn't want her was intolerable. "I want this. I'll take on the entire tiger shifter population if that's what it takes. I don't care about that. I just want to make sure you know what you're getting into, and that you're doing it for reasons you won't regret later."

"They're going to complicate things for us. To start. They'll eventually move on to some other issue, but at the start, they will be an issue. The elders are a pain in the ass. And they'll want to meet with us. And they'll argue over us without actually talking to us much. And the bastards make me stand still for way too long during these things. And it will be a real bore."

His lips twitched. "I'll make sure you get plenty of cake after."

Her eyes widened. "How did you know that's what I'd need?"

"You like cake," he said, tugging her a little closer. She softened against him, her arms coming up to wrap around his neck. "And you don't like being still."

The only time she wasn't moving her hands or tapping her foot or doing something physical was when she was deep in thought. And even then, her eyes moved as if she were looking at something only she could see. He loved watching her think for that reason. She settled physically, but he could still *see* her mind working.

"I hate it," she said. "It actually sort of hurts to stay still if I'm not concentrating on something."

Even as she said that, her fingers were moving against his neck, tangling in his hair. Those particular restless movements were sending little jolts of awareness and lust arrowing through him, a distraction she didn't intend but one he savored. He was perfectly content to be the object of her restless movements. Though he did start wondering what happened to all her restlessness during orgasm. Did she go still when she came? Suddenly, finding out seemed imperative to his existence.

"It uses up a lot of energy for me," she said. For a split second, he thought she was talking about orgasms, until she said, "Forcing myself to stay still does."

And he had to pull himself out of his train of thought before he got so distracted by the idea of watching her come, he lost track of what she was saying.

"So if I'm forced by circumstances to stay still for too long," she said, oblivious to his reaction, "I usually end up starving and have to eat a lot to make up for it."

Her smile, a little shy at the edges, went right through him. Without thinking, he hugged her closer.

"So offering to feed me cake after a meeting with the elders is just…perfect."

"Does this mean you want to keep me around?" he asked. He felt a little breathless looking down into her glorious smile, her dark eyes twinkling in the afternoon sunlight, so his voice sounded gruffer and deeper than he'd intended. "Because of me and not the tigers."

"I do," she said.

She rose on her toes to meet him as he lowered his head to her, and her kiss was so full of sweet longing he groaned. He knew then he'd do anything for her, even face the tiger elders.

And he might have to learn how to bake cake.

2 5

C at went into her tent to call Amy, an attempt at some semblance of privacy even though she knew Dylan could hear the conversation if he wanted to. She just thought this discussion would probably go better if she wasn't staring at him while she had it. Staring at Dylan was too damned distracting and she was likely to wander off the point with her sister as she contemplated how best to strip him out of his t-shirt and jeans.

Which wasn't something she wanted to accidentally end up discussing with her big sister.

She smiled as the phone rang, knowing that a purposeful discussion of just how sexy Dylan was wasn't beyond their relationship. But she just had some other things she needed to tell her sister *first*.

Amy answered after two rings. "Are you okay? Are the tigers bothering you?"

"Wow. Hi to you, too."

Amy snorted. "You aren't calling me just to say Hi or check in and you know it."

This was true. She'd warned Amy she'd likely be too preoccupied by the eclipse stuff to call while she was here. She'd rang after arriving at her hotel in Portland, just so her sister knew she was safe. And she'd intended to call right before flying back. After what happened to their parents, they both made an effort to check in with each other regularly. But Cat also knew herself well enough to know she'd forget to call *during* the festival, and she'd made sure to warn Amy of that ahead of time.

Which meant her sister's reaction to this call was probably justified.

"I'm fine," she said, with a minimum of little-sister exasperation. Then smiled when Amy harrumphed at her tone. "But yeah, some tigers did follow me here."

"Should Ethan and I come out there? Do you need backup?"

She shook her head. "No, of course not. I'm good. It's just… I have something to tell you, and it's important, and it's going to change a lot of things."

"Is this the Cal Tech job? Are you taking it finally?"

Cat let out a little breath. She hadn't realized Amy wanted her to take a job all the way on the opposite side of the country, even though it was Cat's top choice. She'd told Amy it was her favorite offer. She just hadn't realized Amy would be okay with her moving so far away. Until that very moment, she'd been afraid she'd have to convince Amy that Cal Tech was the right choice.

She should have known better. Her hesitance all these months—to take any of the job offers, to move, to get on with her future—had always had more to do with her own fears than what her sister would want for her. More to do with what the world expected of her than what her sister hoped for her.

"Actually," she said, "I have decided to take the Cal Tech job, but that's not why I'm calling."

She straightened her shoulders, even though her sister wasn't there to see her, and then she told her everything. Dylan. The mate bond. The confrontation with the tigers. Her conversation with Elizaveta. All of it. And by the time she'd finished, she felt like a weight had been lifted, a weight she hadn't even realized she'd been carrying. She was relieved her sister knew everything now. Like… Like she was ready to move forward, but she'd just needed to cross this one last bridge.

"Well," Amy said after a long pause. "That's going to be a little difficult for a few months."

"Yeah."

"The tigers are going to hate this."

"Already do."

"Cool."

Cat chuckled. "Better warn Ethan, though. And the rest of the clan. There's likely to be pushback."

"We'll take care of that. Don't you worry. But…" She let out a breath Cat heard clearly through the phone. "I have to be big sister for a moment and ask this. Are you sure about this Dylan guy?"

"Surprisingly sure," she said. She was absolutely still surprised by her certainty. It felt sort of like when an elegant solution to a particular equation turned out to represent actual reality and wasn't just a neat mathematical trick. The elegance, the simplicity, and the *rightness* of it just felt so satisfying. And that's how she felt about Dylan.

"You've always known your own mind," Amy said. "I trust you to know it now. But I will need to keep checking in to make sure you're safe. And if you need me. Us. We're here to kick his ass for you. The entire clan will join in. I'm sure they won't mind."

Cat laughed. And the idea that she had that big of a family to call on started to sink in. She was used to thinking of her family as Amy. Neither of her parents had had siblings so when they'd died, her family had contracted to just her sister and her. But then Ethan joined. And he fit in well and became family. Even Spike liked him, and their badass poodle was a good judge of character. Then Ethan's multiple siblings became part of their family. And their partners and children. Which included the Chernikovs. And all of them were great and fiercely protective of each other. Which now included her and Amy.

"Wow," she said aloud after a moment. "It's happened so gradually over the last four years, I'm only just realizing… We have a big ass family now, don't we?"

Amy's chuckle sounded as startled as it did amused. "You're right. I hadn't really noticed either. But it's…"

"Nice," Cat finished for her.

"Yeah. It is."

A beat of silence filled with a lot of contentment before Cat broke it with, "For the record, though, Dylan's mother is apparently a big deal on this coast among the leopards, enough so that the one tiger I didn't know had heard of her and was terrified. So, probably, even if things go sideways with Dylan, we shouldn't beat him up. Maybe just negotiate an out so everyone stays whole and intact."

"If you insist. But if he hurts you, I don't give two fucks who his mother is. I will rip holes in him with my bare hands."

"I will pass that message on to him." Cat grinned for no real reason but that she was happy.

"You're good with this, though." There was statement and question in the comment.

"I'm good. I'm amazed that I'm good. But I'm good. I… I like him. A lot. And I see a lot of potential in front of us."

"Even though you've only known him a couple of days?"

"You were obsessed with Ethan on sight if I remember correctly."

"Yeah, well, I just thought he was a muse. Or a god. Or you know, something equally out of reach and awesome."

"Right. Except he was in reach the whole time, and that's all worked out just fine for you two."

"Our relationship was never about a chemical bond that would be impossible to break eventually, though. It was a choice all the way down."

"This is my choice. Okay, the chemistry is pretty intense. But… Amy, this man… The chemistry would be intense anyway."

Amy laughed. "Fine, fine. I'll stop nagging. Just… Keep me in the loop. And get him here to New York soon so we can meet him, and I can get Ethan to suss out his scent."

"Absolutely. Also Spike. If he can't get along with Spike, we may have some issues."

"Spike stays in New York, by the way. She is a New Yorker, through and through, and will not do well in California."

Cat had anticipated that but still let out a dramatic sigh and a little humph of a pout. "She likes me better, you know. Our hair matches now."

"I don't care. She stays here. With her people."

"Fine." She pretended at reluctance but in all honesty, she couldn't picture their spike-collar wearing poodle in California either. "But I get custody for the holidays."

"Only if you spend them here." After a pause, Amy said, "When *will* we see you? Are you coming back as planned or…"

Cat straightened a little. She hadn't actually thought about that yet. "I'll let you know. I guess I'd better make a decision soon, though. My flight back is Wednesday." She'd given herself an extra day so she could explore Portland. But she and Dylan needed more than a day after the eclipse to…make a plan. "I don't have to settle things with my university or the Cal Tech job this week. I'll talk to Dylan, and I'll let you know what the plan is as soon as I have one."

"Fair enough. If you need me, I'm here. And if you just need to talk more, call."

"I will. And…thanks. Thanks for not trying to talk me out of this or treating me like I've gone silly-buggers." One of their mom's favorite phrases she'd picked up traveling in the UK and Ireland.

"Oh, I still think you've gone silly-buggers," Amy said with a laugh. "But I trust you to know it's the right kind of silly. And frankly, I'm glad all this got you to settle on a job and a move forward. I was half afraid you were going to come to me in the next couple of weeks and announce you were going for a third Ph.D."

Cat pressed her lips together to keep from admitting she'd intended to do just that.

After they'd said their goodbyes and Cat promised to check in soon with her plans, she sat in the tent for another long moment. The noise outside was growing as the afternoon heat faded and people starting moving around more or returning from the festival, getting ready for dinner and sky watching. The atmosphere around the site had been spinning up with more and more excitement as the day wore on. They were all ready for the big event tomorrow morning. And the sounds of that excitement made Cat smile. She was excited, too.

She was also a little worried about the future, though. About the way the tigers were going to react to this. She was hardly the only woman—hybrid or human—who they could pursue, and there were some unmated female tigers still. Not a huge number of them, but there hadn't been large numbers of female tigers in two centuries so that was just normal. It shouldn't be a big deal that she was moving on with someone not a tiger shifter.

But it would be. And that sucked on multiple levels. Still, she couldn't lead her life to accommodate the tigers, and she didn't want to. Sympathy for their reproductive plight did not have to mean sacrificing her own future for theirs.

And, though she was still a little amazed by it all, she was certain in her bones that Dylan was her own future.

When she emerged from the tent, he was standing at his telescope, talking with Tom who'd returned with extra beers for them—he was such a sweet man!—and attempting to give her privacy for her call. He could hear the conversation she'd had with her sister at that distance. Shifter hearing was an awesome thing to behold. But she did appreciate that he'd tried not to eavesdrop.

She joined the men, taking one of Tom's offered beers, and gave Dylan a "later" look when he raised a brow in question. With Tom there, she didn't want to talk about her conversation with Amy. So they chatted for a while about the eclipse and telescopes and which planets and systems would be visible tonight. And Cat let herself just enjoy the moment. She enjoyed it even more when Dylan, seemingly without much thought, wrapped an arm around her shoulders and pulled her close even as he answered a question Tom had about his larger scope.

She leaned into him, savoring his heat and that delicious earthy scent of him that made her toes curl. Had any man smelled quite so delicious in the history of men? Probably not. The possibility seemed highly improbable. She just wanted to live inside that wonderful scent, with his magnificent arms wrapped around her, the brush of his roughened finger tips against her skin. That sounded like a glorious place to live.

Tomorrow, after the big event, she could worry about tigers and the world beyond this little campsite. Tonight, she intended to explore the more appealing and delicious complexities of her mate.

Dylan waited well past dinner, when they'd settled in with their night scopes for a little stargazing, before he brought up the call to her sister. He'd made an effort not to listen in, focusing his hearing on other things. It was harder than it should have been because everything in him gravitated toward her, like she'd somehow become the sun in his solar system and he circled her now. Without even meaning to, he listened for her and tested the air for her scent. Even when she was sitting right next to him.

Fortunately, the camp noise and Tom arriving with beer and a desire to talk meant Dylan had other things he could focus on to keep him from accidentally eavesdropping on her conversation. He did catch the part where she told her sister she was taking the Cal Tech job, though, and for some reason that had left him a little lightheaded. She'd said that out loud to her sister. That meant she did intend to move to this coast. She still intended to give him a chance, to give them a chance.

His continued need for reassurance on that point was humbling.

When the camp had settled into the nighttime routines—stargazers by their scopes; groups talking and laughing loudly at their camps; someone nearby playing music which competed with the music coming from the opposite side of the park; the TV from the camper next to his site; the family group across from Cat trying to settle their kids in for the night—he finally broached the subject of the call to her sister in the most obvious way possible.

"So what did Amy say about you having a mate?" He winced a little, hoping she forgave him the less than gentle lead up.

She grinned, but her gaze stayed on her eyepiece. She was standing tonight, her foot tapping as she adjusted her focus. "That this would make things difficult with the tigers but whatever happens she has my back."

Her response was as complete of an answer as he could have hoped, hitting almost all of the important points in one go. Except… "But how does she feel about you…well, believing me? About the mate bond."

She turned her head just a little to meet his gaze. "She trusts me and my decisions. But she intends to kill you if you hurt me so, you know, typical sibling stuff."

He let out a slow breath. "She didn't try to talk you out of moving?"

"No. She wants me to take the job." She rolled her eyes. "She'd already been worrying I'd decided to go for a third degree rather than take one of the offers, so I think she was relieved."

"She obviously knows you well."

Cat huffed and refocused on her scope.

More relief rushed blood to his head. If her sister hadn't been happy about all this, it would have made their lives a lot tougher. He'd have gone to New York to meet Amy, to convince her he was sincere. But still…

"She expects you to come to New York soon, though," Cat said, almost as if she'd picked up his thoughts.

Which she couldn't possibly have. Could she?

"She wants Ethan to sniff at you and make sure you're not lying." She chuckled. "Shifters." This last she muttered quietly so only he'd be able to hear.

If it meant his future brother-in-law could vouch for his honesty, he was willing to go through the trouble.

The fact that he was thinking of her sister's husband as his future brother-in-law brought him up short for a moment. Somehow, the seriousness, the…permanence of the bond settled on him in a way it hadn't before. He'd been mostly concerned with just ensuring he and Cat found a way to be together, to stay close enough that he didn't lose his mind while the bond tightened. But he'd missed the fact that after that happened, there would be other parts of a long term relationship they'd have to consider. Mates were permanent, and among the leopards, that was enough of a commitment. It wasn't like they could back out once they'd allowed the mate bond to strengthen. At least not without a lot of pain and suffering. But there were human social conventions to take into consideration with a human mate who had human family.

Like marriage.

He studied her in his peripheral vision, and wondered if she'd want that eventually. He'd better ask. Though, maybe not immediately since that might just scare her off. He had to keep reminding himself they'd only met a couple of days ago. That even though his shifter nature was settled with all this, she needed more time to come to terms with the mate bond. He couldn't rush her or these long term conversations. They had time now, because she'd accepted this enough to stay with him. And they still had so much to learn about each other. He could ask where she stood on the whole marriage formality after he'd passed her brother-in-law's sniff test.

He snorted at that, and Cat glanced at him, her eyes narrowed. "What?"

"I was agreeing with your earlier assessment." He lowered his voice. "Shifters." And rolled his eyes.

She laughed, the sound a delicious rub against his nerves. She glanced around, the look suspiciously shifty, and then abandoned her scope. To his utter surprise, she settled on his lap, wrapping her arms around his neck. His arms came up around her, pulling her close before his brain had fully processed what she'd done.

"What's this for?" he asked, his voice low and rough.

"For making this easier," she said, and she leaned in and kissed him.

He wasn't about to argue with her. The brush of her lips, so soft and full and lush, robbed him of thought anyway. His hands flexed on her waist and he angled his head to deepen the kiss, groaning quietly at the perfection of her taste on his tongue. Just a hint of the sugary sweetness of the funnel cake she'd had for dessert mixed with her natural lemon and lightning flavors. His body tingled with that combination, reaching, straining for more.

More of her taste, more of her touch, more of her... Everything.

He cupped the back of her head with one hand, tunneling his fingers through the silky softness of her hair. With his other arm, he pulled her even closer, as close as their position in the camping chair would allow. It was a little awkward in the soft chair, but she fell against him so fully, fit with him so well, he barely noticed. He just needed to have more of her pressing tight into him. If there'd been less clothing between them, he would have been even happier.

His cock would most definitely be happier with less clothes. The bump of her hip against his erection made him groan. His fingers tightened in her hair before he forced himself to relax his grip. She might be his mate, but she was also human. He'd have to pay attention to his own strength so he didn't hurt her.

The realization that he might dampened some of his raging need, at least enough for him to pull away from the kiss. "Warm me if I'm being too rough," he said, his voice so gravely he hoped she understood him. "Shifter strength," he muttered when her eyes widened.

"Ah. Well. I do like a little rough," she said, leaning into him, kissing along his jaw, her lips brushing a spot along his neck that made him groan. "But I'll keep your strength in mind." She dragged her lips along his neck up to his ear. The brush of her hot breath against his lobe set off fireworks in his head. "Though, you should know, I'm not as delicate and breakable as I might look."

His arms flexed without his permission when she nibbled his earlobe, tightening hard and fast right along with every other part of his body. And having her rubbing against his cock, even through his jeans, was almost like torture but the best possible kind of torture he could imagine.

"We should…" He had to swallow to force more words out. "We should probably stop this."

She sat up enough to meet his gaze.

"I'm less…controlled than I would normally be because of the bond. And… I'm trying really hard not to rush you."

"You are very hard right now," she said with such a serious expression he might have laughed, but she also rocked her hip against his cock in the same moment and that scattered any hope of coherent thought. "You do realize, I'm the one who came to sit on your lap, right? Maybe I'm rushing you?"

"No," he said. If it weren't for the seriousness of the bond and the implications of sex, he'd have already carried her to her tent and stripped her naked. "But…once we…" Another hard swallow as her fingers tangled in his hair at the base of his neck, distracting him again. He forced his brain back on track. "Once we have sex, this bond gets almost impossible to break. I doubt one night was enough to really…" What the hell was she doing with her fingers? It was glorious. He didn't want her to stop. He blinked. "I mean, I think maybe a few days at least might be…" He moaned softly when she brushed a kiss along the spot where his jaw met his neck.

"I'm distracting you," she murmured. "Sorry. Please, go on."

Except she hadn't stopped kissing him, or rubbing against him, or doing whatever it was she was doing with her fingers at the back of his neck, and thought just wasn't possible under that onslaught. At least not the kind of thought that would allow him to remember what he was trying to say, nonetheless form actual words. His brain was filling up with thoughts of her naked and stretched out under him, moving his mouth from her breasts, down her stomach, to between her legs… He had lots of room in his head for those thoughts apparently.

Just not words. "Mm," he managed before capturing her mouth again.

He felt her smile, and he was pretty sure if he could think and focus he'd recognize the smugness in it, but he just couldn't seem to care. She had him wound up tight, ready to break, and he didn't give a fuck about anything but getting her into her tent in the next few seconds.

He stood abruptly enough to make her gasp and to knock over his chair, keeping her in his arms with one hand at her back and one under her legs. The same way he'd carried her back from the fields last night.

"The telescopes?" she said, sounding less interesting in them than she was in toying with the edges of his t-shirt's collar.

"I'll hear if anyone comes too close to them." Although, he was so wrapped up in her, he wasn't actually sure he would. Or that he'd care. He'd replace her scope if it got stolen. He just needed to get her alone. Now. Before he lost his mind.

"Your eyes are glowing," she murmured.

That gave him pause. "Does that bother you?"

"No. Not even a little." She cupped his jaw in one hand. "You have beautiful eyes."

The acknowledgement of his nature, and that she *liked* that part of him, did something to his insides, in the area of his chest, some strange change he'd have to analyze at some point. But the warmth of the feeling, the rightness in the change, filled him right alongside the heat and lust thrumming through his blood.

He set her on her feet outside her tent, again a mirror of last night, but this time she tugged at his t-shirt before ducking inside. And he followed her without argument. He'd lost track of the argument for resisting this anyway. He was pretty sure he'd had reasons, but none of them surfaced.

The inside of her tent was basic enough, with a backpack tossed against one curved nylon wall and a sleeping bag stretched out in the middle of some thicker blankets on the ground under it. The extra blankets made him smile. They'd have more cushion beneath them than just the rocky ground.

She settled back on the slippery surface of the sleeping bag and reached for him. He went, stretching out beside her and rolling her into his arms. Damn but she felt good. Her small breasts pressed into his chest, a softness he'd been craving more than air. His kiss turned desperate now that they were alone, as he tried to taste her more deeply, memorize the feel of her.

She tugged at his shirt again and dragged her mouth from his long enough to demand, "Off."

Her tone made him smile as he stripped his shirt over his head without comment. She reached for him as soon as he'd tossed the shirt aside, her hands gliding over his bare skin leaving sparks of heat in their wake. He closed his eyes, his full focus on the brush of her fingers as she explored, the way she scooted down enough to place a kiss against his collarbone, then lower on his pectoral. Her scent filled his head until there was nothing but her. When her hands slipped to his waist, to the waistband of his jeans, he pulled her close for another kiss, needing his mouth on hers.

She managed to open the top button of his jeans before he stopped her, tangling his fingers with hers when she tried to pull away. "You first," he said.

He slid his other hand up under her t-shirt and the heavier zippered hoodie she had on against the night chill. Her skin was warm and so so soft. She sighed when he pushed her shirt and hoodie higher, dragging his hand up along her waist. She shivered when he brushed his thumb over her breast, across the top of her bra. There was definitely too much material in his way, though. He tugged her into a sitting position and without even unzipping the hoodie pulled her shirts off over her head. She grinned when he tossed them to the side of the tent to join his.

She stripped off her own bra without ceremony, tossing it to join the rest of their clothes, and then shivered. The tight buds of her nipples drew his full attention. He cupped her breast, rubbing his thumb over the hardened nub in a circle of pressure that made her moan and press into his hand. He watched her face as he flicked his finger against her nipple, watched her eyes drift shut and her lips part on a quiet sound of need.

Her skin was cool, silky soft, but little goosebumps raised along her arms and stomach. The air inside the tent was chilly, maybe even a little cold still as their body heat hadn't had time to warm things up. He did not want her getting cold. He pulled her back into his arms, wrapping her in his heat. The instant they were skin to skin, though, the idea that she might be chilled vanished because her skin felt like fire against his, like the silky burn of delicious flames. He was so hard, so tense from wanting her, he barely recognized himself.

His kiss turned frantic again, the need to claim her mouth, her body so strong it overwhelmed his urge to savor. He didn't want to rush, though. He wanted all of her. And he wanted her as mindless for him as he was for her. He shoved at the waistband of her jeans. "These need to go."

"You too," she murmured against his mouth even as she scrambled out of her hiking boots. They made a thud when they hit the ground at one side of the tent. "Naked. I need you naked now."

"Yes." The deep gravely sound of his own voice, strained with his desire, might have surprised him more if he'd been able to think. As it was, he removed his own clothes and shoes without noticing what he was doing because his entire focus was on her as she wiggled out of her jeans, shucking her underwear with the pants in one move. For a moment, as she stretched out against the sleeping bag, fully naked and open, he could only stare.

She was beautiful, lush and delicate at the same time, a pixie temptress with purple and blue streaks in her hair. Her skin glowed faintly in the muted light coming through the tent walls. It was dark enough inside he wasn't certain how well she could see, but his night vision was spectacular and he'd never been so grateful for that fact as he was in that moment, drinking in the sight of her.

He realized with a start he'd stripped fully and hadn't noticed when she reached out and wrapped her hand around his cock. The sensation drew a hiss from him and he wrapped his own hand over hers to keep her from pulling away. The intensity of feeling her fingers squeezing him left spots in his vision.

"You feel so good," she murmured, the sound of her voice like another caress along his already sensitive nerves.

"Having your hands on me might just kill me, but I'll die very happy."

"How about my mouth on you?"

He groaned and actually had to bite the inside of his cheek to keep from losing control completely. "That would definitely kill me. Ending all this too soon." Reluctantly, he eased her hand off his cock. "And I have plans that require I don't die just yet."

She chuckled, even as she pouted a little when he kept her hand tangled with his and wouldn't let her stroke his cock anymore. "I promise to be gentle and not kill you," she said.

"Not yet." He wasn't sure what he was saying no to. Her being gentle or her mouth on him. He wanted both eventually. But he didn't want to come too soon. And he was wound so tight her mouth on him would send him careening over the edge in minutes.

But sending her over the edge…

He kissed her, deeply, in a bid to distract her, smugly triumphant when it worked. She melted into him, her arms wrapping around his neck, her fingers tangling in his hair again.

"What do you want?" he murmured against her neck. "What do you like?"

"Everything."

"All at once?"

She hummed and chuckled but the sound turned into a groan when he palmed her breast and pinched her nipple. "I don't expect… Except you to bend spacetime…" She gasped when he kissed a particularly sensitive spot on her neck, where her throat met her shoulder, and he memorized that spot.

"I would for you if I could," he said. "But I'm afraid I can only do so much at once."

"That's good." She was panting as he brought his mouth to her breast, taking one nipple in and biting gently. "I'm good with… with…" She trailed off, her fingers tightening in his hair.

"Good with?" he teased before biting her gently again and tugging at the same time.

She arched under him, the sound of her hiss of pleasure filling the tent. He wanted more of that. He swirled his tongue over her nipple, sucked once more, deeply, then moved to her other breast, watching her face as he teased and nipped. She had her head back, her eyes half-closed, a flush warmed her pale skin. She looked glorious and he would never get enough of this.

"You never finished your sentence," he said as he moved his lips down her stomach, over her ribs, savoring her every gasp and shiver.

"Huh?" she asked.

He grinned against her skin. Pushing her beyond thought felt like the greatest triumph of his life. "What do you like? Where do you want me?" He licked a path along her waist to her hipbone, tasting the delicate skin just there, and her hips bucked up.

"There… Good. All of it…" Her words fell out on her gasps and pants, her desperation thick in her scent, as well as her desire.

Dylan had never encountered anything in his life he wanted more of than her scent in that moment. Lush and delicious with the flavors of lemon, lightning, and the sharp tangy spice of her lust. "Where?" he asked again, brushing his lips low on her abdomen.

"God," she gasped. "There. On me. On my pussy. Your mouth."

He growled in satisfaction as she opened her legs further, letting him settle between her thighs. She was beautiful. And he couldn't resist anything his mate wanted from him.

Cat slapped one hand over her eyes and gripped the sleeping bag next to her in a tight fist as Dylan's mouth closed over her, his tongue slipping between her folds. She was so desperate, her nerves so sensitive, her body so tight and ready to explode, she was almost in pain. But it was the most exquisite sensation she'd ever experienced. And when he tongued her clit, she nearly came apart.

Oh but she wanted this to last just a little longer, because the feel of his mouth on her was perfect, and she didn't want it to end. He squeezed her thighs in his big hands, his roughened finger tips making her skin sing, adding an extra, almost unbearable level of sensation to the stroke of his tongue. A part of her recognized he was holding back a little, his touch careful, and she'd have to talk to him about that later. But most of her was too damned focused on his tongue, and the way he licked and sucked at her clit and she didn't want to do anything but feel.

And then she was all feeling, all tightening, building pressure, all her awareness focused on his mouth, her body, the overwhelming plea-sure. She was panting with it, gasping, straining. A flick of his tongue and her hips bucked against his mouth, demanding more. She dropped her hand from her eyes to look at him, realized he was watching her, his eyes glowing just a bit yellow in the dark tent. The golden color, the intensity in his expression robbed her of what little breath she had.

He was probably the sexiest man she'd ever known and watching him pleasure her broke the last of her control. She tightened her jaw to keep in a scream that would startle the rest of the camp and her body exploded in waves of sensation that careened through her, breaking through her with such release of pleasure she actually saw spots.

The orgasm left her so sensitive that when he licked one more time she jerked and gripped his head. "Need…" She could barely speak, she was too busy trying to relearn how to breathe and be in her body. "Just…" She pulled at him, tugging him upward. He obeyed her barely coherent request, sliding along the length of her, the rub of skin doing nothing to calm her nerves.

His heat enveloped her, and his scent settled around her like a blanket, mixing with the scent of her own lust and sweat. She was only a little surprised at how much she liked that combination.

Her muscles were so lax and shaky it took her several long moments and a few gentle kisses, tasting herself on his lips, before she could move to wrap her arms around him. "I'm going to want to do that a lot more," she murmured.

His gravely chuckle sent a tremor of desire warming low in her abdomen. The brush of his rough fingertips over her waist, settling on her hipbone, made her shiver.

"Also," she said, still breathless. "I think you need to be inside me now." She reached down and gripped his still very hard cock, savoring his quickly indrawn breath and the way his jaw tightened.

"Condoms…" He trailed off as she stroked over the head of his erection, taking some of the moisture there and using it to slick her hands as she ran her palm up and down his shaft. "In my truck."

She gestured to her backpack. "I come prepared too," she said.

He raised his brows. She grinned and shrugged. "I'm a safety girl."

His surprised laugh sent a giddy dance of delight along her nerves. "I love that movie."

"I can't believe you got the reference." He didn't seem like the type to have seen *Pretty Woman* enough to know lines from it.

He rolled over to her backpack, a move that sadly drew his cock from her hand. She'd have pouted about that but given where she wanted his thick length, she was willing to make that sacrifice.

"It's my sister Brigit's favorite movie. She watched it so much I soaked it in, like osmosis. I'd have been disowned as a brother if I hadn't learned the important lines."

She laughed as he turned back to her, condom packet already open. She bit her lip and watched him roll the condom on, distracted by the sight of his big hands, his very capable fingers, and his beautiful, thick cock.

He settled onto his back and pulled her over the top of him, with an easy show of strength that made her shiver. Her need built again, despite the earthshattering orgasm she'd already had. She almost felt like her desire wasn't entirely in her control, like someone a lot lustier and hungrier than her had taken over. She wanted *more*. More of him in every way possible. Like she'd never be finished or fully sated.

The idea might have worried her if she didn't also feel so safe with him. So free. So completely able to be herself. She couldn't remember the last time she'd been with a man and felt so…relaxed, while also feeling so wound up and ready to fuck her brain wasn't functioning properly. Everything about him and this moment felt *right*.

A strange thing for her, to toss aside logic for intuition. But with Dylan beneath her looking all gloriously male and sexy and delicious, his blue eyes glowing in the dark, his jaw tight as she straddle him, his expression intent, logic didn't seem to make much sense anyway. Who needed logic?

She rubbed against his cock, rocking her hips as a tease to them both, grinding on him without taking him inside just yet. He growled, low and quiet, and his fingers tightened on her hips. Ah, she loved seeing him like this so much. She took him in her hand and guided him inside, slowly easing down, adjusting, stretching, the slide onto him a delicious build of friction and tension. When she dropped the last inch, her hips bumping against his, his cock fully inside, she groaned.

"You feel so good," she murmured.

"Yes." His word sounded strangled, gravely. "Fuck."

She met his gaze. The glow was brighter in his eyes. His nostrils flared and his fingers clenched her hips tight enough she knew he was barely in control of himself. She also knew, if he hurt her on accident, he'd beat himself up about it, and she did not want this glorious moment disrupted by anything as nonsensical as regret. She grabbed his hands in hers, tangling her fingers with his, and leaned over him, bringing his hands to the sleeping bag beside his shoulders. Pinning him there as she lifted her hips and slid down. The friction of the downward glide made her groan, her eyes closing without thought as she enjoyed the sensation. When she opened them again, she was staring into his eyes. So much heat, so much pleasure and intensity. Sucking her into the whirlwind of need.

She set a slow rhythm, watching his face as she rode him, the way his fingers clenched around hers when she dropped a little harder against his hips, the way he sucked in a breath when she came nearly off him before sliding back down hard. She could watch him for the rest of her life, just like this.

The slow pump of her hips sent her spiraling up again, tight and desperate. And when she slammed harder downward, he growled. "Yes. Harder."

She couldn't argue. She couldn't speak anymore. She slammed down, the pressure built, and she gasped as her body tightened.

"Let my hand go," he said.

And when she did, he licked his thumb, then set it against her clit, adding just enough pressure to send her mindless. Careening. Over the edge with her teeth clenched again so she wouldn't scream.

He held her hips with both hands—she'd released the other without realizing it—and held her as he pumped up hard into her once, twice, and then he let go with a groan she'd hold in her memory always. His muscles all tightened, his head thrown back, his shoulders and neck straining. The pulse of him inside her. She was so sensitive his release triggered a wave of mini aftershocks of pleasure through her, leaving her in a state so mindlessly pure she felt like all of spacetime stilled. When she collapsed against him finally, she was a trembling heap of jumping nerves and giddy satisfaction.

He wrapped his arms around her, holding her close, his heat better than any blanket. So warm. And he smelled so damned good. Like the sex had intensified his already delicious scent and it filled her with contentment right down to a cellular level. She buried her face against his neck, something she'd been wanting to do since meeting him—wow, had that only been a few days ago?—and breathed him in.

"So," she murmured against his warm sweaty skin. "That was perfect."

His laugh, dark and rich, vibrated against her chest in a way that made her breasts tingle.

"Yes. But very soon we need someplace where you can make all the noise you want without holding back. I want to hear those screams."

She grinned, her face still pressed against his neck. "Noticed that, huh?"

He slid his big palm in a gentle stroke down her spine and she shivered in response. "I noticed everything," he murmured. "Including that you kept me from hurting you."

"You wouldn't have, not much, but you'd have worried if you'd left bruises. Couldn't have that." She levered up just enough to meet his gaze. "For the record, going forward, I won't mind a few accidental bruises. But I will mind if you beat yourself up over them. Trust me to tell you when it's too much."

He nodded, cupping her cheek in one hand. "Can I kiss your bruises better if I do accidently give you some?"

She grinned. "I would enjoy that very much, yes, please, and thank you."

He smiled and kissed her and she hummed as she melted against him again.

"I'm not too heavy?" she asked after a few minutes of just sprawling across his chest.

"Not even a little bit," he said, patting her ass. "But I do need to clean up."

She did, too.

The cleaning was a little awkward in the small confines of the tent, and resulted in some laughter over the washcloth and bottled water that they used up so they'd have a place for the used condom.

Then they had to get dressed enough to put the telescopes and equipment away—which for Cat involved getting fully dressed and pulling on her hoodie again, and for Dylan involved putting on his jeans. She envied his metabolism. After they'd secured the scopes, and without needing to discuss it, he returned to her tent with her.

She stripped off everything but her t-shirt and underwear, he shucked off his jeans, and they laid down together on top of her pile of blankets, underneath the opened up sleeping bag and an extra blanket for her against the night chill—she'd brought a bunch and bought an extra one in Portland before driving to Madras. The tent had cooled a little after they'd left but was still warmer than outside and felt cozy with Dylan next to her.

She snuggled against his side, and her eyes drifted closed almost immediately. "I'm going to sleep," she said as she pulled in another deep breath, memorizing his scent and the way he smelled on her skin. The whole tent smelled of their sweat and sex and she'd have never guessed that would be such a comforting scent.

"You won't be crowded if I stay the rest of the night," he said against her hair.

"I will kick your ass if you leave. You're very warm, and I'm very comfortable. Does that answer your question?"

"That was a perfect answer, yes. Because I really don't want to leave."

He tugged her closer, pulling the spread sleeping bag up a little higher. She sighed in contentment, deciding his chest made an absolutely perfect pillow. She tangled her legs with his to ensure he remained securely in place next to her, then she succumbed to sleep.

DYLAN STAYED AWAKE AS LONG AS HE COULD AFTER HE FELT CAT relax fully next to him, her breathing deep and quiet. Her very slight snore was an adorable distraction for several long moments.

But he couldn't keep himself distracted from reality for long. The reality that being with her felt more right than anything else in his life. But also the reality that they'd stepped over a line tonight, the line between being able to break their mate bond or not.

At least for him.

She was human. She could still walk away, despite the sex and the tightening bond. That knowledge was…difficult. Uncomfortable. On a level he hadn't realized was there. Knowing she wanted to be with him was glorious. Knowing she could leave easier than another mate, though, left his leopard edgy and nervous.

Edgy and nervous shifters were dangerous shifters.

But for now, she wasn't leaving. She was here and she'd wrapped herself around him like she intended to keep him. So for now, he'd let go of the worries. They had a few hours to sleep and then the eclipse, the entire reason they were both here in the first place.

Afterward, they could talk about what came next. A trip to New York, obviously. He had to pass her sister and brother-in-law's sniff test. And if he went with her to Portland—which of course, he would because he couldn't be separated from her now—he probably shouldn't avoid Deacon and Caitlin, although introducing Cat to his older brother and sister before telling his twin probably wouldn't go over well. He'd better call Julia first.

His parents would expect to meet Cat sooner rather than later. His arm tightened around her in an instinctively protective gesture. Maybe his parents could wait a few months.

Some schedule changes would have to be made so he could helped Cat move to California for her new job. And he'd have to reorganize when and how he worked so he wasn't forced to be away from her for too long at a time. At least not for the first few months. Mostly, he was writing up his thesis now, and he could do a lot of that from just about anywhere, so he could be flexible.

When he realized how much planning he was doing already, after just one night with her, he scowled up at the tent roof. The thought of throwing himself into this thing so fully didn't scare him nearly as much as he'd thought it would. So long as he could be with her, the rest of it was just…logistics.

He'd never have guessed he'd view the complete upheaval of his previous life as just logistics. But he supposed that's what happened when a leopard met their mate. He pulled in a deep breath, filling himself with her scent and the scent of them together, mixing in a deliciously perfect combination of smells. The rightness wrapped around him like a blanket. For the first time since meeting her, his leopard quieted, content and settled.

And Dylan finally slept.

2 8

The morning was gloriously clear, blue skies, light breeze, warm and fragrant in the fallow fields beside the campsite. Cat couldn't have been happier. The area was crowded with eclipse watchers, some sitting on blankets, some standing with telescopes, all of them with various types of eclipse sunglasses and eye protection. There was some music in the distance, and the group with the tinfoil hats wandered past and waved while Cat was adjusting her filters.

The atmosphere was sharp with anticipation and excitement, the feeling sweeping her up into the giddiness. She'd been excited about the eclipse before. But sharing it with all these other enthusiastic watchers just made it all better.

"Some party," Dylan said quietly from beside her, smiling at the tinfoil hat people as they were cheered by another group.

"What time is it?" she asked. For the fifty-third time in twenty-three seconds.

"It's eight fifty," he said. "Only sixteen more minutes until first contact."

She bounced on her toes and couldn't figure out what to do with her hands because sixteen minutes felt like ages and she was *excited*.

His laughter made her tingle in all her sensitive places, which were a lot more sensitive this morning, in a very good way. He'd woken her with his mouth on her body, moving in a lazy, delicious path down to between her legs, and she'd decided that was the perfect way to wake up in the morning, bar none. She was still a little tingly from the orgasms, and that only added to her general happiness.

She knew they had things to discuss, mostly logistical stuff. But by unspoken agreement, neither of them had brought up the future, their plans, what they'd do next. She was aware, maybe more than he realized, that they'd crossed a line last night. A line of no return. For him at least. She'd been listening closely when he'd explained the mate bond and the permanence of it. She wasn't treating that lightly or dismissively. She just…wanted the bond.

She wanted him.

In her life from this point forward. She'd never been one to believe in instant love or anything like that, and they hadn't even discussed the whole love thing, but a part of her that worked more on instinct than logic—a surprisingly larger part of her than she would have expected —the part that knew how to breathe and demanded she eat even when her brain was engaged elsewhere, that part of her knew this was right and wanted it. Wanted it with the same sort of determination she felt when she was on the edge of unraveling a particularly difficult problem. She *knew* she was on the right path here, and she intended to follow that path to the end.

From her peripheral vision, she caught sight of Dylan moving his tripod to a slightly better position on the uneven ground, his bicep muscles flexing as he did, and she sighed. The fact that she found him gorgeous and sexy did not hurt. She suspected she'd have found him sexy no matter what, given they were mates, but even objectively speaking, he was a pretty glorious sight to behold. And honestly, she could live on his scent alone. Well, that and cake. But definitely his scent would give her sustenance. She wasn't sure what it was about the way he smelled—and that was probably a mate thing too—but she just couldn't seem to get enough. Even now, when the breeze shifted and she caught just a hint of him in the air, she wanted to move closer and bury her face against his neck.

He caught her staring, and the heat in his eyes, the way his lips curved in a private little smile, made her toes curl. Her tummy danced and she had to look away before she did something embarrassing, like wrap herself around him and start making out in front of all the other eclipse watchers. If they weren't careful, they'd melt their scopes. He was just so damned hard to resist. And he likely knew how she felt because he could pick it up in her scent.

The fact that he could do that didn't bother her nearly as much as she'd have thought. At least not anymore. Not as much as it had after she'd learned he was a shifter. She'd always found the fact that the tigers could read her scent so easily annoying. But with Dylan, she kind of liked it. She didn't have to explain things in words if she didn't have the right words for the explanation. He'd just know how she felt. The fact that most of her current thoughts were happy, lusty ones didn't hurt.

Maybe that was why her sister didn't mind that Ethan could basically read her mind through her scent.

She was excited to introduce Dylan to Amy. And to gloat smugly at her sister when Dylan passed Ethan's sniff test. She understood Amy's protectiveness and was grateful for it, but it was her duty as a younger sister to gloat when her sister's worries proved unfounded. She'd be skirting her obligations as a little sister if she *didn't* gloat.

A few quiet murmurs and a general feel of settling came over the crowd. People sank onto the ground, or straightened a little in their seats, chatter quieted to a low hum. And more and more people, protective glasses firmly in place, started to look up.

Without needing another time check, Cat knew first contact was upon them. She grinned at Dylan once before turning to her scope. She checked some of the settings on her tablet, adjusted the eyepiece on her scope, then settled in for the show. Her heartbeat hammering as the dark leading edge of the moon touched the edge of the sun, a little curve of darkness against the glow.

First contact.

For the next hour, Cat watched the dark shadow of the moon slowly creep across the face of the sun, listened to the quiet murmurs around them, the occasional loud bark of laughter, or a surprised comment from one of the many kids in the crowd. She took a steady stream of pictures, hoping for a good compilation shot when she was done. In that time, the breeze remained steady, the clear morning remained bright. Without looking at the sun through the filtered glasses or telescope, it was impossible to notice an eclipse was happening. Nothing changed in the quality of the air or light…

Until totality approached.

In those last few moments, as things around her got even quieter, the breeze died down and the light started to feel shadowed, dimmer, almost like sunset but not quite because the *time* felt wrong for sunset. The change didn't feel like the usual fading at the end of the day, though she'd have had trouble putting that into words. The sounds of birds, something she hadn't paid much attention to in the background, quieted, and in that quieting, she realized how much noise there'd been. But as the sky began dimming, as the shadow reached near full coverage and the air cooled noticeably, everything from people to traffic to nature seemed to pause and take a breath.

The final seconds, the flash of the diamond ring effect, the Baily's beads around the edge of the shadow—the last bumps of bright bright light surrounding the dark shadow, and then…

Totality.

Darkness settled over the field as people pulled off their protective glasses, and for a full ten seconds, everyone was silent. Then the cheers, the claps, the sounds of awe and wonder.

Cat continued to take pictures, hoping to catch the distant stars behind the sun so she could still do the light bending calculations later, but the sight of totality, of the flickering light of the corona around the black disk covering the sun, caught her breath and left her feeling a kind of quiet awe. The same sort of awe she felt when contemplating the size of the universe and all the things they still had yet to learn.

She paused long enough to walk away from her telescope and pull Dylan into a hug, kissing him soundly once. He grinned down at her, hugging her tight before releasing her so she could return to her scope.

On her other side, Tom let out a long sigh and a quiet chuckle.

He'd removed his protective glasses to look up at the eclipse. "Beautiful, isn't it?" he said to her, the quiet awe in his tone matching her own.

"Beautiful," she agreed. Without really thinking about it, she reached out to him and he took her hand, also without looking away from the eclipse, squeezing her fingers in a surprisingly strong grip before releasing.

She spent the rest of the minute of totality, protective glasses off, alternating between taking pictures and just staring at the glorious sight.

And then the minute was up and the first bubbles of light appeared at the opposite side of the sun as the moon moved on. Glasses around the site returned to faces, and another general cheer went up as the sun's light returned. Somewhere across the crowd, she heard a loud, chanting prayer go up, and closer she heard more gasps and sighs of awe.

"Beautiful," Tom murmured again as the sky brightened once more to early morning glory.

Cat continued to take pictures throughout the last phase of the eclipse as the moon moved away. When the last contact happened, when the final curve of shadow moved away from the sun, she sigh in pleasure.

"That was definitely worth the trip," she said to no one in particular.

"Definitely," Tom said with a chuckle.

"Without a doubt," Dylan murmured.

Around them, people began gathering up their gear and moving back toward the site.

"The rush to leave is going to be a mess," Tom said, his gaze moving out over the flow of people. "Think I'll wait for the worst of it to clear out first. How about you two?"

She hadn't really considered what she'd do the minute totality ended, but Tom was right, things were going to be crazy for the next hour as people packed up and hurried to leave, trying to beat traffic that was inevitable.

"Pack, obviously," she said, then frowned at Dylan. "But I'm not in a hurry to get back to Portland." The fact that they hadn't discussed next steps became abundantly clear in that moment.

"We can discuss it while we're packing," he said, as if he knew what her hesitant frown was about.

Huh. It really was nice not to have to put everything into words before someone understood what you were trying to say.

When she glanced back at Tom, he was smiling at them a little. He winked at her. "Ah, young love."

She rolled her eyes but felt her cheeks heating, which seemed a little ridiculous, but it was an autonomic reaction, and she didn't have control over the sudden flush of shyness that swept through her. Tom's grin as he turned back to his telescope to lift it off the tripod didn't help her sudden flush.

Maybe it was his mention of "love" that triggered the physiological reaction in her?

She mulled that over as she disassembled her scope and tripod, settling the scope back into its case and minimizing the tripod so she could easily carry everything back to the campsite.

Dylan joined her as she hefted her tripod and chair under one arm, carrying her telescope case in the other. "You need help?" he asked.

He'd asked on the way out to the fields, too. Which was sweet, but she had the same answer as she had earlier. "If you carry some of my gear as well as yours, it's too obvious you're stronger than you look," she murmured quiet enough for just him to hear. "You have a very big scope in that case, and glass isn't light."

He leaned in to speak in her ear. "Sometimes, having to hide my nature is a pain in the ass, because my leopard would like nothing better than to show off by helping you carry your gear."

She laughed at the "showing off" part of his sentence but the feel of his breath on her cheek and neck made her shiver. "I appreciate the offer," she said, "but I've got this."

"I know." He brushed his lips against her cheek, and she sighed, leaning into him without meaning to.

She hurriedly turned back toward camp, walking maybe a little faster than she needed to. She was afraid if she didn't, she'd drop her gear—not good for the scope!—and embarrass herself by pulling him into a big sloppy kiss.

Dylan kept pace with her easily, which was kind of nice. When she got into her fast walk, people always told her to slow down. Yet another nice thing about a shifter boyfriend.

She nearly stumbled over the term boyfriend. How weird. It sounded wrong for someone she'd just met a few days ago. Yet, she'd accepted he was her "mate," which was a lot more serious than just a simple boyfriend.

This whole thing was going to take some time to get used to.

2 9

To reach their respective sites, they had to dodge around hurrying people and already moving vehicles. The two men across from Cat's site had already packed up and left. The family were nearly loaded and just chasing down the kids to get them into the cars. The camper next to Dylan's site had the motor running, but the couple were still adjusting things on the outside, getting it ready to leave. Various vehicles drove down the dirt roads between the rows of campsites, all heading toward the exit and the highway.

"This really is going to be a mess," she said as she realized the road to Portland would be packed, even if they waited to leave until most of the campsite had cleared out.

"And not many directional options that won't be just as bad," Dylan said. "You said you weren't in a hurry to get to Portland."

"I did want to arrive sometime today, though," she said as she carefully packed her scope in the trunk of her rental car. Her stomach grumbled and she sighed. So long as there was someplace to get food along the way, she supposed she could deal with the slow traffic.

Dylan joined her by her car just as she was turning to take down her tent. He brushed a finger over her cheek, pushing some of her hair that had escaped her clip back behind her ear.

"We haven't talked about…what happens next."

She'd kept assuming they'd have plenty of time for that. But now that the time was *now*, she was strangely nervous about this conversation. It brought this whirlwind process into the real world in a way she'd only barely allowed herself to consider.

"My flight to New York is in a couple of days, but I can change the departure date if necessary." She pushed out the words that left her feeling vulnerable for reasons she couldn't entirely explain. "I'd like you to come with me if that's possible."

His slow smile made her stomach dance even as a sense of relief moved through her shoulders. "I do need to pass your brother-in-law's sniff test."

"Yes." She grinned. "But…you have college soon and…"

"And we have a lot of logistics to sort out," he said. "First, we make sure your sister is comfortable."

"Your family?"

"Will be fine waiting. They understand the mate bond in a way your sister doesn't, so this isn't unfamiliar ground for them. I need to tell my twin so she doesn't kill me when we do show up together, but the rest of them can wait."

When he frowned a little, she said, "What?"

"I have a brother and sister living in Portland. They'll be a little… annoyed if I avoid them while I'm there. Maybe not surprised, but annoyed."

"We don't have to, you know. I mean… Maybe it's like a Band Aid. Rip off all the uncomfortable first meetings quickly so that part is done and we can focus on…figuring out all the rest." Like her moving all the way across the country for work, and figuring out how to finish her thesis remotely, and where they'd live, if they'd live together or not right away.

Oh. They might have to live together because he couldn't be away from her for long. That felt…too fast. Her heart started thumping again as the reality of all this really sank in. For some reason—probably related to wanting to fuck him—she'd thought the logistics, the realities would be trifling after adapting to the fact that the mate bond was real. Now faced with those logistics, a lot more panic set in than she'd anticipated.

"Do you need to sit down?" Dylan asked, sounding suddenly very concerned. "You're really pale all of the sudden. Do you need something to eat?"

She forced a smile at that last. "I do actually, but that's not what caused…" She gestured at her face. "Panicking a little is all. No problem. I'll adapt. Just…"

He took her face in his hands. "We'll go slow. It's okay. You don't have to panic." He pressed a kiss to her forehead. "How about this? One step at a time. First, the gauntlet of families. Then we'll figure out our respective academic adjustments. Then you can tell me what you need for the move to California, and I'll do what you need. And—" he brushed another kiss against her temple, "—we don't have to do anything that makes you uncomfortable. Separate places to live is fine. I will manage being away from you as much as you need me to so you can feel safe and comfortable. That part's on me. Not your responsibility. Even as my mate. Okay?"

"You reading my mind?" she asked, her tone a little shaky as the panic eased.

"'Fraid I can't help it." He brushed his fingers over her neck, and she shivered, leaning into him. "I seem more attuned to your scent than I am anything else around me. Does it bother you?"

"Not like I thought it would. Easier if I don't have to find words sometimes. I'm better with math."

His quick grin made her breath catch. Wow, he was handsome. And the tease of lust that rolled through her blood helped push down the panic.

"Listen," he said quietly, cupping her face in his big palms, "I will do whatever you need me to do. And if that means you want me to stay away until you're settled in your new job and have had time to adapt, I will. If that means you want me with you at every moment to hold your hand while you start your new job, I will. You set the terms of this, and I'll abide by them because I want you to be happy."

She let out a low breath. "What about how you can't be away from me or you lose your mind? That part of the bond. You can't just ignore it."

"No, but there are ways to deal with it." He shrugged. "If you need me to stay away from you for an extended period of time while you adjust to things, I can, but I'll have to stay with my parents so my mother can help control my leopard."

Her eyes widened. "There's a lot in that sentence. First, you really will lose control being away from me."

"Yes. But again, that's my responsibility to handle, not yours."

"And your mother can help you with your control, so you're not…dangerous?"

"Yes." His expression turned wry. "It won't be the first time she's had to do that for one of us. My oldest brother was a mess after meeting his human mate."

"I don't want you to be a mess."

"Again, I can deal with it. It'll be fine."

"Right." She wasn't so sure about that, not if he needed his mother's help just to deal with distance between them. But knowing it was possible and that he was willing to give her any space she needed was a relief. Knowing he *would* do that for her made it feel less necessary that he *did* do that for her. A not entirely logical conclusion. But a helpful one.

"I think you needing to stay in Oregon while I move to California might be unnecessary," she said. "But I thank you very much for being willing to do that."

Her stomach choose that really inopportune moment to grumble because breakfast had been quick and many hours in the past. She raised her brows at the interruption, and then started to laugh. Such a serious conversation to have it interrupted by a bodily function.

"Guess I need to eat soon," she said. "We need to pack. Our chance to leave will open up soon."

"Okay. But before we finish… I do still want to come back to New York with you. That's okay?"

"Yes."

"And when we get to Portland, I would very much love to stay with you there. If you'd be comfortable with that."

She narrowed her eyes. "If I said no, where would you stay?"

"With my brother. He's barely home anyway—he stays with his mate."

She considered that option but realized, with no little surprise, that she'd be very uncomfortable sending him to stay with his brother when she had a perfectly good hotel room. With a very large and comfortable bed in it.

"I'd rather you…didn't stay with your brother."

His slow smile made her toes curl. "I'd rather stay with you too," he said before kissing her.

The kiss fogged all her thinking, her worries, and left her with just lust and wonder. She liked lust and wonder. Lust and wonder felt amazing. She pressed into him, wrapping her arms around his neck, and for a long moment, forgot about everything else—including the fact that they were supposed to be packing up their campsites.

Then she realized that the sooner they got to Portland, the sooner they'd get into that hotel room. The sooner she could strip him naked and take advantage of that big hotel bed.

She patted his chest as she leaned away. "We need to get on the road soon." She met his gaze, letting him see the heat curling through her system, sure he could pick out her intent in her scent. His nostrils flared and his eyes darkened, confirming her guess.

She was grinning in anticipation as she took down her tent and got all her stuff neatly packed into the trunk of her rental car, happy to focus on the lust over the logistics.

The site was nearly cleared out by the time she'd finished breaking down her site. Everyone on their row had already left except for Tom. The dust of the hurried exodus had settled. And now she was anxious to get moving, too. It was after noon, the day's heat blanketed the emptying campsite, making her sweat as she tucked the last of her equipment into her trunk and closed the lid. She turned to check on Dylan, excitement thrumming through her blood.

Only to be pulled up short.

As the three tiger males appeared at the edge of her site.

Dylan was at Cat's side almost before he registered that the tigers were there and had appeared suddenly, moving at shifter speeds when there were still too many humans around for that. Most of the site might have emptied, but Tom was still just across from Dylan's truck, packing up his camping seat. If Tom hadn't noticed the tigers seeming to appear out of nowhere, it would be a damned miracle.

Dylan hissed at the three men, his tone low but full of warning. They were acting recklessly and endangering more than just themselves. But more than that, they were a threat to Cat, a threat in a way he felt in the very marrow of his bones. And he would not have his mate threatened.

Cat crossed her arms over her chest as she faced the three. "I thought you'd have scattered to the wind." She focused on the twitchy tiger who couldn't seem to stop moving and glancing over his shoulder. "You especially," she said. "I called Elizaveta. She's aware of you now, and that you're no longer welcome."

"You told her about him," Lenny said without looking at Dylan. His eyes were fully yellow now, his tiger right at the surface.

"I did. And she approves."

"She doesn't," Rick said. "None of us do."

"None of you are my concern," Cat countered. "Not even Eliza-veta. But she knows it's a done deal."

"You've fucked him," Lenny said. Not asking a question.

"None of your business what my mate and I do together."

"He's not your mate," Lenny said. "Or he won't be for long."

"A threat?" Dylan asked, his voice very deep.

"A challenge," Lenny said, finally meeting his gaze. "You want one of our females, you fight for her."

"Ugh. No." Cat pointed a finger at Lenny's chest. "First, those challenge fights aren't allowed. Second, no. Just no. Third, ew, I'm not one of your 'females,' and if you call me that again I'm gonna pepper spray you."

"A fight to the death," Lenny said, ignoring Cat.

She set herself in front of Dylan and growled. A growl to rival any big cat. For a beat, he had to fight down a smile. His mate was fierce and he loved that.

"No fighting, no fighting, no death, no fighting. Or I swear I will chop off your balls myself. I will not have it. Do you understand? I will not have it."

"You don't get a say in this," Lenny said, his gaze never leaving Dylan's.

"Of course she does," Dylan said. "This is about her. And her choices."

"And you better bet your ass I get a say in what happens to me." Cat snarled.

"You don't get a say in if I kill your mate or not," Lenny said. His voice had dropped to a lower register. He was right on the edge of releasing his tiger.

The twitchy tiger behind him kept glancing over his shoulder and his scent was full of a combination panic and blood lust that wasn't going to help anyone. The big man, Rick, held his place behind Lenny, his expression neutral. But there was a lot more uncertainty in his scent than there had been during the earlier confrontations. He wasn't nearly as committed to this challenge idea. Dylan got the feeling Rick would have let all this go. And the twitchy guy was just here to see the blood but not actually get involved. That boded well, because it meant there was just one of them he'd have to actually fight if it came to that.

The problem was he couldn't fight one tiger and protect Cat from the others. And she didn't want a fight, which meant he didn't want a fight. He'd defend himself if Lenny actually let his tiger out. But there would be no challenge because his mate most definitely did not approve.

Her scent spiked with her fear and anger was like lightning on the dry grass, sparking a fire Lenny shouldn't have started.

The reality that she was still very human in the middle of this shifter pissing match crawled through the back of his mind. A distraction if Lenny attacked. They both knew it, too.

"Elizaveta will have you all thrown into tiger jail for this," Cat said.

"You gave up your protections under our laws when you refused a tiger mate," Lenny snarled. "You want him? He's got to fight for you."

"No. And *no*. And again, one more time because you seem to be missing this key point, no!"

Dylan's lips twitched. God, he adored her.

More than adored, he realized. Though maybe too early for that realization, but it was there. The possibility of it. The truth of it creeping into his bones. Love.

A love he intended to protect no matter what.

The shotgun under his front seat was too far away, unfortunately, but if he could get to it, he'd put an end to this instantly. An old trick his mother taught all her kids. Shifters rarely considered protecting themselves from mundane weapons. Especially when facing other shifters. It was a weakness he could exploit now. None of the three had weapons beyond their own shifter natures on them. But his shotgun was safely locked in its case under his seat, making it a lot less useful just then.

He glanced toward Tom, whose back was to this standoff. He was leaning into the back of his rental car, finishing his packing. He was another human Dylan would have to protect if Lenny didn't control his anger.

If Lenny had been a leopard, the threat of Maria Jones's retribution would have been enough to send them all running—but then, a leopard shifter wouldn't be denying a mate bond this way. They didn't technically fall under his mother's domain as shifters. But they did have to follow the rules in this part of the country. All the shifters did.

"There are no shifter challenge matches allowed in the Pacific Northwest," Dylan said, realizing his voice had dropped as his leopard rose to face the threat. Damn, he hoped Tom didn't look this way. The signs of something he wouldn't consider part of the natural world were way too fucking obvious.

"I don't follow your rules, leopard," Lenny hissed.

"You don't follow any rules, you son of a bitch," Cat snapped. "If you did, you would have fucked off months ago."

Lenny's upper lip lifted in a snarl he didn't quite release, but it was enough to flash his teeth for a brief moment, enough to show his threat.

"That last human leaves," Lenny said, his voice low, "and we fight, leopard. You don't fight, you die."

"My mate doesn't approve," Dylan said. "Your challenge is refused."

"She's your boss?"

Dylan raised his brows at that. Was that supposed to be a taunt? What a stupid fuck this tiger was. "If I'm a good mate to her? Yes, her wishes in this are my top priority."

Cat smiled up at him. "Ah, I like that. The fucking tigers never take my wishes into consideration. Thank you."

"Of course," Dylan said, though he didn't take his eyes off Lenny.

Rick huffed out a sound like annoyance or a curse, but he didn't elaborate. Twitchy guy just twitched.

And from the corner of his eye, Dylan saw Tom getting into his car. Finally. And thankfully. He liked Tom. The farther away the older man got from all this, the better.

Dylan kept his gaze on Lenny as Tom's car started, but he opened his senses to the rest of the campsite. It wasn't empty yet, though the exodus had been quick and was nearly complete. But there were still parks personnel taking down the food tents and hooking up the shower trucks for removal. It sounded like the crew responsible for cleaning up the site had already moved into the far section of the camp as well.

Still too many humans around. Still too much light and open space. It was the middle of the day, in the middle of a human population. The traffic on the road out was loud and steady. There weren't any big enough wooded areas for them to hide a fight. And Dylan couldn't guarantee all the eclipse watchers had cleared out of the fields, which were too open in the middle of the day anyway.

Most importantly, though, Cat didn't want a fight.

Tom's car crept down the road away from them. Dylan watched and waited. Tom didn't pass them or even wave goodbye, which a part of Dylan recognized as strange, but he was too focused on Lenny to consider that and what it meant. Lenny's snarling increased and he released a low hiss that wasn't a sound a human could make. His eyes were almost entirely yellow now, not much sign of his human-self left.

Like it or not, Lenny was going to attack. And he'd have to protect himself. And more than anything else, he was pissed off that Lenny was going to force his hand to do something his mate didn't want.

"Don't," Cat said, pointing at Lenny, as if speaking to a misbehaving animal—which at the moment, Lenny was. "Don't do it. Elizaveta—"

"Isn't here," Lenny interrupted. "No one's here but us. And he's one against three."

Dylan snarled at the three tigers, holding Lenny's gaze as the tension of the tiger's threat brought Dylan's leopard closer to the surface. He could take on three tigers if he had to, but he was still very aware that Cat didn't want this. Still, now that Tom was gone, and the other humans in the campsite were still some distance away, he let the animal side of his nature rise.

"There are two of us," Cat answered Lenny's threat. She pulled something from the pocket of her jeans. "And I told you, I will not hesitate to use my pepper spray."

Dylan and Lenny broke their staring contest at the same moment to look at Cat. He raised his brows at the little canister she held up in front of Lenny's face. Twitchy guy hissed and leapt several yards away in one move. Rick glanced at Lenny, a question in his frown. Dylan tried not to smile.

The breeze had died down. She could easily use that toxic gas in her hand without it accidentally blowing back on her.

"And if the spray isn't deterrent enough," Cat continued. She pulled something from her back pocket that Dylan assumed was her phone. Until he got a closer look at it.

"A Taser gun?" he asked. "How long have you been carrying that?"

"Most of the time since they first showed up. As well as the pepper spray."

"Tasers won't stop us," Lenny snarled.

"No," Cat said reasonably. "Neither will the spray. But it'll irritate the hell out of you, make your face sting and burn. And the Taser will make your muscles bounce around so much you won't be able to fight. I have it set to high. And for the record, Victor Romanov tweaked it for me. So the charge is sufficient to light you up, Lenny." She grinned as she said this last.

Rick took a step back.

"Who's Victor?" Dylan asked.

"Tiger in charge of security for the elders. Mate to a legendary Tracker named Alexis Tarasova."

"Tracker?" he asked again. Wow, he knew a lot less about tiger shifters than he'd thought.

"They're like tiger police. Sort of." Cat waved that away. "I'll explain later." To Lenny, she said, "You're a fool to think I haven't prepared for you guys to be assholes like this. From the beginning. And you're even stupider if you think I haven't had help. You want to take a chance with Victor's souped-up Taser, that's up to you. I wouldn't recommend it. But then, I'm a genius, and I know how to calculate odds."

Dylan had to work really hard not to smile at that last sentence. He loved her brain so much.

"Although," she said as if it just occurred to her, "if you want me to go into details about how the upgraded Taser works, I'd be happy to. It's fascinating really. Electricity is fascinating in general. Well, I should be specific, I mean the force particle that carries the electro-magnetic force is really fascinating."

She fell into her lecture voice and started down the road of a brief history of electromagnetism. Dylan watched Rick roll his eyes and twitchy guy, from his safe distance several yards away, let out a noise that was hard to interpret but it sounded almost like a suppressed yawn.

How the guy could not appreciate a smart woman telling him cool things Dylan didn't know. He'd have enjoyed listening to her longer—

he knew most of what she was telling the tigers, but he loved listening to her talk science—but Lenny cut her off.

"Enough!" The man's voice had gone gravely. His tiger still right under his skin, ready to burst out. "You think you can stop us with human tools?"

"Yes, actually." Cat raised her weapons in each hand and aimed them at Lenny.

Rick, apparently with more self-preservation instincts than his partner, took two steps back and looked like he might join Twitch soon.

Lenny snarled, and in a move so fast and sudden Dylan almost didn't catch it despite watching closely, lunged toward Cat. Dylan dove forward, without thinking, and grabbed at the man before he could reach her. Cat shouted something he didn't hear just as Lenny turned on him, and all Dylan's focus went into fending off the tiger's attack.

The man hadn't been trained to fight. He fought instinctively, letting his tiger take control. All speed and anger and vicious intent. But no plan. Just claws out and attack. He was fast, though. Faster than Dylan would have given him credit for. And the viciousness made him dangerous.

Dylan dodged and avoided most of Lenny's punches and swipes, but not all. The fight was a grappling of swings and hits in close proximity that didn't give Dylan time to do more than bat and duck and avoid. He lost ground, moving back as Lenny charged hard at him and didn't give him a beat to breath. Dylan took the attack, letting Lenny push them both farther from Cat. So long as she was safe… That was the one thing he could focus on outside Lenny's attack.

That and letting Lenny push him closer to his truck.

He heard Cat shout again, the sound of her anger and a hint of fear distracting him. Lenny got in a jaw punch that made Dylan see stars. Using his own anger, he dove head first into the tiger and hefted him up over his shoulder, tossing him up and over so Lenny flew into his truck, slamming hard against the side of the truck bed.

The tiger slipped to the ground, momentarily winded. The pause wouldn't last long but it gave him a moment to check on Cat.

She stood with both her pepper spray and Taser out. The Taser, she'd shot into Rick, who was now laid out on the ground convulsing as electricity coursed through his body. Whatever this Victor guy had done to the Taser, he'd made it capable of taking out a full grown—very large—shifter. Thank the fucking universe.

She had the pepper spray aimed at Twitch, but he stood at a distance with his hands raised. In the split second Dylan had to take all this in, she didn't lower her spray, despite Twitch trying to show he meant no harm.

Smart woman.

Before he could ask if she was okay, Lenny hit him in the side with a full body tackle, taking them both to the ground. The fall left him on the bottom of a raging tiger taking swings at his kidneys. Dylan gritted his teeth and grappled for purchase, the struggle again formless and wild, without any room for him to get in more than a couple of hits to Lenny's jaw. The man had a face like granite, though, taking the shots to the head and barely slowing down.

Dylan needed more space, room to bring the fight to Lenny. He managed to get a solid grip on Lenny's shoulders and jam one of his feet up under Lenny's hip, letting years of his parents' fighting lessons sink into his actions. He used his leverage on the enraged tiger to dip him closer before putting all his strength into pushing out.

The move sent Lenny flying again, this time over the top of Dylan's truck. The crash on the opposite side was loud enough to make Dylan wince.

He didn't waste the advantage this time, though. He had to trust Cat had the other two in hand. He jumped over his truck, not even pretending at human speed and strength, landed on the roof of the cab in a crouch long enough to take in where Lenny had fallen, then dropped on the other man just as he was attempting to climb to his feet.

Before Lenny could do more than raise up to his knees, Dylan had an arm around his neck, pulling him back into a choke hold. He hooked his free arm to his choking arm and used that leverage to squeeze tighter. Lenny frantically clawed at Dylan's arms, leaving bloody gouges. Dylan didn't loosen his grip.

Lenny tried to kick out backward, but Dylan had hit him in an awkward position from which he had no leverage and the desperate lunge only increased the pressure Dylan had on his neck.

Choking a shifter into unconsciousness was even more difficult than choking a human to death. Short of breaking Lenny's neck—which he could from that position—the best he could do was knock the man out long enough he could get his shotgun from his truck.

When Lenny's struggles grew weaker, Dylan increased the pressure at his neck. Lenny's body slumped, heavy against Dylan's arm, and might have pulled him over if he hadn't braced for the extra weight. He held his chokehold longer, until he was certain Lenny was unconscious and not just pretending. The moments ticked by as he counted in his head, knowing just the amount of time this took after the body went limp to ensure the shifter was out cold.

He finally released his hold on Lenny and pushed him to the ground. The tiger landed face down into the dirt and dry grass, his body sprawled out. Dylan didn't pause to check for a pulse or make sure Lenny was out. He leapt back to his truck and pulled his shotgun case from under the front seat.

He had it unlocked, the break-action double barrel gun out, and two buckshot shells ready to load when Lenny groaned and lifted onto his hands and knees.

He loaded the shells, snapped the gun closed, and swung around to face Lenny just as the tiger threw himself at Dylan. His attack left Dylan no time to fire, and instead, he found himself on the ground again with Lenny on top, grabbling for the gun barrel.

The sudden, earsplitting retort of a single shot echoed across the site.

3 2

Cat froze at the sound of the gun shot. Shit.

Without releasing her finger on the Taser as it continued to flood Rick with an electrical current that kept him immobile—it took a *lot* to keep a tiger shifter down—she turned, desperate to find Dylan.

He was on the ground, Lenny on top of him, a shotgun gripped between them.

And over them stood Tom Baxter with a very large shotgun of his own.

"That'll be enough of that young man," he said to Lenny. He motioned with the gun barrel. "That was a warning shot. Up. Off. Now."

Lenny snarled and didn't release his hold on the shotgun he and Dylan both held.

Tom shook his head. "If you think you're fast enough to reach me before I can fire, you'd be wrong. Been practicing with Alexis, so I can hit a shifter dead center before they reach me. She's good at more than hand-to-hand fighting, you know."

Cat blinked several times at the older man. He knew about shifters? And did he just say...Alexis? Did he mean Alexis Tarasova? The legendary Tracker married to Victor Romanov. The one who taught all the female tiger shifters how to fight. The adopted daughter of Elizaveta.

He couldn't mean *that* Alexis. Could he?

And how the hell did he know about shifters?

Lenny narrowed his eyes at Tom. "How do you know Alexis?"

"Funny enough, not all hybrids are women," Tom said, his tone affable. "Though some of us are too old to be much use in the whole reproduction issue." He winked at Cat.

"You're a hybrid?" Cat said, finally releasing her finger on the Taser button, stopping the flow of current to Rick. He collapsed against the ground with a groan. She mostly ignored him, though she kept him in her peripheral vision in case he moved. Shifters were fast, but he still had the little metal prong in his neck. She just had to depress the button again to shoot him with another jolt of shifter-stopping electricity.

The jumpy tiger was still several yards away, his hands raised, his gaze moving between Rick on the ground, Lenny still crouched over Dylan, and Tom holding a pretty sizable gun.

She pointed to the jumpy tiger with her pepper spray. "Don't you think about interfering."

He shook his head. "Think I'll tap out of this one," he said.

And Cat realized it was the first time she'd heard him speak. His voice was a lot deeper and resonant than his jumpy, twitchy presence made her think it would be. He also had a distinct Russian accent which, for some reason, she hadn't been expecting either.

She shook off the distraction because Lenny still hadn't released the gun.

"You think even Alexis can change physics," Lenny said, his lip lifted in a snarl. "I move too fast for an old human's reactions."

"Maybe," Tom said, stills sounding matter-of-fact and reasonable. "But I'm betting my finger against your speed cause I'm pretty nervous right now, as you can no doubt smell, and I'm going to fire this gun soon on accident when my nerves make my finger jump. If you're not very careful, I'll shoot you even if you don't try to attack me."

"You'll kill him too." Lenny nodded down at Dylan.

"Oh, my fingers may be effected by my nerves, but my aim is not. I've practiced. A lot. And I'm aiming real good at your head right now. You've given me a great angle."

In the distraction caused by Tom's presence and his own weapon, Cat watched Dylan. He'd frozen at the sound of the gun shot, but he wasn't watching Tom during all this. His gaze was firmly on Lenny. Narrowed on the tiger's face. Dylan's eyes were fully yellow now, his own shifter nature right on the surface.

The fight had been a horrifying thing to watch because shifter speed meant everything had blurred. She hated that. It wasn't the first time she'd seen a shifter fight, though she'd been saved from having to witness too many of them thanks to her age and status as a protected human within the community. But this was Dylan in the middle of the fight, and watching him in danger had terrified her.

And there hadn't been a damned thing she could do to help him because she'd had to deal with Rick almost immediately. He'd lunged for her while she was distracted by Dylan's fight. Her finger flexed against the Taser button. She was tempted to run another current of electricity through him again. She wasn't sure what he'd intended when he'd tried to reach her, but she didn't really care. The fact that he'd forced her to pay attention to him so she couldn't help Dylan had pissed her off, and she had no sympathy for his groans.

As she watched Dylan now, she realized he wasn't as still as he seemed. He'd moved his hands very subtly along the barrel of the shotgun. The dangerous end was, fortunately, pointed at his truck, not at any people. He'd lose a tire if the gun went off, but that was the worst that would happen. Still, he didn't release his hands from the weapon, and had in fact slid his hands into a position that ensured he had it braced in a better grip.

A grip with leverage, she realized.

She studied his position relative to Lenny's and the position of the gun between them. The placement of Lenny's hands. She did a quick calculation. And straightened her shoulders. If she was seeing this right…

That could work.

But only if Lenny didn't notice.

Thanks to Tom, all Lenny's attention was on the older man. "You aren't cut out to kill me," Lenny was saying. "You're already shaking. That gun will get too heavy for you in about two seconds."

"You think, so huh?" Tom let out a long sigh. "Well, it's possible. Possible I don't have the reaction time I've trained to have. Possible I'll let Elizaveta down. But even if I do, she's already sent Trackers. There's one on this coast. He'll arrive before you three can get far enough away to hide. So… I'm betting on the good guys here."

Lenny's eyes narrowed. "A Tracker?"

"She sent for him yesterday. If I've got my times right, he'll likely be here any minute."

That news seemed to be enough for the jumpy tiger with the Russian accent. He glanced between Lenny and Rick. "This wasn't what I was told. Or promised. I want no more of this."

In a blink, he was gone, moving at that speed that made him blur.

Cat wanted to ask what he'd been promised—because if Lenny and Rick had promised something to do with her she was going to tell Tom to shoot Lenny and she was going to run more electricity through Rick.

Too late now. She'd have to leave…whoever the hell he was to the Trackers.

From his prone position on the ground, Rick raised his hands. "I wasn't going to hurt you, you know," he snarled up at her. "I was trying to keep you out of the fight so you didn't get hurt."

"Right. Because you care so damned much about what happens to me the person. If that were true, Rick, you wouldn't be backing Lenny."

"I just want a mate. A family. Is that so much to ask?"

"When the person you're pursing is unwilling? Yes. Yes, it is. Fucking hell, man, just find a willing mate."

"Tried that. There aren't enough of them."

"Then find a nice human you can love and adopt babies, you asshole. Stop stalking people for their wombs. Stalking is bad. Also, you're not entitled to anything, not a family, not attention, not anything at all, and thinking you're owed what you want 'just because' is fucked up. This is not rocket science."

"And she should know," Tom answered, "given how she's smart enough to do rocket science."

She grinned at Tom. "Thank you."

"Only the truth of the thing," Tom said with a wink.

Lenny's low hiss broke through the conversation. The skin along his face was jumping as if he was on the verge of shifting. Shifting shapes took time and left him vulnerable. He couldn't *want* to shift in that moment, not if he had any sense at all. But since Lenny had proved himself low on sense lately, she wasn't sure that would deter him.

His voice so gravely it was almost unintelligible now, Lenny said, "This was none of your business. This was none of anyone's business. This was between me and the woman, and you will pay dearly for your interference."

"The woman? The woman?" Cat snarled. "I have a fucking name. This is why you're still alone. You're an asshole."

Lenny finally looked away from Tom to growl at her. "I'll deal with you soon," he said in his guttural tone.

She raised her pepper spray in warning.

And in the next instant, Dylan moved.

Cat watched, frozen in place, as Dylan swung the long barrel of the gun around and slammed Lenny in the side of the head with the butt. Even at a distance, Cat heard the crack of bone.

Lenny hadn't noticed the change in Dylan's grip, or that it left him in no position to prevent the swing. His hands were all wrong and he had no purchase to keep the heavy base of the gun from smacking into him.

The hit stunned Lenny and he wobbled a little to one side. Dylan continued to take advantage, slammed him with the shotgun again, and then leverage up and over so he was the one straddling Lenny now.

He pressed the barrel into the tiger's throat, pushing down with his weight. Lenny scrambled at the barrel, trying to push it up. The gun lifted off his throat an inch. Dylan released the pressure suddenly, which brought the gun up so fast Lenny's grip on it slipped.

And then Dylan swung the barrel around to point it at Lenny's face.

"I won't miss at this range," Dylan said, the front of the shotgun resting on Lenny's forehead.

Lenny raised his hands, palms up, and relaxed back into the ground, snarling, but the glow in his eyes finally, finally dimmed.

In the distraction, Rick had removed the Taser prongs. Cat swung back to him as he rose on his elbows, prepared to spray him with the pepper spray if he lunged for her again.

He raised his hands, palms out in a mirror of Lenny's pose. "I'm done," he said, though he sounded bitter. "All I wanted was a family. Not a stint in confinement."

"Should have thought of that before stalking me across the country," she said with no sympathy.

"She's not yours to keep," Lenny said to Dylan, his voice more normal now.

She swung back to them but kept Rick in her peripheral vision and her pepper spray trained on him.

"She belongs to the tigers," Lenny said.

"No," Dylan and Cat said at the same time.

"And I'm done with the tigers now," Cat added. "No more. From any of you."

"Or you'll answer to the leopards," Dylan said.

"You don't want to do that on this coast," a new voice said.

Every gaze turned to face the newcomer. Though Dylan didn't move the barrel of his gun from Lenny's forehead, Tom swung his around to face the potential new threat.

He was the first to let out a breath and lower his weapon. "You're the Tracker," he said.

"How can you tell?" Cat asked. Then she remembered. "You're a hybrid. You can sense the tigers."

Tigers sensed other tigers, where they were, sometimes even what form they were in, even when they weren't visible or they'd kept downwind so their scents didn't carry. And it turned out, hybrids could sense other tigers, too. She wasn't hybrid, so she'd never had that advantage, but she realized Tom did. Amy did as well.

The other tiger could have been another irritating male come to join Lenny. But now that she paused to study him, she was sure Tom's guess was right. The new tiger had that…thing she'd never been able to explain properly in words that most of the Trackers had. A kind of confident stillness. To be fair, the hot assassin who'd come after her sister all those years ago had had that same stillness. He'd been a

Tracker before turning assassin, so that made sense. Amy's biological father—also a former Tracker—had the stillness thing, too. It wasn't like they looked like statues. And it wasn't like they didn't *move*. But there were no extra movements. They seemed to take in everything around them without appearing to look. And when they did move, it was with purpose.

"I'm Nick Lee," the Tracker said.

Outside of his stillness, he was a pretty average looking man. Not unattractive at all. He was actually handsome, with black hair cut short and very dark brown eyes, but he wasn't *obvious* either. Not the way Dylan was sort of smack-you-in-the-face handsome and sexy. Nick Lee was more subtle. Like you had to look at him twice before you'd notice him. She realized that was probably pretty useful for a Tracker.

"Sorry I wasn't here earlier," he added. "Got caught in the traffic leaving the place."

Cat groaned and looked at Dylan who was still straddling Lenny and hadn't moved the barrel of the gun from his forehead. "We're gonna get stuck in that too on the way to Portland."

"Sounds like," he said, sounding resigned and normal and not like he was holding a tiger down at gun point. Though his eyes continued to glow faintly. He was very still now too, coiled, like he was ready to act at any moment. And while he had the gun on Lenny, his gaze was steady on Nick.

She faced Nick again. "There was a third tiger but he took off. I didn't know him. He's not one of the males who's been harassing me for months."

"Lenny and Rick have been?" Nick asked.

She didn't have to ask how Nick knew their names. She'd told Elizaveta who they were. If she sent a Tracker, she'd have given the Tracker all the information he needed.

"They wrapped it up in pretty words, but yeah, they've been persistently pestering me back in New York. More so than the others."

"Others?" Nick asked, raising his brows.

She rolled her eyes. "Too many males thinking my womb is open for business." She snarled at that. "You know, you people have a serious issue with this, right? The way your males act." She realized she was talking to one of those males as she spoke, but she didn't care. She hadn't cared from the beginning.

Too many of the young tiger males acted this way. It was a really serious issue in the tiger society. And it felt like no one did anything about it. The Mate Run—their standard answer to keeping the males in line, allowing the female tigers choice, but still giving the illusion of competition—had been breaking down for the last twenty or thirty years, maybe longer. Maybe it hadn't ever really been a great solution.

Cat hadn't been around two hundred years ago, when tiger society had fallen into blood and death and chaos. She couldn't judge their solution at the time because it had worked—enough to keep them from complete extinction. But it wasn't working anymore. Hadn't worked well in years. The males had grown entitled. And the fact that they now felt entitled to *any* possible person who might be able to bear them children only compounded the problem.

"For the record," she said, "I'm not eligible for this weird tiger version of courting anymore. Spread the word."

Nick nodded. "Elizaveta said as much. The word is being spread." He glanced at Lenny and Rick. "The rest of the males will abide by your choice."

"You sure?" she said with no little annoyance.

"If not, they'll have to face the full force of our laws," Nick said, sounding very matter-of-fact.

"And ours," another new voice said into the quiet that followed his statement.

Now who was joining the party? Cat turned to face yet another newcomer.

The woman was average height, maybe five foot six, with thick brown-black hair pulled up into a bun. She was dressed elegantly in wide-legged pants and a button down shirt, yet still managed to look like she fit in the campsite surroundings. Which was a strange contrast that would have sent Cat down an analysis hole under different circumstances. The woman held herself almost regally, but with a calm quiet that nearly matched the Tracker's stillness.

Dylan sighed loudly enough for the entire site to hear. "You didn't need to come all this way," he said to the woman.

"Of course I did. You're my youngest. You might be an adult, but you're still my baby."

Cat pressed her lips together even as Dylan rolled his eyes. This was Dylan's mother? Shit. Dylan's *mother*. She hadn't anticipated meeting this powerful woman so soon.

The woman's dark-eyed gaze moved to her, and she smiled very faintly. "Catalina Donovan. I'm Maria Jones. It's a pleasure to meet you."

"You too. I think. Depends on how all this goes." Cat gestured at her surroundings.

Maria showed no reaction to that comment. She faced Nick. "Elizaveta was kind enough to call me, too. The tiger in this territory that was involved but ran away, he'll be watched."

Nick tilted his head down in a brief nod. "Seems fair. Let us know if he causes any more trouble. We'll take care of him."

"Will my son's mate have any more trouble from the tigers?"

"No." Nick stared at Maria's raised brow. His confidence meeting hers.

Cat watched, fascinated. If she hadn't been the center of this conversation, this all would have been even more interesting.

"I'll take these two back to the elders to face trial," Nick said. He glanced at Lenny. "Attacking another shifter, in broad daylight when humans could witness the fight is against our laws."

"He challenged him," Cat said, not even a little sorry to throw Lenny under the bus. "To a death match."

That was *very* illegal in tiger society, among other tigers. Ending death matches was the reason the whole Mate Run thing had been instituted. Starting one could get a tiger sent to confinement for months, sometimes years depending on the outcome. She wasn't sure what happened when they challenged other shifters, but she imagined it was a similar offense. And Lenny officially deserved to be locked up because he'd tried to hurt Dylan. She had no sympathy for the asshole at all.

Nick's gaze moved to Dylan and Lenny. "This true?" he asked Dylan.

Cat scowled. "Of course, it's true. You think I'm lying?"

Nick had the sense to look chagrinned. "Sorry. Force of habit to confirm information."

Cat made a disgusted noise. "If I say it, it's true."

"She's very smart," Dylan said. "I wouldn't argue with her."

That mollified her irritation.

"I've heard," Nick said, giving her a slight smile. "Sorry to cause offense."

"You're forgiven. This time."

"Fair enough." He gestured at Dylan. "I'll take him now, if that's okay?"

Dylan rose slowly, but he kept the gun pointed at Lenny even as he moved toward Cat.

Nick gestured at Lenny. "Up. My car's this way. Do I have to bind you or will you face the elders freely?"

Lenny snarled at Cat. "This is your fault."

Argh, she was going to lose her shit with these guys. Seriously. "Why? Why do you all *insist* on blaming other people for your actions? You did what you did and now you have to pay for it. All you. *All. You.*"

"Some men never learn," Maria said, her tone philosophical. "It's a problem." She shrugged.

Since Maria was the only other woman present, Cat appreciated the support.

Lenny rose to a crouch, his stare on Dylan. "I'll be seeing you again," he whispered in a quiet hiss.

Cat blinked and Maria was standing beside Lenny, his head pulled back sharply by his hair, and her *claws* against his throat. Tiger shifters didn't do partial shifts. They couldn't actually let claws out of their fingers without changing into their animal form. Maria was still very much in human form, but the claws that had erupted from her fingertips were all big cat. Sharp and deadly. She tapped one of those claws against Lenny's jugular.

"My son has a large and very dangerous family," she whispered, but loud enough for the others to hear. "His mate is part of that family now. And we kill to protect family." She dragged her claw gently against Lenny's throat and a thin line of blood appeared in its wake.

The wound healed almost immediately, but a few drops of blood remained to prove Cat hadn't imagined the injury.

Maria's voice dropped further. "I take threats to my family very seriously, young tiger. You'd do well to keep away."

"I wouldn't upset her anymore," Nick said. He hadn't moved from his spot several yards away, but he'd crossed his arms over his chest, looking perfectly at ease with Maria threatening to kill Lenny.

"Wow," Cat said in a whisper to Dylan. "Your mom is impressive. And scary."

He nodded. "Tried to warn you."

"I like it," Cat said.

This earned a faint smile from Maria, though she didn't loosen her grip on Lenny. To him, she said, "I will release you to your people's justice. But know, Catalina Donovan is protected by the leopards now."

She stepped away from Lenny in a graceful move that appeared effortless and yet Lenny still ended up on his face in the dirt.

"Yeah, I like her a lot," Cat said to Dylan, grinning at Maria.

Maria raised her brows in response, her only show of reaction.

3 4

Nick wasted no time scooping Lenny off the ground. He wrenched his hands behind his back, a move that made the tiger wince and snarl in response. The Tracker ignored Lenny's quiet curse and glanced at Tom. "Elizaveta sends her thanks for everything. She'll be in touch later."

"Always a pleasure to work with Elizaveta," Tom said.

Cat felt her own brows rising to her hair line at Tom's quiet smile as he said pleasure, his gaze turned inward. There was a story there between Tom and Elizaveta. That was very interesting. Her curiosity nearly had her blurting out questions but she figured she better let Nick haul Lenny and Rick away first.

Cat plucked at her shirt as sweat trickled down her back. She wasn't sure if the sweat was from the climbing mid-day heat or her earlier fear and anger. Either way, the knowledge sunk in that she wasn't exactly at her best for meeting Dylan's mother. Too late to change that now. But she would have preferred to at least have her hair combed and be less sweaty in front of a shifter who could smell her emotions.

Rick dragged himself to his feet as Nick approached and walked ahead of the Tracker without argument. He gave Lenny a sour look, and glanced back at her once. But he didn't comment as he stalked away.

She'd half expected a parting insult or something. That Rick didn't do that made her think better of him. Not much better. But better than she thought of Lenny.

"Well, this is an interesting first meeting," Maria said into the ensuing silence.

Cat huffed out laugh. Dylan's mother was good at understatement.

Dylan shook his head at Maria. "Thanks for the backup. I had this, though."

She shrugged. "I know. I taught you well." She nodded at his shotgun. "But as I said, you're my baby." She glanced at Cat. "And I wanted to meet your mate. I didn't want a repeat of what happened with Deacon."

Cat frowned up at Dylan.

Dylan said, "My oldest brother took months to introduce his mate to the family. My mother was less than pleased."

"Yes," Maria said dryly.

That was the mate who was also a human. Had Deacon delayed introducing his mate for so long because she was human and not a shifter?

Maria was a strong and scary matriarch. It was important to know where she stood with the woman. And Cat liked to have as much information about a situation as possible.

So she asked, "Do you have an issue with me being human?" Curious but not accusatory. If Maria had a problem with her being human, that would just be something they had to deal with going forward. But she did want to know before they went any further.

And fortunately, because she was dealing with shifters, Maria would smell her emotions and know the question wasn't an accusation. Cat almost smiled. She was finding it surprisingly nice to talk with beings who wouldn't misinterpret her intent. She asked a lot of questions. It was in her nature. But frequently, people misinterpreted what she meant, or got the wrong idea from her tone. Maria wouldn't read her wrong simply because her tone might be hard to gauge. She'd understand what Cat meant.

This was a bonus of having a shifter mate that she really hadn't counted on.

"I have no issue with my son having a human mate," Maria said, her expression gentle. "Though, it will be difficult as you age. He will live longer than you—significantly so, if he doesn't get himself killed." She directed this last part at her son with narrowed eyes. He didn't rise to the bait. "But other than that, no, you being human isn't a problem." She sighed. "Though children might not be possible."

"Brigit already gave you grandchildren," Dylan pointed out. "You don't need more."

"Yes, but I *want* more."

She said this with such an obvious huff of maternal exasperation, Cat laughed. She couldn't help it. Dylan just rolled his eyes.

"Obviously, this is a conversation for another day," Maria said. "You still have a dangerous period of time ahead of you, when Dylan is…less controlled than normal. Has he explained the mate bond to you? How it works, and what it takes for his leopard to feel settled in the bond?"

Cat nodded. "That a lot of sex is required for the bond to solidify. We've gotten started on that. Should make progress on his control soon."

Maria blinked very slowly, then looked at Dylan. "I like your mate."

Dylan finally laughed. "I'm glad to hear it. Now, can you leave so we can settled some things? I have to fly to New York to meet her sister. Who's married to a tiger shifter, by the way. We'll be tied to them going forward."

Maria shrugged. "That's fine. Elizaveta and I have always had an understanding. We'll have a meeting and adjust that arrangement. All will be well. And no tigers should bother you anymore." This last she said to Cat. "That will be a requirement of our new arrangement. Elizaveta has already indicated she'll be amenable."

"She's not happy about me not choosing a tiger, though," Cat said.

"Do you know why?" She'd explained to Dylan. And Tom obviously knew since he was a hybrid and had some sort of interesting relationship with Elizaveta. But had the elder let a leader of another shifter species know that the tigers were in trouble?

"Not in detail," Maria said. "Elizaveta keeps most tiger business to herself. And that's acceptable so long as it doesn't impact my people." She glanced at Dylan. Then back to Cat. "Will it impact my people?"

"Not so long as Elizaveta has accepted this and makes sure the other elders accept." Cat shrugged. "She will. She's pretty good at ensuring she gets what she wants. And she's not above a lot of manipulation when it suits her purposes."

"I've always liked Elizaveta," Maria said. Her only response to the tiger issue. "I'll leave you then. I'd like for you to meet the rest of the family when you can," she said, raising a brow at Dylan that, if Cat was reading her right, was more of a command than a request.

Dylan leveled an even look on his mother. "Once we've settled some things and Cat has gotten moved to her new job in California, we'll arrange something. But don't expect a full family dinner by the end of next week."

Maria's lips flattened. "You could stay in Portland for a few extra days. That wouldn't be too much to ask."

"It would. She can meet the family later. When she's ready. We haven't even discussed all this yet and rushing my mate is a bad idea."

Cat smiled up at him and took his hand. She wouldn't mind meeting his family right away—the typically scary part, meeting his mother, was already over. But it was really nice that he wasn't trying to unilaterally arrange things without discussing them with her. That boded well for their future.

At Maria's continued stare, he let out a sigh and squeezed Cat's hand. "We *will* discuss it, though. Soon. Good enough?" he asked his mother.

Maria shrugged, gracefully giving ground. "Good enough." She nodded at Tom. "Thank you for your help."

Tom tipped an imaginary hat at Maria. "My pleasure. You have a good son there."

That earned a smile from Maria. A full one, not the more contained smiles she'd shown so far. "I think so too." She gave a little wave, and then she just…

Vanished.

Cat blinked. Even after four years of watching shifters come and go at those speeds, it still left her a little startled when they did it while other non-shifter people were around.

She gave herself a little shake and faced Tom. "So… You and Elizaveta?" She raised her brows, waggling them.

Tom's soft smile was accompanied by a charming blush. "She's a good friend."

"Uh huh." Cat grinned. "So she sent you to keep an eye on me, did she?"

He shrugged and for the first time looked a little hesitant. "She knew the young ones were…getting a little intense in their attempts at courtship. She wanted someone who wouldn't arouse their attention nearby to keep an eye on things. And being a hybrid myself, I could sense them, but they wouldn't be able to pick me out of the crowd. Seemed like a good idea at the time. Especially since I'd intended to travel for the eclipse anyway."

"Are you really a high school science teacher in New Jersey?" she asked.

"I am. All true. Just left out the part about knowing tiger shifters."

"You heading home now?" she asked.

"Gotta make a stop in West Virginia first. Then heading back to Jersey. The school year starts soon."

He made a face that ensured Cat laughed. But she wasn't distracted from the fact that he was heading to the same place where the elders' US compound was located. A visit to Elizaveta herself no doubt.

She couldn't wait to tell Amy about this bit of gossip.

"Stay in touch," Cat said. "We hybrid and hybrid-adjacent humans should stick together. Elizaveta has my cell number. Text me when you're home and let me know how your meeting with her went."

"Will do," he said, without showing any sort of flinch that she'd guessed he was going to see Elizaveta. He nodded at Dylan. "When you get a chance, be sure to ask your mother about some of her arrangements with Elizaveta. Should make for some interesting stories." He glanced between them again, his smile wide. "They didn't expect this, though. Take care of yourselves."

He gave them a little salute and walked away, his shotgun resting gently between his hands.

Cat watched him leave, presumably heading back to wherever he'd left his car before he'd circled back on foot to help them.

"I have a feeling there are going to be a lot of interesting stories and revelations in our future," she said.

"What do you think he meant by that last comment?" Dylan said, frowning as he gazed after Tom.

"Got me. Better ask your mother."

He faced her and pulled her into a tight hug. "You weren't hurt, were you? Rick didn't get close enough to do anything?"

"I'm fine," she assured, wrapping her arms around him and settling her head against his chest. His smell filled her with a sense of warmth. And a strange feeling of coming home. That was new. She'd have to study that more. "The Taser worked perfectly. And he really wasn't going to hurt me. I don't even know why he lunged at me. He said it was to keep me from stepping into the middle of your fight with Lenny."

Dylan leaned back enough to meet her gaze. "You were going to?"

"Of course. That's what mates do, right? Have each other's backs."

"It is." His smile was slow and sultry and she felt the look in every part of her body, but most especially in her core. They'd already packed the tents, which meant unless she was willing to fuck him in the backseat of one of their cars, they'd have to wait until Portland. But the thought of having him all alone in a room with a big bed was enough to keep her from stripping him naked just then. She was going to enjoy him on that bed.

He raised his brows. "I'm not entirely sure what you're thinking right now, but I like the direction. Too much. I'm going to be distracted driving now."

She leaned into him. "I'll explain everything when we get to the hotel."

He made a deep, rumbling noise that vibrated against her breasts where she was pressed against his chest. "I'm looking forward to that."

"Oh, me too. But in the meantime, we'd better face the traffic before the cleaning crew kicks us out." They were already late leaving the grounds. Most of the place was empty now.

He brushed his hands through her hair, pulling her face close for a deep kiss that left her giddy and tingly all over.

When he lifted is mouth, he murmured, "There's a lot still. A lot to discuss."

"There is. And I'm still a little nervous about some of it. I've never lived so far from my sister. I'll miss Spike."

"You aren't arguing for custody with Amy?" He sounded amused.

"I will. But Spike is getting too old to move so far. She's a New Yorker anyway. I don't think she'd like the California scene as much."

He laughed.

"But all the logistics aside, there's one thing I'm sure about."

"What?"

"That I want to be with you. That this is right. All the other stuff… I'm still nervous because this is the first time I've been anyone's mate." She shrugged. "And there's a lot we still need to learn about each other. Like… I get really distracted when I'm working and thinking. I might not pay attention to you or even notice you're there for days if I'm really on to something."

"Can I be around to make sure you eat and watch you think?"

"You won't mind my ignoring you?"

"So long as you talk to me once you've had your breakthrough so I can hear all about it, I'm good with it. I'm not good with you not eating while you think, though, so I'd like permission to ensure you get food to fuel your brain."

Something in her chest softened and turned all mushy at his words. Probably her heart. Was this falling in love? Interesting…

She nodded. "I'd be good with that. More than good. And I'd *love* having someone to talk to after I come out of those thinking stints.

Amy and Spike don't understand what I'm saying when I try to explain what I've been working on."

"I can't guarantee I'll understand, but I'll be fascinated."

"You're sure?"

"Of course. First, I love your brain, the way it works, and listening to you expound on science."

More mushy softening around her chest.

"Second, your stuff is close enough to my field, when you have a breakthrough, it'll affect all of us in the field. I will be overjoyed to be on the front line. To be able to say I was there when she made that breakthrough. I mean… It'd be like watching Vera Rubin figuring out the galaxy rotation problem and confirming the existence of dark matter. Who wouldn't want to be there for that?"

He said that last so seriously, not like he was joking, not hyperbole. He really wanted to be there if she made a major scientific breakthrough. *When*. He'd said when.

And he didn't mind that she'd ignore him for days when she got focused. He said he wouldn't mind. Others had said that to her before and then gotten offended when she'd completely ignored their existence for days at a time. Worse with attempted boyfriends than friends, but everyone took some level of offense. Yet, he said he wouldn't.

Did she trust him? Believe he meant what he was saying? She couldn't analyze his scent to be sure. But…

She breathed him in, and while she couldn't do what he and other shifters could do, something about his scent, that heady male musk of him, left her feeling…certain. Certain he was being honest. Certain he meant everything he was saying.

Certain, yet again, that this mate bond between them was right.

"You're making me feel very happy and mushy inside," she said. "I think that's a good sign."

He smiled, leaning his forehead against hers. "You make me feel that way too. Might be because I've fallen hard for you. And not just because you're my mate."

"Oh well, that just did me in for good." She cupped his cheeks in her hands. "This is good. And we're going to work. And all the rest will be fine."

"Glad to hear you agree." He kissed her, lightly, then deepened the kiss.

And for the first time in a long time, Cat was excited to step into the future.

Dylan stroked Cat's bare shoulder, listening to her quiet breathing as she slept. A thin line of light peaked between the hotel curtains but otherwise the room was dark and cool. They'd been here for two days already, and they'd barely left the bed in all that time. One more night before their flight to New York. He rolled just enough that he could see her in the faint light.

His mate.

He wasn't sure he'd ever get over the awe that thought inspired. His leopard was certainly pleased with the situation. Which meant his control didn't feel nearly as shaky as it had when the tigers had confronted them. He knew things wouldn't always be this easy—especially all the moving and new jobs and adapting academic schedules.

But for these few days, he was beyond content and just happy to have her in his arms.

She moved a little in her sleep, rolling toward him. Even in sleep she wasn't still. She turned and moved and adjusted herself all night. He'd have thought that would make sleep difficult, but instead, he slept more peacefully than he could remember. Her every little movement confirming to his subconscious that she was still there, still beside him and safe, and he could rest.

All these new discoveries. So much still to uncover.

Her lemony lightning scent filled him. He nuzzled her neck, smiling against her skin when she mumbled something in her sleep and pressed closer. The feel of her soft breasts against his chest had him hardening instantly. She snugged her thigh against his, pressing into his growing erection which made him groan.

He had a delicious way to wake her up.

He kissed his way along her shoulder, over her collar bone, her body soft and warm against his lips. So soft. She tasted like she smelled, the lightning flavor stronger on her skin. There was energy and power in her he wasn't sure he'd ever get enough of. Down across her breasts. Her nipples hardened as he lowered the blanket slowly, exposing more of her to the cool room. She made a little grumbling noise in her sleep. He grinned as he pulled her nipple into his mouth. The grumble turned to a soft sigh and she pressed into him.

The moment her breathing changed, he knew it. When she moved from full sleep to almost awake, to fully awake. But her eyes remained closed. He moved to her other breast and her hands came up to tangle in his hair as he pulled gently at the little bud with his teeth.

"I love the way you wake me up," she murmured, her voice husky from sleep.

"Good because I love waking you up this way," he said, before sliding his lips down her stomach.

Her breath caught as he kissed low on her abdomen, swirling his tongue against a particularly sensitive spot he'd discovered near her hip. She shivered and her grip in his hair tightened. But she didn't push him away or rush him. Just held on.

When he settled between her thighs, she was already panting and had moved one hand from his hair to cover her eyes. He noticed she did that when she was starting to get overwhelmed with sensation. A way to focus her concentration, she'd said when he'd asked. The fact that she was concentrating on how he was making her feel delighted him. The sight of her open and eager for him, made his leopard roar in satisfaction in his head. *His mate.*

He kissed her inner thigh, rubbing his morning scruff against the sensitive skin because he'd discovered just last night how much she loved that. He was rewarded with her deep groan. Her hips lifted with a small gasp of impatience when he skimmed over her wet heat but didn't immediately settle in.

"Impatient," he murmured, blowing hot breath against her wetness.

She whimpered. "Yes. It's too early for patience."

He chuckled and she shivered. "It's probably ten in the morning."

"See," she said, her voice breathless, "too early."

"So you'd like me to…get on with things then?" He nibbled her inner thigh again, a quick bit that made her gasp.

"Lick me," she moaned. "Please."

"Yes," he growled. He ran his tongue over her outer lips, then slid between her inner lips and finally allowed himself a taste of her. She was sweet and musk and spice and that lightning flavor that was so uniquely hers and so so wet. He could live on her taste, the sounds she made when he circled her clitoris with his tongue, the way she writhed and ground up against his mouth.

He licked and sucked and indulged his need for her until her entire body went stiff and taunt under him, and then she cried out as her release took her, her body quaking as she came.

"I love the way you sound when you come," he murmured. Another gentle lap made her hips jump and her fingers tightened in his hair, urging him up.

She dropped her hand from her eyes, pulled him over her, wrapping her legs around his hips. "I love waking up this way," she said. "With you. With you making me come. I could do this every morning forever."

"I would enjoyed nothing more," he said, very seriously.

He rolled away long enough to slip on a condom and then he settled over her again, sliding into her like coming home. Her heat surrounding his cock was so fucking perfect, it felt like she was made for him.

And since she was his mate, really, she was.

They rocked together gently at first, a steady rhythm that built, intensified by quiet kisses and soft moans of pleasure. The hotel meant they didn't have to be quiet, at least not as quiet as they'd been in the tent, and he loved the way her voice hitched when he hit a particularly sensitive spot. The way she cursed and her fingernails dug into his back when their bodies slammed together. The way she cried out his name when he moved harder, faster. And best of all, the keening sound she made around panting breaths as another orgasm took her, shivering through her, the waves pulsing against his cock in a rhythm he couldn't have resisted if he'd tried. His own orgasm took him in a powerful release that left him limp and breathless and trembling.

She wrapped him close, kissing his temple as he collapsed against her, settling his head on her chest as he caught his breath.

"Good morning," she murmured.

He kissed her breast. "Very good morning," he agreed. Which made her chuckle.

The quiet sounds of the air conditioner and her slowing heartbeat nearly sent him back to sleep. But he roused himself when he heard her stomach grumble.

She laughed and pressed a hand to her stomach. "Guess all this sex is revving up my appetite."

"I love feeding you so this works out well on all levels for me." He sat up and pulled her gently up with him. "Shower first. Then room service."

"I love room service."

THEY'D JUST SETTLED DOWN TO A BRUNCH-LIKE MEAL, A MIX OF pancakes, eggs, and roast beef sandwiches, when a knock on the door had them both frowning at each other.

"You suppose we've been too noisy and the manager is here to tell us to keep it down?" she asked.

She didn't seem bothered by the idea, which amused him. But since he was still a little leery about the tigers, he approached the door cautiously. He was within a foot when a very familiar—and familial—scent reached him through the door. He groaned and dropped his head back.

"What?" Cat asked, coming up behind him.

"I haven't talked to my sister yet. She's gonna kill me."

"Is that her?"

"No." He sighed. "It's my oldest brother. And the fact that he's meeting you before she is will turn into a thing." He opened the door. "Deacon, what the hell are you doing here?"

"Checking on you, what else?"

His brother stood in the hall looking as controlled and serious as he usually did, but there wasn't nearly the level of iciness in his demeanor that had been there before he met Cary. He was still more controlled than the rest of them, more like their mother in that way. But he'd relaxed that strict control in the last few months, seeming more at ease than Dylan could ever remember seeing him before.

"Why?" he asked his brother, then glanced around Deacon and grinned. "Hey Cary. Why'd you let him do this? I haven't told Julia yet."

"I *told* him to leave you alone," she said. "But did he listen? No. Your mother was worried because of that whole tiger thing so of course she calls Deacon and he has to rush over here to check on you even though you were safe. And you are safe, by the way. I'd know otherwise." She grinned past him at Cat. "Hi. I'm Cary Redmond. This is Deacon Jones. Sorry to interrupt."

Cat smiled back. "Nice to meet you. How do you know we're safe?"

Cary waved a hand. "Just a knack I have for that kind of thing. We interrupted your breakfast."

"It's okay." She glanced between him and his brother, a slight frown creasing her brow. "Is your entire family this…impressively handsome?"

"They are," Cary answered for him. "It's scary. They're all unnaturally gorgeous. You met Maria?"

"She was impressive beyond just being beautiful," Cat said. Then she frowned again. "Cary with a 'c' or a 'k'?"

"Cary with a 'c', why?"

"This is going to get confusing at family gatherings. All the 'c' and 'd' names in one place."

Cary laughed and nudged Deacon. "I like her." She faced Cat again. "You're human. That's unusual."

"Dylan told me. I need to do some research once we settle some things."

Dylan let his mate and his brother's mate talk while he moved Deacon to one side. "Why was Mom worried?"

"The tigers."

"Did Lenny or Rick escape the Tracker?"

"No. Just that one that disappeared. We're looking for him but can't find him. She wanted to make sure he hadn't circled back to bother your mate."

"I doubt he will. He understood what it meant to get on Mom's bad side. He's probably disappeared into the mountains by now." But since Deacon was here... "Hey, will you take my truck and telescope equipment back to your place? I'll pick it up sometime soon, but I'd rather not haul the scopes all the way to New York with me right now."

"I'll take care of it."

Dylan grabbed his telescopes from where they rested next to Cat's and handed the heavy cases to his brother, who hefted them easily.

"You're moving to New York?" Deacon asked.

"No, she's moving to California. She has a job there."

"Convenient."

"I would have moved to New York."

"I'm glad you didn't have to."

That gave Dylan pause. "You are?"

There were a lot of years between him and Deacon in a very large family. By the time Dylan and Julia had come along, his oldest siblings were adults out doing adult things. They got along. He loved his brother. But it hadn't occurred to him Deacon cared one way or another where he lived.

"Hard enough having Jocelyn on the other coast. It takes a long time to reach her if she needs us. I'd hate to see more family scattered that far."

Huh. "Cary's having an interesting effect on you."

Deacon's expression turned rueful. "You have no idea." He raised his brows. "Although, I suspect you will soon." He nodded at Cat.

Just as Cat turned and said, "Your mother named her three oldest and her two youngest with names that started with the same first letters on purpose? Why?"

"She's never told us," Dylan said with a shrug.

"It's because of her brothers," Deacon said.

Everyone in the room turned to look at him. "What?" Cary said. "You knew and didn't tell me?"

"I'm not supposed to know," he said, surprising Dylan with how defensive he sounded. Deacon never let others see him defensive like that. "She doesn't talk about her brothers."

"What were their names?" Cat asked.

"Diego and Javier."

"And Maria," Cary murmured. "Ah. Now that makes sense."

"What?" Cat asked, looking between them all.

Dylan explained. "Deacon's twins are Michael and Jocelyn. If Julia and I had had another twin, they'd have had an 'm' name." He glanced at Deacon. "She named you three and us after her and her siblings. Why keep that from us all these years?"

"You know how she is. She refuses to talk about her past and her life in Guyana before coming to the US."

"Her brothers both died there," Cary said quietly to Cat.

Cat nodded, and the sympathy and understanding in her scent made Dylan's chest tighten for reasons he couldn't quite place. Since she knew what it was like to lose close family members, he realized she could relate to his mother's loss even more than the rest of them.

"So there's an explanation for all your names matching," Cat said after a moment, ending the short silence. "And just coincidence my name and Cary's start with the same letter."

"Weird, but yes," Dylan said.

"I need to calculate the odds of that," she said, her gaze moving inward.

He grinned.

Deacon frowned at him. "Is she really…calculating that?" he murmured.

"Yes," Dylan said. "I'll let you know the odds when she works it out."

He waved his brother and Cary away, closing the door behind them with promises to call and text and generally keep everyone updated on his movements until they were sure the tigers were no longer a problem.

When he had Cat alone again, he pulled her close. "Still calculating?"

"I'll have it soon," she murmured, her gaze still distant, her eyes moving back and forth as if she was actually looking at the numbers on the air.

He gently led her to their table by the window, and their waiting feast, and happily watched her work while he made sure she ate.

The flight to New York was uncomfortable—seats on airplanes were way too close together for someone his height—but uneventful. The fact that he and Cat survived their first trip through the annoyance that was airport security and an overnight flight without biting each other's heads off boded well for their future together.

Exhausted after the red-eye and waiting in a long line for a taxi at JFK tested them further, and Dylan was delighted with the fact that he only snarled once when a stranger tried to cut in line in front of them.

The all new noises and scents of New York were an assault on his shifter senses, though, and the August humidity made the air oppressively thick, heightening the stench of too many human bodies and sweltering tarmac.

By the time they reached Cat's apartment, blessedly close to JFK, Dylan was ready for a few quiet moments alone with her. She turned her window air conditioner on the instant they walked through the door, dropped her bags—including her telescope—into her bedroom, then pushed him against a convenient wall for a kiss he welcomed with every ounce of his being.

It was like breathing, he needed her so much. Like if he didn't have her in his arms, his mouth on hers this very instant, he might have just died from the lack.

When he finally lifted his mouth from hers, he was breathless and hard and not in any shape to meet her protective older sister yet. Or her big sister's tiger shifter husband.

"How long do we have before we have to go back downstairs?" he asked.

Amy and her husband lived on the first floor of the same apartment building, which made this meeting both easier and more awkward because he and Cat couldn't hide for long.

"When I texted her that we'd landed, I said it would be a few hours before we could stop in." Her grin widened even as her gaze settled on his mouth. "I said we'd need to shower and sleep after the overnight flight."

"Sleep? Yeah, we can do that." He lifted her into his arms because it made her gasp and laugh. "Later."

THEY DID SHOWER AND EVENTUALLY SLEEP, AND WHEN HE WOKE, HE finally took in her apartment. The place looked like her. Posters of scientists and bad science puns decorated the walls. Whiteboards covered in formulas and scribbled writing were scattered throughout the apartment. A bookshelf against one wall was stuffed with paperback Romances and Mysteries next to science textbooks and popular science books. There was a desk in her living room but it and the chair in front of it were covered with books and papers and charts so that he was pretty sure she never sat there to work. She was too restless to sit still while working anyway.

An empty dog bed sat by the bedroom door, and Dylan could smell Spike underneath Cat's scent throughout the apartment. The kitchen was small and serviceable but there was a stack of takeout menus on a table by the door that looked well worn. And there were sweaters stored in her oven.

"Amy likes cooking more than I do," she said when he raised his brows at the sweaters. "And I go down to her place when I feel the need to bake cake. She has a better kitchen."

"She doesn't mind?"

"I'm making cake. Who would mind that?"

He pulled her into a hug. "You're going to miss her."

"A lot. But that's what video chat and direct flights are for."

He kissed the top of her head. "Ready to face the gauntlet?"

Well, really, he was the one facing the unknown. And his future brother-in-law's sense of smell. But the fact that she'd be there with him, that she had his back, made him feel happy and content despite the "gauntlet" ahead.

The sounds of a frantically barking dog greeted their knock, well before the door opened.

"Spike?" Dylan asked.

"Spike," Cat said. "And she'll be as important to impress as my sister." There was warning in Cat's voice that made him reassess the bark on the other side of that door.

The minute the door opened, a miniature poodle burst out, barking loudly at Dylan's legs. He stared down at the fluffy beast. She had white curly fur under a few rainbow stripes of color that reminded him of Cat's hair, and was wearing a black leather collar with spikes on it.

"Spike," he said, nodding. Then he squatted down to let the poodle sniff his hand before gently scratching her behind the ears and under the chin. "Nice to meet you, Spike," he said. "I'm Dylan Jones."

Spike pushed her head into his hand and let her tongue loll out as she leaned into his scratches.

"Huh," Cat said.

He glanced up, his brows raised in question. Cat grinned at him.

"No problem with your cat smell." She sounded a little amazed. "She was really uncomfortable around Ethan at first."

"Told you our family business involved animal rescue. I'm good with dogs."

"Welcome to the family then," said a new voice.

Dylan finally looked up at the human who'd opened the door and released Spike. The family resemblance wasn't immediately obvious.

Amy was a little shorter than Cat, had dark, curly hair, and her eyes were blue instead of brown. She wore loose-fitting white linen pants with paint stains on them that matched the paint under her fingernails. And she smelled distinctly of oil paints and turpentine with a hint of her tiger mate on her skin underneath that.

But there was something about the way she raised her brows and held her mouth that was very definitely similar to Cat. When she shook her head and laughed at the dog, Dylan heard hints of Cat's laughter. The way she leaned against the doorframe and gestured at the dog also reminded Dylan of his mate. Once you got past the superficial outer differences, the sisterly resemblance became obvious.

He started to rise to greet the most important person in Cat's life, but Spike protested with a little nipping bark, so he stayed where he was, continuing to scratch the poodle's head.

"Apparently, this is where I live now," he said. "Sorry I can't shake your hand. But it's nice to meet you."

Amy smiled, her gaze dancing between him and Cat. "I don't think we need Ethan," she said to Cat. "Spike's character reference should suffice."

"Do I smell pizza?" Cat asked, bouncing on her toes.

Amy rolled her eyes. "You think I'd put you through this meeting without feeding you? Come on in whenever Spike allows it."

She left them at the doorway, disappearing back into the apartment. Inside, Dylan heard a deeper male voice ask quietly, "Good?" And Amy's answering, "Spike likes him."

That was met by a grunt of acceptance.

"Well," Dylan said to Cat, "that went well."

"Except I'm not sure Spike wants to let you go anywhere."

Dylan glanced down at the poodle who'd now rolled onto her side so he could scratch her stomach. "You think she'll let me pick her up and carry her inside?"

"You can try," Cat said, sounding both amused and wry.

Dylan looked at the poodle. "Okay, Spike. I need to go in and make sure the rest of your family likes me since I'm going to be around from now on. You mind if I lift you up?" He moved his hands around and gentle picked the poodle up, standing at the same time.

Spike wiggled a little in his arms, rearranging herself to face him, then she licked his face.

A gesture that made Cat laugh. "Wow. I can't believe she likes you so much already. She's usually less of a hussy." Cat's gaze turned speculative. "Maybe she could travel with us to California after all."

"No," Amy shouted from farther in the apartment.

Cat sighed dramatically. "Fine," she shouted back. Then to Dylan, "Spike shouldn't travel that far at her age anyway. But..." She met Dylan's gaze. "Maybe we could get a dog of our own?"

"I'd love that. A shelter dog."

"Absolutely." Her gaze jumped toward the inside of the apartment and then she met his gaze again. "I don't want to keep the pizza waiting, but I need to say something before we go inside."

He leaned closer when she rose up to whisper in his ear. Spike wiggled around to lick at Cat, too.

"I know we're just at the beginning of this," Cat said, her voice very quiet, so only he would be able to hear her. "But I feel like you should know, I'm pretty sure I'm already in love with you, so I think this is going to work out really well, and I'm relieved Spike loves you, too."

Dylan's pulse pounded hard as her words sank in, a rapid beat of happiness unlike anything he'd ever felt. When Cat dropped back and gazed up at him, open and sweet and beautiful, he thought his heart might burst apart with joy.

He set his forehead against hers and whispered, for her—and Spike's—ears only, "I love you, too. And I'm relieved Spike approves."

Spike yipped loudly, her tongue hanging out in a happy doggy grin where she was firmly secured between them.

Cat glanced at the poodle long enough to chuckle, then rose up to kiss him.

And Dylan knew, no matter what they faced ahead, he was the luckiest, happiest man alive to have found such a perfect mate.

EPILOGUE

Maria settled on the large, comfortable couch in her favorite room in the family home. The library was a soft family place, with worn rugs and furniture, shelves lined with beat-up paperbacks, a corner of the room specifically for children full of kids' books and toys, and an air of relaxed negligence permeating the air. Even the scents here were familial and relaxed. No excess of cleaning chemicals, just a light undertone of wood polish, a bit of dust, and a hint of the fruit punch one of the leopard children had spilled in the corner yesterday.

The library always felt carefree and a little chaotic. Everything that her life outside this room was not. Outside this room, she had to always be controlled and careful. If she wasn't, people—her people—could be hurt. But here… Here, she could relax.

At least as much as she was able.

She'd sent her mate, the love of her life, down to the kitchen—his favorite place in the mansion—so she could take this very private phone call. She didn't even check the caller I.D. when her cellphone rang. She didn't have to. This particular caller was always on time.

"Elizaveta," Maria greeted, genuinely pleased to talk to the tiger shifter matriarch.

"Maria. Thank you for speaking with me."

"Of course." It was rare to have even an acquaintance who understood Maria's life and responsibilities completely. Elizaveta Chernikova was one of the rare few who could. Which made their association something Maria wished to maintain.

"I wanted to thank you, again, for our arrangement," Elizaveta said. "Though, it did not work out the way I anticipated."

"Neither of us could have guessed she'd be his mate. Why would we? She's human. And with ties to your people…" Maria shrugged even though Elizaveta wouldn't see her. They preferred phone calls to video chat—for reasons Maria couldn't explain even to herself, she found video chats distracting and irritating in a way she didn't phone calls. "And I already have a son mated to a human. It's so rare among my people, there was no way to anticipate this."

"Still…" Elizaveta sighed and her Russian accent deepened. "I will consider it one of the few failures of my life."

"Catalina is alive and safe. I wouldn't call that a failure."

"Ach." The sound was a combination of annoyance and acceptance. "I am glad she's safe. But something must be done about our males soon."

"Will you ever explain what the issue is? Maybe I could help."

"You have helped enough. You sent a member of your own family. I could not have asked more from you."

Their arrangement had been made more than a two years ago, when it was clear Catalina would come to this coast for the eclipse. Elizaveta worried some of the tiger males would bother her once she was out of her own territory. According to the scant details the elder provided to Maria, the males hadn't begun to "court" Catalina yet, but by the time the eclipse happened, she'd be of an age that they would start. And Elizaveta worried for her safety so far away from the rest of her family.

She'd asked Maria to arrange for one of her own people to camp close enough to Cat to deter any interested tiger shifters from bothering her, reasoning—quite rightly—that the tigers would be aware of the leopard's presence and wouldn't want to start trouble with another shifter in front of so many humans.

Elizaveta said she'd already arranged for another person who was close to the tigers to watch over Cat, but she'd feel better if another shifter was nearby. Just in case.

And since Maria's youngest son had already been hunting for a place where he could also see the eclipse… Well, the arrangement had seemed perfect and fortuitous. Even if it had taken a considerable amount of money and maneuvering to get the three people so close to each other in a single campsite at one of the best locations on this coast for the eclipse.

Of course, neither she nor Elizaveta had anticipated that the tigers who followed Cat to Oregon *would* be willing to fight in front of humans—going so far as to issue a challenge to a male outside their own people—or that Dylan and Cat would be mates.

But Maria couldn't claim to be upset by the outcome. She really did want more grandchildren in the future. Life was not eternal. Only one of her fourteen offspring had given her grandbabies so far. She stood a better chance at having more with more of her children mated. Even if two of their mates had turned out to be humans.

And at least Catalina didn't have a dangerous job—unlike her oldest son's mate.

She brushed away that worry to address Elizaveta. "We haven't found the third male yet. When we do, I'll let you know where your people can find him."

"Thank you. There have been far too many incidents of this kind in the last few years. The last twenty years really. It's past time we put a stop to it with harsher punishments. Especially now."

Maria had her suspicions about the difficulties faced by the tigers. She kept track of the shifter world, and it was hard not to notice that there weren't very many tiger females. It was always possible the females simply kept to themselves better than the males and went through life without allowing other shifters to be aware of their presence. But Maria doubted that explanation held up to reality.

"When you feel able to confide in me," Maria said, "do. The leopards are prepared to help if we can."

There was a beat of silence. And then, "Thank you, Maria. For everything."

Maria smiled. "Thank you," she said in turn. "For the potential grandchildren you've arranged for me."

"Ha!" Elizaveta snorted. Then her voice softened when she said, "Grandchildren are a delight. So are great grandchildren. You'll learn that sooner than you like, young one."

Maria's turn to snort. By human standards, and even leopard standards, she was anything but young. But she got the impression the tiger elder was her senior by at least fifty or sixty years. Which, she supposed, gave Elizaveta the right to toss around "young one" epithets.

"Will you be…okay? Settling all this with the other elders?"

"Of course. Those old men. They think they're so clever. They've no idea half the time what I do behind their backs."

Maria chuckled.

"Now," Elizaveta said, her voice firming, "while I'd love to discuss grandchildren more, I'm afraid I must go. I'm expecting a guest, and I believe he's just arrived."

"I liked Tom," Maria said, her smile turning smug. "He seemed a very nice man."

"He is," Elizaveta said. "He very much is."

Maria continued to smile after she disconnected the call and leaned back into the overstuffed couch. She could sense her mate approaching. With luck, he'd brought food—hopefully not pizza, though. They'd eaten far far too much pizza of late.

A quiet night in with her mate, and a moment of peace knowing her family was all, currently, okay.

That sounded like a very nice night.

THANK YOU

Thank you for reading *Romancing the Leopard*. I hope you enjoyed this cross-over between Cary Redmond's world and the Tiger Shifters' world. If you haven't read one, or either of those series, keep reading for an excerpt from the first Cary Redmond book, *The Trouble with Black Cats and Demons*, as well as an excerpt from Cat's older sister's book, *Taming Her Tiger*.

I've just realized as I write this that the heroes in both those books are naked in the first chapters. I didn't do that on purpose, but somehow it seems appropriate. To be fair, though, the circumstances are very different.

For more on my books, occasional free reads, and ramblings about baking and books, you can join my newsletter (http://eepurl.com/Ox-QQL). You can also get updates at my website (https://www.katsimons.com) or follow my author page at your favorite vendor.

Thanks again!

THE TROUBLE WITH BLACK CATS AND DEMONS

CARY REDMOND BOOK 1

EXCERPT

1

"Not again." Cary Redmond ducked as another fireball clipped over her head. "You don't think fireballs are a bit over the top," she shouted up at the ceiling then had to duck again as a dagger whispered past her ear.

Close. Her heart pounded. Way too close.

She needed to find the damned cat and get out of here. She scanned the apartment from her dubious cover behind a table piled high with unopened mail. Fireballs, daggers, gusts of preternatural wind, freezing hail, and the occasional lightning bolt dropped around her, roaring through the living room in a bright cacophony of magical mayhem.

The lightning bolts flashing in the small confines were pretty spectacular. If they hadn't been trying to fry her, she might have enjoyed the show.

"Jaxer, I'm going to kill you for this."

Normally, this kind of thing was just a part of her job. She was a Protector and literally got paid to run around keeping people safe, mostly from magical bad guys. Not that she'd asked for the job, but that was another story. It *was* her job, so she faced off against dangerous stuff because the Nags—her bosses—told her to.

Tonight, however, was not an official assignment. Tonight, she was just doing a favor for her demented faery mentor. The bastard knew exactly how to get to her. All he had to do was mention a defenseless little black kitty cat and she was done for. How could she refuse to help a kitty? People did rotten things to black cats on Halloween.

Except Jaxer had forgotten to warn her about the fireballs.

She screeched through her teeth and dove behind the couch as one of the aforementioned fireballs barreled toward her. She cursed Jaxer as she took a quick look under the couch for the cat. Where the hell was it?

She'd called out to it when she'd first entered the apartment but hadn't gotten any irate kitty responses. After her lurching hunt of the living room and kitchen, the only place left was the bedroom.

She pulled in a deep breath as she contemplated the long space of unprotected ground between her hiding spot behind the couch and the bedroom door. Once she found the cat, this would be easier. When she was actively protecting something, very little of the magical dangers could get to her, and nothing deadly would touch her. She just had to *find* the cat first. And quickly. They had to be out of this cursed apartment before midnight. Before the wizard got home and all hell broke loose.

Again.

She ducked flying objects and ran to the bedroom, squealing when a lightning bolt hit the ground right behind her. Crossing her fingers that there were no nasty spells waiting for her, she lunged through the half-open door and cringed in anticipation of magical repercussions as she fell onto a red-carpeted floor. She held perfectly still, waiting. Nothing. She let out a breath and pushed herself up onto her hands and knees, shaking her head. All this for a cat. That bastard Jaxer had a lot to answer for.

She rose to a crouch, trying to calm her racing pulse, and froze.

In front of her sat a huge bed, which she barely noticed because the naked man lying in the middle of the enormous mattress stopped her heart.

Holy shit.

He was absolutely magnificent. Tanned skin, well-defined muscles, thick, black hair hanging down over his forehead. He was lying against a giant headboard with his head hanging forward so she couldn't get a good look at his face, but his golden eyes seemed to glow up at her from under his brows. Piercing and stunning and breath-stealing.

Cary swallowed. Hard. Because even the captivating gold of his eyes wasn't enough to keep her gaze from wandering over the breadth of his naked chest, the corded muscles of his shoulders and arms, the flat expanse of his stomach. It took a great deal of will power not to follow the line of dark hair arrowing down his abdomen...lower.

The man straightened and Cary heard the clink of chains at the same time as she got a look at his neck—and the thick collar covering most of it.

What the hell had Jaxer gotten her into?

"Who're you?" she asked, breathless and embarrassed.

"Who are you?"

His voice carried a deep reverberation that made her spine tingle. Oh boy.

"I'm looking for a black cat," she said, knowing the explanation sounded inane. Jaxer had told her about Sheldon the Wizard, but this? This was something else altogether. What was this guy doing here? He wasn't Sheldon, she was sure of it. But then who was he? And where was the cat?

She blinked and a black leopard lay on the bed where the man had been. She sucked in a sharp breath, blinked again. And the man was back.

"Whoa." Cary swallowed. "*You're* the black cat I came to rescue?"

Oh, she really was going to kill Jaxer now. He hadn't said anything about a fully grown man who happened to be a leopard shapeshifter. He'd made sure she thought she was after a little, harmless kitty cat, not a deadly dangerous big cat who shifted into a beautiful, naked, very large man.

The faery was dead. Not that she knew how to kill him, but that was beside the point.

"Jaxer sent you?" The man's eyes narrowed and his features took on a dangerous edge. He hissed a curse under his breath and shook his head. "Stupid."

"Hey!" She stood, the better to face his gorgeous disgust. No one should look that good while insulting you. "You could have done worse, buddy."

She took a step toward the bed, wiping damp palms on her jeans. The chains she'd heard earlier linked the collar on his neck to the headboard, which was brass and made-up of a scrawl of symbols she didn't recognize but looked like they might mean something if she stared at them long enough. He wasn't bound anywhere else that she dared peek, and the chains appeared flimsy enough. So obviously the power keeping him confined was in the collar.

"What is that?" She gestured with her head toward the thick band of metal.

"A binding ring," he said slowly, as if speaking to a child.

She frowned, both at his tone and the news. "But you just shifted."

"It's been designed to contain both my forms. Any other questions before you get me out of here?"

"Yeah, what crawled up your butt and put you in such a pissy mood?"

"Being held captive for sacrifice by a wizard and having a child sent to rescue me has dampened my day a bit," he said.

She grinned and enjoyed watching his eyes narrow suspiciously. "Child, huh? You know, at my age that's a compliment."

"How old could you be? Twenty?"

She shook her head. She'd actually turned thirty-one last April. But when she got tricked into becoming a Protector at twenty-five, she'd stopped aging at a normal rate. One of the few things about the job that didn't irritate her.

She took a quick moment to glance around the rest of the room. The red carpet wasn't the only gaudy element. Lots of black leather covered the walls and an animal skinned rug, which she was afraid to think about too closely given the captive on the overlarge bed, was tossed across the floor in front of what she thought might be a closet. A wood and metal trunk sat against one wall, red silk drapes covered the single window, and the overhead light was covered by thick, dark metal chains which gave the room strange shadows.

Fortunately, there were no nasty attack spells in here, which meant Sheldon the Wizard didn't want his captive accidentally hurt by a stray lightning bolt. That worked in her favor, giving her time to solve the binding ring problem without being pelted by hail.

Though even if there had been spells in here, now that she was officially protecting someone, she could keep them both safe.

She did wonder why Sheldon would care if his shape shifting captive got hurt before the midnight sacrifice. Obviously, he didn't want him dead. You couldn't sacrifice something that was already dead. But an additional warning spell in here probably wouldn't have killed his prisoner. Maybe. If Sheldon had enough control.

If he didn't, and was as powerful as Jaxer claimed, they really needed to get out of here. Fast.

She eased up to the bedside, still leery of traps, and leaned in close to the leopard man, trying to ignore the yummy, stomach-fluttering male scent of him as she studied the binding ring. It was a thick band of silver and copper intertwined in a complex pattern of twists and turns. Over the silver, tiny runic symbols danced and shimmered so they were nearly impossible to read.

"Oh good," she said, "a hard one."

The prisoner shivered, a low growl rising from his throat. The sound made Cary's heartbeat jump.

Speaking of hard ones.

She could feel his glare on the side of her face, but she resisted looking. She had other things to worry about at the moment.

Like how the hell she was going to get this damned magical containment brace off his neck without alerting the entire mystical neighborhood.

"You did that on purpose," the man snarled.

"Huh?" She glanced at him. "What are you talking about?"

"Don't breathe on me again," he said.

She scowled. "What am I supposed to do? Hold my breath until I get your collar off? Just relax, big guy. You'll be out of here in a minute." To herself, she mumbled, "Wouldn't have gotten this much grief from a proper black cat."

"You some kind of witch?"

"No." After a moment, she sighed and shook her head. "Well, there's no help for it. I'm gonna have to use brute force. It'll take too long to get this off subtly."

"We don't have much time. It's nearly midnight now."

"Gee, really?"

He ignored her sarcasm. "Brute force?"

"Hold onto your valuable body parts," she said and tried not to think about his exposed valuable parts. Then she wrapped her hands around the collar, easing her fingers gently under so the backs pressed against his neck. His skin was warm and another shiver danced down her spine.

"Wait."

She met his gaze.

"What the hell are you doing? If I can't break that with my bare hands, you can't—"

He stopped short when she tugged and the collar came away with a quiet click.

"I'm not without some talent," she murmured.

"Who *are* you?"

"Come on. We have to get you out of here. I just made a lot of magical noise with that little stunt."

"Hold on."

He grabbed her hand. The feel of his warm palm wrapped around her fingers sent tiny sparks of electricity dancing over her skin. He dropped his hold, but she saw his eyes widen with the same shock she felt. He inhaled deeply, and against her will, she watched the strong muscles of his chest rise and fall.

"What's your name?" he asked.

"Cary."

"Cary. I'm Deacon."

"Nice to meet you." Did that sounded as stupid to him as it did to her given the circumstances?

He smiled, a slow, deadly grin that made her pulse race. "Nice to meet you, too."

She blinked and shook her head. "Come on, Deacon. We need to move."

As he slid to the edge of the mattress, Cary turned her back to avoid embarrassing them both—despite the temptation to look over every inch of him. The sound of material moving over skin behind her didn't help curb her less polite impulses, though, so she hurried to the door to see how the lightning bolts and fireballs were doing.

SLIPPING INTO HIS JEANS, DEACON WATCHED THE WOMAN AS SHE peeked around the edge of the doorframe at the living room and the still popping spells Sheldon had set to keep help from reaching him.

She wasn't the rescue he'd been expecting. He'd expected the damned faery to come himself.

Jaxer had convinced him to let the wizard "capture" him, so they could find out *why* Sheldon was kidnapping shifters. They'd only found a few of Sheldon's victims—their bodies anyway. And they'd been little more than desiccated husks. The rest of the missing shifters... Even their bodies had vanished.

Wizards didn't typically go after shapeshifters for sacrifice. They were too hard to contain, and most of them didn't have the kind of magical energy an average human wizard could absorb through ceremonial magic. Shapeshifting wasn't typically magic. It was just a species trait.

Deacon knew none of the shifters killed so far had had any actual magic. He was a different case, but he was pretty sure Sheldon didn't know that. Jaxer did, which was why he'd come to Deacon in the first place, and Deacon had felt obliged to help even though none of the shifters taken had been leopards.

He suppressed an irritated growl. This was the last time he'd let the faery use him for bait. He'd been chained to that fucking bed all day with no sign of help. Then Jaxer went and made things worse by sending in this...woman to rescue him instead of coming himself. How dare he endanger someone else when this crusade against Sheldon was his own personal business? Bad enough he dragged Deacon into it.

But as Deacon watched the woman straighten away from the doorframe when a lightning bolt flashed, he realized there *was* something about her. He couldn't deny the power she must have to break through the binding ring. Yet she looked and smelled like a normal, human woman.

Her light brown hair hung in long ponytail her back over a battered brown leather jacket. She wore jeans, hiking boots, and a purple t-shirt with a glittery Happy Halloween emblazoned over a maniacally grinning jack-o-lantern. Her blue eyes had sparkled when he'd called her a child, then flashed with irritation when he'd insulted her. And for reasons he couldn't quite understand, he'd found it hard to look away from her, especially when she'd knelt next to him on the bed.

Something about her...something about her scent tugged at his instincts.

Who the hell was she? *What* was she? She had to be more than human, but none of his sense picked up anything particularly preternatural about her. So where did all that power come from?

Jaxer had some serious explaining to do.

Deacon shook off his preoccupation and walked up behind her to stare at the living room over her head. Black scorch marks marred the hardwood floors, and a layer of frost covered one side table. The air was heavy with electricity and the smell of burning ozone.

Despite the multiple magical eruptions, the apartment was in remarkably good shape. As he watched, a dagger flew toward the bedroom, dropped harmlessly a foot from the doorway, and disappeared as if it hadn't existed.

Clever. Less clean up. And a testament to Sheldon's power.

He couldn't blame Jaxer for being worried about the little shit. But given a choice, Deacon would have taken a more...active approach to getting rid of the wizard.

Unfortunately, and he was reluctant to admit this even to himself, his approach probably would have gotten him killed. The bastard wizard was powerful. How Sheldon managed to be so powerful at his age was a mystery. But maybe that was the reason Jaxer was so obsessed with finding out the *whys* behind Sheldon's actions.

If Deacon got out of this apartment alive, he'd ask the faery. In the meantime, he and this very human woman in front of him had to navigate the bespelled living room and get away before Sheldon got back.

Deacon drew in a slow breath and was hit again by Cary's scent. Vanilla and cinnamon. And something else. Something that shot jolts of lust and need through his gut, making him lean closer to her just so he could feel the heat of her skin. He felt a possessive growl rising in his throat and swallowed it back, fisting his hands by his side to keep from reaching for her.

What the hell? He had more control that this. A lot more. He had to or people got killed. Resisting a woman, even one that smelled like heaven, had never been a problem before. With Cary, it took an effort to resist pulling her close and burying his face in her neck to soak up her essence.

If he didn't know better, he'd think she was a witch, casting a lust spell on him.

His nostrils flared. That scent of hers…

It reached down inside him, calling to a deep instinct. As he breathed her in, his leopard whispered, *Mine.*

Out in the living room, wind-lashed hail whipped toward the bedroom without actually coming through the doorway. And behind that, a lightning bolt sizzled the floor.

"Sheldon didn't make this easy," he said, quirking a brow when she jumped at the sound of his voice.

"Are you dressed?" she asked without turning around.

He couldn't help smiling at the slight panic in her voice. "Yes."

"Okay. Stick close. Stay behind me and don't try to dodge around me. Got it? That's how we'll get out of here alive."

He frowned down at the top of her head. She must have some pretty powerful shields to get through that mess. But she wasn't a witch?

He grunted a noncommittal response, and she swung around to face him. The flash of heat in her eyes made his pulse kick.

"Listen, buddy," she said, her chin tucked back as she glared at him, "if you don't let me protect you, we're both dead. Okay? Don't go trying to be a hero. Just stay close and let me do what I came here to do."

She mumbled something unflattering under her breath as she turned back to the living room, and he had to fight a completely irrational urge to kiss her.

Over the course of the long day, with no sign of help from Jaxer, he'd had to face the possibility of his own death. His reaction to Cary might be a result of that, a need to reaffirm he was alive.

But as he breathed in the heady scent of her again, he wondered…

TAMING HER TIGER

TIGER SHIFTERS BOOK 9

EXCERPT

1

Amy Donovan hurried up the wooden stairs to the fifth floor of the Brooklyn art studio, out of breath and trying not to panic about being late. Damned weekend subways. She cleared the huge, rolling steel doors and stepped into the brightly lit, high-ceilinged loft, winter sun pouring in from the wall of windows opposite her. The gray sunlight was augmented by the overhead lights, reflecting off the scuffed pale wood floors and bright white walls.

She sighed in relief when she saw the open session hadn't started yet.

The familiar smells of the art studio—paint, solvent, charcoal, paper, and canvas—filled Amy with that sense of belonging, settling into her bones. The familiarity helped slow her racing, panicky heartbeat as she made her way across the room to a free space. Easels, chairs, and tables were already arranged in a rough semi-circle around a central model platform, the piles of pillows in the middle of the platform were draped in neutral, tan sheets. A dozen artists, the monitor, and the model coordinator all hovered around the room. A few people stood in small groups, chatting and drinking take-away cups of coffee and tea. Others were already at chairs or easels, setting out their materials or flicking through their sketch books.

She waved at acquaintances and other studio members as she wove past a section of seats to her easel. This was the final long-pose session of a four-week cycle, her last opportunity to have the figure model in front of her while she finished her oil painting.

Thoughts of said model scattered her focus and she nearly tripped over someone's bag. Apologizing, she hurried to her spot, pushing the momentary lapse aside. She was a professional; this was a professional setting. She refused to entertain the strong feelings and longings she'd experienced when Ethan Gupta had first taken the dais three weeks ago.

It hadn't exactly been a sexual reaction, though that was part of it. She'd done so many life drawing sessions over the years, she didn't really view the nude models that way—she saw lines, shadows, proportion, perspective, angles, and light contrasts. Or at least she had before Ethan.

But her reaction to him had been a lot more than just the sexual punch of seeing a man as beautifully masculine and perfect as Ethan was in real life. It was more stunned shock, a realization that she was staring at an actual muse. Her brain had exploded with images, colors, a longing to capture…something. *Him.*

She didn't believe in muses, exactly. Not in the mythical sense of the word. She knew a good figure model could inspire and energize her and her art. She'd had the experience on numerous occasions. But with Ethan, everything was different. More instant, more overwhelming, more…vivid.

That first time, she'd even sensed him before he'd come into the room, as if he projected an aura of creative inspiration she could feel along the length of her spine without having to look at him. The fact that she could sense him now, even though she couldn't see him, even though she knew the feeling was just a figment of her imagination, left her edgy and anxious.

After that first three-hour session, she found herself counting the days until the next one, and the one after that. Yet a part of her also dreaded each session, dreaded that sense of being overwhelmed and awed. The sense that her skills would never be good enough to capture the purity of the inspiration he offered.

Settling into the area she'd used for the last three sessions, she focused on putting out her supplies, collecting her canvas from one of the storage lockers provided to regular members, organizing her brushes, setting up her palette, studying her progress on her painting, determining where she needed to make adjustments and what she'd need to do to get the work done today…

One of her dearest friends, Reese Jordan, sat down next to her in a place already set up and ready for the session to start. Reese was a superbly talented sketch artist, oil painter, and sometimes sculptor. He was also the person who'd originally directed Amy to this studio and encouraged her to become a member. They'd known each other since Amy had come back to the art world two years earlier, and now she couldn't imagine her life without him. At forty-three, Reese tended to treat her like a little sister, and he'd become the big brother as well as the art mentor Amy had never had.

He kissed her cheek. "I thought you were going to miss the class."

"Subways," she growled, making him grin.

On her other side, Devine, artist, gallery manager, and another of Amy's good friends, settled into her station, rubbing Amy's arm by way of hello. Despite being in her mid-thirties, Devine was ageless, with flawless, smooth skin, hair that changed colors and cut frequently —that week it was a beautiful pale lavender shaped to imitate a 1950s flip—and blue eyes she accented with perfectly penciled black liner drawn to make her eyes look tilted and cat-like. She'd confided to Amy once that her ever-changing look was designed to appeal to her clients because they expected artists to be eccentric and "artsy." Devine ran a gallery in Soho that catered to art collectors of the rich-but-not-very-knowledgeable type. She could sell sand in the desert and ice in the arctic.

And for reasons Amy had never figured out, Devine kept encouraging Amy to take her art more seriously, turn it into an actual career. Despite Amy's insistence that it wouldn't happen anytime soon. Her refusal to accept the possibility of art as a career had never deterred Devine from nagging her about it.

Before Amy could say more than hello, the shuffling, shifting sounds of people settling into their seats distracted her. She looked past Devine…in time to see Ethan step out of the bathroom at the rear of the studio, near the storage lockers and slop sinks. He'd changed out of his street clothes and into his simple dark blue robe, a color that did fantastic things to his wavy dark hair and eyes. He paused at the back of the room to chat with the coordinator and monitor, smiling and relaxed.

Amy caught herself staring, her gaze drawn to the perfect shape of his mouth, the solid line of his jaw, the way his hair curled around his ear. She blinked a few times, trying in vain to look away. She felt like such a fool, such a cliché, becoming obsessed with a model. But once he came into the room, she had trouble concentrating on anything else. To her embarrassment, he glanced up and caught her staring. His soft smile and nod of greeting only humiliated her more. She nodded back and turned to face her canvas, heat crawling along her skin and making her scalp prickle. He wasn't on the dais yet. He wasn't hers to study. He was a skilled human being who deserved her respect and admiration—not her obsessive ogling.

"He's magnetic, isn't he?" Reese leaned closer and said. "I can't stop watching him either."

His voice was quiet, but Amy still looked around to see who might overhear them.

"He's just so damned good at holding these long poses and still being…present, isn't he?" Devine said. "It's like watching performance art every time he hits the platform."

"I keep forgetting I'm supposed to draw and not just stare," Reese said, chuckling. "If I don't sell this piece, the world has no taste whatsoever."

Amy smiled at that. Reese's oil paintings and charcoal sketches were displayed in galleries across Manhattan and Brooklyn. He was one of the most gifted artists she'd ever encountered, and his work sold regularly even in the competitive New York market.

"The world doesn't have taste, darling," Devine said. "That's why I have a job."

Reese snorted. "And we're all very grateful for the job you do."

Devine nodded at Amy's unfinished painting. "That'll be worthy of sale, too, when you're done."

Amy stared at the canvas, at the way Ethan occupied the scene she'd built around him, the long, muscled lines of his body draped across the pillows like an ancient god. "Maybe," she said noncommittally. More than her resistance to considering art as a profession, the thought of parting with this particular painting actually caused something tight and painful to collect in her chest.

The final shuffling and noise of preparation settled and silence descended around the room as Ethan stepped up to the platform and dropped his robe.

ETHAN SETTLED ONTO THE PILLOWS, USING THE TAPE SET DOWN BY THE moderator after the last session to resume the exact position he'd held for the last month. The pose was comfortable, his upper body resting against the piled pillows, one knee bent and one arm resting on that knee. He could recline like this for the thirty-minute period without it hurting too much and without drifting off to sleep.

He concentrated on his own body, putting himself in exactly the same angles as the weeks before. Keeping his mind off the beautiful artist just to his right.

Amy Donovan.

She caused him more difficulty than he'd ever had during a life drawing class. Usually, he let his mind drift into a zone that embodied the pose, managing to remain present without focusing on any of the artists around him. But an *awareness* of Amy kept him on edge the entire time. He'd been hyper attuned to her for the last four weeks, and it was all he could do to keep his body from showing just how much he wanted her.

After seeing her, catching her scent at the first session, he'd very nearly backed out of this job. It wouldn't have done his reputation in the art world any good, but for the sake of self-preservation, he'd almost made the sacrifice. Only a keen sense of wanting to finish what he'd started kept him coming back. That and sheer, stubborn pride.

By the end of the first session, he'd managed to convince himself that his reaction was just because Amy bore a resemblance to a woman Ethan didn't want to remember. The thick dark hair, the blue eyes, the pale skin were superficially the same as Siya's. Amy's hair was curly where Siya's had been straight. Amy was a little taller and curvier than Siya. But the similarities in appearance were hard to ignore. And they made a great excuse for dismissing his reaction to Amy. Nothing he had to worry about. He'd be over that superficial attraction by the time he saw her again.

Unfortunately, when he'd shown up for the second session, he'd had to admit he wasn't just struck by Amy's beauty. She *drew* him the way a magnet pulled metal. He found himself overly focused on her, aware of where she was even when he couldn't see her, conscious of the subtle shifts in her scent—honeysuckle and art studio and woman. A combination that set his blood on fire.

He'd had a very similar reaction to Siya. And that was the real danger.

He hadn't had that kind of reaction to any other woman before or since—until Amy. It felt a little like obsession, impossible to control, overwhelming and consuming. Like being around Amy was as necessary as his next breath. He hated that feeling more than just about anything he'd ever experienced before. The same kind of preoccupation with Siya had almost gotten him killed. He could *not* do that again. He'd come to New York to escape the memory of Siya and what she'd done to him. He'd refused to have anything to do with the tiger shifter world, outside of his immediate family, after that.

Amy was human, which should have made her safe. But she called to his tiger so strongly it reminded him of being around a tigress. Which meant he should avoid Amy Donovan at all costs.

And yet, he couldn't bring himself to cancel the remaining two sessions. He was a professional, it was just once a week for a few hours, and for the most part, Amy seemed intent on avoiding him. He assured himself all of that would make it easier, and he wouldn't have to sacrifice his reputation just to avoid a human woman who didn't seem particularly interested in interacting with him anyway.

Unfortunately, his keen sense of smell picked up her attraction, the spice of desire in her scent, the way it enhanced the womanly musk that was part of her essence. He wanted to disregard that flavor, to pretend he didn't know she wanted him, too. She never showed any signs of acting on the chemistry and lust. He didn't have to act on those feelings either.

But his tiger saw her resistance to her own desire as a challenge—a challenge that was impossible to ignore. So hard he'd found himself walking past her during each break at the third session, making excuses to exchange small talk with her, to pass a comment on the progress of her painting. Despite his efforts to resist, he still pulled in her scent, holding his breath to keep the flavors on his tongue as long as possible, savoring the complexity. And more often than he cared to admit, his mind wandered to more erotic thoughts, musings that had been invading his dreams during the intervening week. What her skin might taste like, feel like, what she'd look like stripped out of the loose jeans and t-shirt she always wore to the studio, what she'd look like in the throes of orgasm...

Those thoughts during a nude session were *not* good. The entire room would notice his erection, which wasn't exactly the look he was going for with this pose. It happened to male models sometimes, and artists generally ignored it. But as a tiger shifter, Ethan rarely noticed being nude and never had trouble controlling his body while he was. He'd spent his life taking his clothes off in front of other shifters so he could let his tiger out. Unlike most humans, Ethan was as comfortable without clothes as he was with them.

Except with Amy Donovan in the room.

Even now, during what was thankfully the last session of the four-week cycle, it took a concerted effort on his part not to let his awareness of Amy show. The room was mostly silent except for the sounds of brushes lapping over canvas and pencils scraping across paper, or the occasional groan of a seat as someone adjusted their position. His pose kept his focus on a point in the room where the steel frame around one window butted up against the white wall, so he only caught glimpses of Amy from the corner of his eye. If he didn't focus on it, her scent blended in with all the other smells in the large, open space, just one more part of the complex essence of an art studio.

But even without trying, he still ended up parsing her scent out from the more complicated background. And her lust was there, tamped down by her concentration but still there, heady and rich…and tempting.

If it wasn't so quiet in the room, he might have groaned out loud.

This was the last session, he reminded himself. After this, he wouldn't see her again, and he'd go back to living his life without this preoccupation. He couldn't afford to lose his heart and soul to a woman again. In fact, he wasn't sure how much he had left to lose after the damage Siya had done. Amy called to that part of him, and he just couldn't give in to the desire and risk any more pain. So lust or no lust, Amy Donovan was off limits.

At the first break, he donned his robe and made a circuit of the room, stretching and loosening muscles that had gotten stiff over the last half hour. Some of the artists stopped him to make small talk. One or two gave him their cards, offering the possibility of future work. He managed to keep his distance from Amy, but only barely. His tiger kept urging him to walk past her, test her reaction to him, see if he could make her desire overcome her focus on her painting…

His focus on keeping Amy at a distance while still being utterly aware of her was his excuse for missing the feel of another tiger shifter nearby.

He frowned and glanced at the huge windows. What the hell was another tiger doing in this area?

Settling back onto the dais, Ethan opened his senses to that other shifter, trying to get a sense of who it was.

There were two other males in the city. When Ethan had moved here, they'd met to set up territorial boundaries which would allow them to remain neighbors without conflict. Of necessity, they did occasionally have to move through each other's territories, but those incursions were overlooked if they didn't last long or happen too frequently. Ethan specifically chose modelling jobs that avoided the other males' territories—usually in places that were neutral. His freelance work as a tax accountant rarely brought him into contact with the others either.

He'd never sensed one of the other New York males nearby during his previous sessions here, but he supposed it wasn't out of the question for one to have come into Brooklyn for personal reasons. This was neutral ground, so there was no reason for one of the other males to avoid the area. And being New York, tiger shifters from other places did make their way into and through the city on business, travel, or just as tourists. But this area of Brooklyn wasn't on the typical tourist routes, and it was a Sunday afternoon, so there shouldn't be a lot of reason for a tiger to be here for business.

Despite his senses being fully open, the other shifter remained just at the edges of his awareness, too far to give Ethan much information. He couldn't even be sure if the tiger was male or female. He kept his attention on the shifter throughout the next half-hour period, and the tiger remained in the same place the entire time—maybe eating at a local restaurant?

When the break was called, Ethan blinked in surprise. He hadn't even noticed his wrist on his bent knee falling asleep. He rose, slipped into his robe, and wandered close to the big windows in his circuit to stretch his muscles. Glancing outside in hopes of catching sight of the other tiger didn't help. Whoever it was, they weren't in plain sight from the studio.

With his mind on the mysterious shifter, Ethan didn't realize he'd wandered close to Amy until her scent hit him hard. He fought off a scowl when he noticed he'd stopped just behind her. She didn't glance back at him, but she did sit a little straighter on her chair.

Cursing his unconscious pull to her, he made an effort to look at her painting so he could pass a comment as an excuse for why he was just standing there.

For a long moment, he stared at the painting, unable to actually form a coherent word. When he could speak, he said, very quietly, "That's magnificent. You're amazing."

Pleasure and surprise filled her honeysuckle scent with citrus and a touch of vanilla. He edged closer, unable to resist her, wishing there weren't so many people in the room watching this exchange.

Wishing he could back away before he lost his mind completely.

"Thank you," she murmured. She glanced over her shoulder, smiling shyly at him, her blue eyes sparking with pleasure through the fringe of her long lashes.

The sexy look combined with the husky sound of her voice hit him hard, right in the gut and lower. His blood pounded, his breathing sped. In that moment, he was extremely glad to have his robe on because his body reacted instantly. He took a half step closer to her when she faced her painting again, raising a hand to test the texture of her hair before he realized what he was doing. He snatched his hand back and with a grunt, he spun away from her and stalked to the farthest end of the studio.

Damn but she was dangerous. Without even trying. Even the puzzle of a strange tiger in the area couldn't fully distract him.

If he wasn't careful, he was going to give in to this lust, and to hell with the consequences.

He sighed when his tiger growled in his head—in approval.

BOOKS BY KAT SIMONS

THE CARY REDMOND SERIES

1 – The Trouble Black Cats and Demons

2 – The Trouble with Ghouls and Serial Killers

3 – The Trouble with Leopard Queens and Shifter Wars

4 – The Trouble with Baby Gods and Vampires

5 – The Trouble with Magic and Faery Curses

6 – The Trouble with Wizards and Old Enemies COMING SOON

CARY REDMOND SHORT STORIES

When Cary Met Jaxer

When Cary Met Pickles

When Cary Met Marianne

When Cary Met Lucy

When Cary Met Angie

Cary and Deacon (Try to) Go on a Date

Date Night Take Two

Third Date's the Charm

Cary vs the Goblin King

Dinner with the Jones

Cary and the Cursed Jack-O'-Lantern

When Cary Met the Good Guys (Collection 1)

Romancing the Leopard: A Tiger Shifters-Cary Redmond Crossover Novel

ABOUT THE AUTHOR

Kat Simons earned her Ph.D. in animal behavior, working with animals as diverse as dolphins and deer. She brought her experience and knowledge of biology to her paranormal romance and urban fantasy fiction, where she delights in taking nature and turning it on its ear. Her Tiger Shifters series combines romance and the otherworldly with heart-pounding action adventure. Her latest urban fantasy romance series follows the adventures of Protector Cary Redmond as she tries to manage her personal life while saving the world. A lot.

For something a little different, Kat also publishes fantasy romance, science fiction romance, and the occasional hockey romance under the name Isabo Kelly (http://www.isabokelly.com).

After traveling the world, Kat now lives in New York City with her family. She is a stay-at-home mom and a full time writer.

For more on Kat and her future books:

Website: https://www.katsimons.com
Newsletter: http://eepurl.com/OxQQL

www.ingramcontent.com/pod-product-compliance
Lightning Source LLC
Chambersburg PA
CBHW021302190726
48288CB00003B/656